W9-CCZ-996

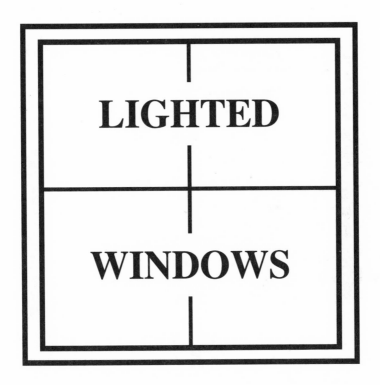

LIGHTED

WINDOWS

Emilie Loring

G.K. Hall & Co. • Thorndike, Maine

Loring

Published in 1999 by arrangement with Little, Brown & Co., Inc.

G.K. Hall Large Print Paperback Series.

The text of this Large Print edition is unabridged.
Other aspects of the book may vary from the original edition.

Set in 16 pt. Plantin by Rick Gundberg.

Printed in the United States on permanent paper.

Library of Congress Cataloging in Publication Data

Loring, Emilie Baker.
　Lighted windows / Emilie Loring.
　　p. (large print) cm.
　　ISBN 0-7838-0342-7 (lg. print : sc : alk. paper)
　　I. Title.
　[PS3523.O645L54   1999]
　813'.52—dc21　　　　　　　　　　　　　　　98-49475

4137726125

Dedication

To the readers of my stories
who, by spoken or written word,
have recognized beneath the
magic glamour of romance and adventure
the clear flame of my belief
that the beautiful things of life
are as real as the ugly things of life,
that gay courage may
turn threatened defeat into victory,
that hitching one's wagon
to the star of achievement will lift one
high above the quicksands of discouragement

1

Fifth Avenue. In that quiet hour before dawn when for a trilling interval the city dozes, it never sleeps. The gleaming asphalt, blanched to silvery whiteness by arc lights, stretched ahead illimitably between looming sky-scrapers, phantoms of concrete and steel, brick and glass, shadowy and unreal as the back drop in a pantomime. In the middle of its polished surface, like a dark isle in a glistening ribbon of river, rested a slipper. Black, satin, buckled with brilliants which caught the light and threw it back transmuted into a thousand colorful sparks. A slipper of parts, unquestionably.

Bruce Harcourt stopped short in his long stride to regard it incredulously. How had it come there? He looked up and down the broad deserted avenue before he salvaged it. A spot of red light was dimming eastward.

Back on the sidewalk he turned the bit of satin over and over in his hand. It was warm. The feel of it sent a curious glow through his veins. It must quite recently have covered a slender foot. Dropped from the now distant automobile? He

7

remembered the gay party of men and girls who had been leaving the hotel as he came out. Why hadn't the owner stopped to pick it up? The hundred eyes of the rhinestone buckle blinked at him with a what's-the-answer challenge in their shallow depths.

He thrust the disturbing bit of foot-gear into his top-coat pocket, gravely regarded the glittering avenue before he entered the Club door. Twenty-four hours more of this and he would be on his way to the wilderness. In his room he set the slipper upon the dresser. From the depths of an easy chair he contemplated it as he smoked his pipe. Too late, too early in the day to go to bed. It seemed such a waste of time to sleep in New York. Soon he would be seeing only forests, glaciers, fields of snow, rails, steam-shovels and the paraphernalia of engineering.

He was not sorry to go back. His college classmates who had given the dinner for him tonight wouldn't believe it, though. They had treated him with the considerate attention due one about to be exiled. It was exile in a way yet — how the dickens could that slipper have been dropped in the middle of the Avenue? The girl who had lost it — its slenderness proclaimed it a girl's possession — would have known had she dropped it from her foot. What was she like? Dark? Fair? Hard? Tender?

Tender! Harcourt shrugged and refilled his pipe. From his observation they didn't make them tender any more. He was thirty-five. Since his sophomore days he hadn't seen a girl who had touched his heart with flame. An intangible presence had seemed to stand between him and love. He was ashamed to acknowledge it even to himself, but it was there. A psychoanalyst would doubtless diagnose it as the subconscious guarding his profession, for he certainly couldn't take a wife into the wilds of Alaska railroad building. He had been given a corking chance to make a name for himself in his profession of engineering, but it meant cutting out romance. From what he had heard of the marital experiences of some of the men who had dined him so royally, he wasn't missing much.

He sat speculating about the slipper and its owner till dawn stole over the roofs he could see from his window. Rainbow colors, violet, indigo, lemon, melted into blue in the eastern sky. Outlines sharpened. The mists of the city fled. The lights in the room paled to ineffectual blurs. Creaking noises in the hall outside. Faint bells in the distance. From the streets ten stories below rose the murmur of a waking city.

Morning and his last day in New York. He stretched his long, lean body. His last day in New York and a full one. Before he left on the midnight train he had to keep innumerable business appointments, confirm orders for materials, and hire a secretary. His brows, a shade darker than his hair, met over his clear gray eyes, the clean lines of his mouth tightened. Why couldn't Tubby Grant have found one for himself on the coast?

Returned from his shower he regarded the slipper on the dresser. What should he do with it? He turned it over in his hand. The eyes of the buckle winked at him, brilliantly but colorlessly now that the lights were out. It was a gem of a buckle. A buckle of value. He knew that, because he had bought several pairs for his sister who had a buckle complex. Would the owner advertise? He'd take a look at the evening paper. Perhaps he would have a chance to return it before he left. The interview might put a decided kick into his last evening. The slipper suggested adventure. He had fought off all invitations. He hadn't known at what time he would finish the business of a full day.

The following eight hours proved more crowded and the search for a secretary more futile than he had imagined. The mere mention of the word Alaska set the prospects he interviewed into shivering refusal.

"Tubby'll have to get one for himself on the coast," he concluded as he opened the door of his room at the Club. As he snapped on the light the eyes of the buckle on the dresser flashed into prismatic glitter.

"Good Lord, I'd forgotten you!" he exclaimed aloud, in surprised response to its almost human appeal. "Let's see if we can find your owner."

He shook out the evening paper, located the Lost and Found column and ran his finger down the list. "Here it is!" He read the advertisement through twice.

LOST. Monday evening on Fifth Avenue, black satin slipper with rhinestone buckle. Reward, if returned at once to J. Trent, 0001 Madison Avenue.

J. Trent. J. Trent. He had heard that combination before. He turned the name over and over in his mind. Click! It slipped into place. Janice Trent! Billy Trent's sister "Jan." He remembered her as a leggy child of twelve when he had spent his last college vacation before the war at the Trents' country place. She had exasperated her brother and himself by tagging after them on fishing expeditions. She had been particularly annoying when sitting on the veranda steps personifying furious rebellion as they shot off in the roadster to pay tribute to neighborhood girls. Funny little thing, naturally timid, always forcing herself to be brave. She had inspired a protective tenderness. His eyes shadowed with regret. Darn shame that he and Billy, who had meant so much to one another, had drifted apart. He had gone to Trent's office at once upon his arrival in New York, only to learn that he was out of town.

He stared unseeingly at the advertisement. Last night at the dinner when he had regretted Billy's absence, Silsbee, the class gossip, had confided.

"Trent's a little gob of gloom these days. Can't blame him. His father played the market, lost practically everything he had and passed out.

11

His sister Janice is to be married in a week. Marrying a multi who's got a way with the ladies. The two are at a prenuptial blow-out in this very hotel now. Confidentially, Billy heard that Paxton — that's the prospective bridegroom's name — had been making whoopee in an adjacent city and he has gone to investigate. Gosh, how do these sheiks get away with it!"

Harcourt looked at his watch. He would change for the trip — no, he wouldn't, he would dress for dinner; no knowing what adventure might be lurking round the next corner. Doubtless, there were a dozen J. Trents in the city, but if the owner of the slipper proved to be Janice he would persuade her to play round with him until his train left. Silsbee had said last night that she was being entertained in the same hotel; he had seen a gay party leaving only a few moments before he picked up the slipper. Those parts of the puzzle fitted perfectly.

An hour later, in answer to his ring, a trim maid admitted him to the Madison Avenue house, a slice of old-time aristocracy sandwiched between new-time shops. He gave his errand, not his name. As he waited in the cheerless reception room, where pictures leaned dejectedly against the walls, where chairs were shrouded in ghostly covers, and furniture was crated, he heard the murmur of voices in a room beyond, the imperative ring of a telephone. Someone answered. Harcourt looked at his watch impatiently. Would J. Trent keep him waiting while she gossiped? He couldn't help hearing the frost-tinged voice.

"No. . . . It was unpardonable. . . . I shall not see you. . . . Don't come. . . . I have said my last word. . . . You should have thought of that before. Good-bye."

The receiver clicked on the hook. Could that have been a prospective bride speaking, Harcourt wondered. Her voice had given him the creeps. Of course there could be two J. Trents in the City of New York, but —

"You have my slipper?"

He curiously regarded the girl on the threshold. Little Janice Trent grown up. The same boyish croak in her voice that he remembered. Who would have thought that the angular child would develop into beauty? Her glinting brown hair waved softly close to her boyish head. The ardent curves of her lips showed vividly red against her pallor. He was vaguely conscious of a beige frock, the yellow of topaz at her throat.

"If this is yours."

The long, gold-tipped lashes flew up. Her eyes were the color of bronze pansies, slightly beaten by the rain of recent tears, he surmised. Incredulity, amazement, certainty followed one another in her voice.

"Why! Why, you are Bruce Harcourt!"

Impulsively she extended her hands. The satin slipper dropped to the floor as he caught them.

"Then you haven't forgotten me?"

"Forgotten you! How could I? Remember how

13

I ragged you and Billy and how furious you boys were when I appeared — how I sulked when you drove off to the Country Club? I was ready to scratch out the eyes of any girl you looked at. However, no matter how obdurate my brother remained, you always relented, and said, 'What's the difference? Let her come along, Billy!' Remember how I clutched your hand when we went through the woods? 'Might see a bear!' was my bugaboo. I shed cloud-bursts of tears when you returned to college. And to think that it should be you who picked up my slipper. Where did you find it?"

She was eager, radiant. Her fingers seemed to cling to his. His hold tightened.

"Winking and blinking in the middle of Fifth Avenue before dawn this morning. I have been consumed with curiosity to know how it came there."

A flame of color tinged her face. She freed her hands.

"I started to get out of a roadster. I had opened the door, put one foot out to jump when —"

"Reckless child! Go on, when?"

"When I — I changed my mind." He had the sense as of a door closing between them. "It's wonderful to see you. I had been told that you were in Alaska."

"Have been for years. I'm starting back tonight."

"Tonight! What a shame that Billy is away. You will stay and dine with me, won't you? This

14

house is a mess. We've sold it and are clearing it, but we still have a cook."

"I have a better suggestion. Dine with me — unless — I was told last night that you were about to be married. Perhaps you are not free."

"I am free to do as I like." The color which the surprise at his identity had brought to her face faded. "I'd love to go, only let it be some quiet place where we can talk."

"Anywhere you say. You know your New York better than I."

She had selected an hotel up town where the decorations, the music, the perfection of the service sank into one's consciousness as softly as the foot into the thick pile of the velvet carpet.

Was this really little Jan Trent facing him across a small, seductively lighted table in the shadow of a spreading palm? She had changed to an evening frock, something lacy and brown, shot through and through with gold. Long, old-fashioned garnet earrings winked countless ruby eyes as they caught the light, six inches or more of the same blinking stones girdled one bare arm. A richly furred, gleaming wrap was over the back of her chair. Harcourt tried to picture the radiant, fragrant beauty of her opposite him at one of the rough tables in the crude log cabin, called the Waffle Shop, at the outfit's headquarters in Alaska. The vision wouldn't materialize.

They talked of her family, the loss of her mother and father, of Billy, of the enormous growth of the city, of the changes in it, in the fashion of plays, of books, of clothes since he was last in New York.

As the gray-haired waiter set the coffee on the table and withdrew to a discreet distance, Harcourt suggested:

"We still have time for part of a show. I don't leave until midnight."

"I would rather sit here and talk."

"Suits me. Will you smoke?"

She shook her head. Elbow on the table, dimpled chin in one hand, she drew hieroglyphics on the cloth with a rosy-nailed finger.

"No. My fiancé so admires the accomplishment in his friends that I wonder he chose a girl so pre-war in her tastes and habits as I."

"And you have promised to marry a man of whom you can speak so contemptuously?"

In the room beyond a violin swept into the music of Scharwenka's Polish Dance, with a swing and fire which set Bruce Harcourt's pulses thrumming to its tempo. She folded her hands — ringless, he noted in surprise — lightly on the table, as she answered his question with another.

"Ever met Ned Paxton?"

"No."

"Then you wouldn't understand. He has attracted me unbelievably, while something deep within me protested, 'You know that you don't trust him.' Moth and candle stuff, I suppose. He has hurt my heart and my pride, yet when he smiled and explained, I would dope my

16

intelligence — instinct, rather — forgive him and remember his good qualities. He has them. Old people adore him, children like him — but he doesn't get on with dogs. Why am I telling you all this, I wonder?"

He answered the troubled sweetness of her eyes, her mouth, so proud, so unhappy, more than her words.

"Because you've reached the point where you've got to talk. You used to tell me everything when we went fishing together. Remember?"

"I remember what a pest I was. All that was needed to make me stick like a leech was to have you say:

" 'You can't do it. It's too hard for a girl.' That settled it. I would put it through or perish in the attempt. I was conscious of my fear complex, though I didn't know enough to call it that. It wasn't fear really, it was imagination plus, which made a specialty of screening disaster. I've fought it all my life but it still gets me for an instant at times. Let's not talk any more about Jan Trent, I'm fed up with her and her problems. How did you happen to go to Alaska — to me it seems the jumping-off place of the universe — you, who Billy claimed were a blown-in-the-glass New Englander?"

"That blown-in-the-glass New England stuff was the answer. I was too darn conservative. I realized that when I came from overseas. Any nurseryman will tell you that young trees grow more sturdy by being transplanted. It was a

17

wrench to tear away from old ties and old customs, but I've never been sorry. The break made me world-minded."

"Does that mean that you're completely depuritanized?"

He laughed. "Not wholly — myself — but I have a greater sympathy for the other fellow's point of view."

"Tell me about Alaska. It sounds so bracing and crisp and clean."

Harcourt lighted another cigarette. "I wish that it always conveyed that impression. I've fought and died trying to get a secretary for our outfit. I'll bet I've interviewed fifty of them, short and tall, lean and fat. The mere name of the country sets an applicant's teeth to chattering."

"I should think there'd be dozens of girls crazy to go."

"Girls! What would we do with a girl in our outfit? We go hundreds of miles into the interior. Ours is no coast cinch. I'm after a man."

"You should have seen the fighting line of your mouth when you echoed 'Girls!' "

He put his hand to his face as though to relax the muscles. "One acquires a fighting line to one's mouth when bridge-building in Alaska."

"Are there no women there?"

"Of course, wonderful women in the cities, cultured, chic, keenly conversant with world conditions, others on remote farms, nuggets of gold, if rough ones; but not in our business. That is not quite true. There are three: Millicent Hale, wife of the chief engineer of the department to which I'm attached, and the Samp sisters."

"Samp! What a curious name. What do they do?"

Her eyes were alight with interest, color had come back to her face. Harcourt was subconsciously aware of an orchestral accompaniment; languorous rhythm, jewels of sound, no measure really begun, no measure really finished for him, just murmurous harmony with a hint of passion running through it all which set an eager pain tugging at his heart, a poignant yearning stirring in his soul.

"Two years ago Mary and Martha Samp appeared at our headquarters on the coast at the mouth of an inlet, and established a Waffle Shop."

"Can they cook?"

"Cook! I'll say they can. The men crowd the shop every night. They would do anything for those two women, who look as though they might have stepped out of the comics of a colored supplement. Martha, the elder, is lean and gaunt, with a tight little top-knot of rusty hair, speaks her mind no matter how welcome or unwelcome her conclusions may be. Mary is round and plump, with big, innocent blue eyes which seem to be eternally interrogating life and being eternally surprised at the answer. They brought an enormous black cat, Blot — he does look like spilled ink when lying on the rug. The Eskimos and Indians who work for us regarded him with the amazement they might have bestowed upon an elephant, don't quite like him. The sisters brought also a melodeon on which Mary wheezes out hymns on Sunday evenings while the men sway, rumble, quaver and soar to its accompaniment."

"And the chief's wife — Millicent, you called her?"

"She has a double interest in headquarters. Her brother Jimmy Chester, is third engineer. He is devoted to her. She is a pretty but pathetic little woman. She has —"

"You needn't describe her. Calling her 'little woman' was as enlightening as sticking up a danger sign on thin ice. I recognize the type. Your description sounds delightfully homey. Not at all like what I thought life in Alaska would be."

"Life — human life in Alaska — is no different from life in other places. People are born, die, marry and divorce, love and hate, the last two a little harder perhaps than when nearer civilization. There are as many people there to the hundred with ideas and ideals as anywhere else. Of course one comes up against raw brutalities and derelicts, but one comes up against them here — in spots."

"Tell me more. Tell me about the country, your work, everything." She was like an eager child begging for another story. "It will keep my mind off my problems."

Her problems! Paxton, of course. Harcourt's heart contracted as though a ruthless hand had squeezed it. The years which had intervened since he had seen her were as a day. Impulsively he spoke to the little girl he had known.

"Be a sport. Acknowledge that you've made a mistake. Don't go on with this marriage, Jan."

Her eyes were intent on a slim finger tracing the pattern in the damask cloth. "Are you suggesting that I back out at the eleventh hour? Think of the stacks of presents! Think of the publicity! Forget me. Tell me about Alaska."

With the sensation as of knuckles smartly rapped, conscious of deepening color, Harcourt acknowledged, "My mistake! Alaska is a big subject. It is our last American frontier. For the first time since its acquisition by the United States there is a program in sight for utilizing great stretches of wilderness. I would advise any youngster in quest of a career to hop on the Alaskan band-wagon. Where shall I begin?"

In the next room a man's caressing voice sang:

" 'Once in a lifetime
Someone comes along
Bringing happiness for two.' "

A foolish little song, yet with a sweetness, a lilt, a minor undertone which gave Harcourt's heart a twist.

"Begin anywhere. Can you get into the

21

northern country at this time of year? Will you go by boat or dog-sleds?"

"By plane. You people in the States don't realize that the development of airways in Alaska is one of the romances of aviation."

"Then you are an aviator as well as an engineer?"

"Rather more engineer than aviator at present. I combined the two professions overseas. Tonight I go to confer with the Crowned Heads of our department. I'm due back at camp before the spring break-up."

"What is that? You see, my curiosity is insatiable. It isn't all curiosity," she admitted, in a voice half eager, half mysterious.

What had she meant by that? "I referred to the breaking up of the winter ice. We've been building a bridge. It spans a river which flows between living glaciers. We've been at work on it two years, two years of the stiffest fighting I've ever known. Great concrete piers, reinforced with steel, begun through the winter ice, were anchored forty or fifty feet to the bottom."

"It makes my teeth chatter. It sounds horribly cold!"

"Cold! I'll say it was cold. Snow storms were continuous. The piercing wind which blew from sixty to seventy miles an hour was laden with fine particles of snow which stung and cut like sleet. This spring will test the bridge. When the ice breaks thousands of bergs will come crashing down the defile propelled by the twelve-mile current of the river. We've been setting ice-breakers this winter."

"How the men must have suffered! Yet you are going back."

"It isn't always like that in winter. There are wonderful nights with their silences and the Northern Lights. There will be days and days — short ones — when the sun comes shining through, when clouds cast purple shadows on snow-capped mountains, when the Stars and Stripes flutter against a clear sky. Most of the engineers are ex-army men, so we raise the flag by Reveille, lower it with the bugle call for Retreat. It reminds us that, frontiersmen as we are, we're still citizens of the good old U. S. A., that we can reflect credit or discredit on our government."

"I love the Colors. Go on!"

"There are days when the banks of streams are vague and misty with young green and you can smell spring in the air. The summers are glorious. Sunshiny days. Birds singing. Long twilights. Ferns and brilliant flowers, fruits and vegetables, double the size of those grown here. An aquamarine sea ruffled into white frills by a soft wind. Over all, a sky like a gigantic turquoise rimmed with dazzling snowy peaks."

"What gorgeousness! What a feast of color! Are you a poet?"

He laughed. "Not guilty. One gets the habit of thinking things through in the immensity of the far North, that's all."

"Do you live in a tent when — when on location?"

"By 'on location' do you mean when I'm at headquarters? A tent! I'm a house-owner. Three years ago a young architect joined the outfit as a draftsman. Someone had fooled him into thinking that the experience in the frozen North would lengthen his life. He came with an outfit suitable for winter sports and a pair of pearl-handled revolvers. The men guyed him unmercifully at first, then they got fond of him. To keep him cheerful and occupied I suggested that he draw plans for a log house for me, he was not physically fit for anything else. He got so interested in the thing that before I knew it I was sold to the idea of building it. The thought of having a roof-tree to return to from the wilderness gripped me."

"What is it like? I'm all excited."

"He called it an H house. It is built of logs chinked with moss. There is a long room in the middle with the length of the rooms at either end going the other way." With a pencil he drew the letter on a card. "Like that. Stone chimneys at each end of the living room provide fireplaces for the other two rooms. We use those in summer; in winter good old Yukon stoves are the only things which will keep us warm. Having gone so far in our plans, we lost our heads, went cuckoo and added a model kitchenette and a bath for each bedroom. Sent for oodles of price-lists and catalogues of fittings. The boy architect and I had the time of our lives selecting them. I spent money like a drunken sailor."

"Where do you get water?"

"This is an engineers' camp, remember. We piped from a stream which is fed from glaciers. As we make our own electricity, warming it after it reaches the house is a cinch. But — oh, yes, there is a but — while it is grand in summer, in winter when the ground is frozen feet deep, the tanks are filled by hand. Not so good."

"Did the boy architect get well?"

"No. 'Twas a tough break for him. He was the nephew of the Samp sisters. That fact accounts for their landing in our particular camp. They came up to take care of him, he was all they had. After he went they stayed to look after the rest of us."

"Your H house sounds marvelous."

"I wouldn't have believed it could mean so much to me. When I mush into headquarters behind my dog-team, I can see, perhaps through falling snow, smoke curling upward from the chimney. The glow from lighted windows sets the icicles which fringe the eaves agleam. Snow piled almost to the roof sparkles like an old-fashioned Christmas card. Although I know that only my husky, Tong, and my house-boy, Pasca, are waiting for me, a sense of home-coming warms me to the marrow."

"That is your winter. Mine is so different. Curious that out of all the world you should have been the one to pick up my slipper. If the incident were used in a story it would be called improbable."

"No such word as improbable now, the war put it out of business. Events which twenty years ago would have seemed unbelievable are all in the day's work. It's not so curious that I should have retrieved the slipper when you consider that we had been dining at the same hotel, that we left at about the same time."

"It seems like — like — do you believe in Fate?"

He considered before he answered. "I believe there is a force in the universe of which, as yet, we know nothing. For want of a better term we call it, sometimes Fate, sometimes the supernatural."

Into the silence which followed boomed the voice of a tower clock. She rose quickly.

"I've kept you here talking and talking. If you don't hurry you will miss your train — I wish — I wish I dared make you miss it."

He caught the glint of tears in her eyes as he laid the costly wrap across her shoulders. A tide of passionate desire to pick her up in his arms and run away with her possessed him. His jaw tightened. Janice Trent in an engineer's cabin in the wilderness? A blind alley. He would better back out.

Only the most casual remarks passed between them as the taxi slithered and serpentined its way through brilliantly lighted streets. At her door he said unsteadily:

26

"You've given me a wonderful memory to carry back to Alaska."

Her face was a pale blur in the dusk of the vestibule as she laid her hand in his. The quick, almost frightened clutch of her fingers touched his blood with flame.

"Don't marry him, Jan. Don't —"

She twisted one hand free to press it against his lips. "Don't say it. Then you'll never be sorry. Good-night."

He kissed the slim fingers fervently. "Good-bye," he whispered huskily, before he bolted down the steps.

2

From a spur on an Alaskan mountainside, Bruce Harcourt regarded the recently completed bridge which straddled the river like a gigantic skeleton. A row of eighty-pound rails set a foot apart all round, bound together with concrete, surrounded the great steel reinforced piers. Above the piers, icebreakers, similarly constructed, were planted. He sniffed the soft wind which sobbed through the thick growth of spruce and cottonwoods behind him. Spring in it. The break-up was due any hour, any minute. Across the canyon sparkled a cave of ice, apparently as green and harmless as a velvet arras. Above, the sky was clear cerulean blue. Below, the frozen scarf which was the river lay gray and hard as granite, with no suggestion of the seething, surging current underneath. The glacier from which it issued five or six miles away was faintly discernible. He sniffed again.

"It won't be long now before we know how good we are," he told himself. He turned at a hail. A man, almost as broad as long in his Eskimo parka, which hung down to meet the tops of his skin boots, was hurrying toward him.

The part of the face which the fur hood left uncovered was russet-apple brown from exposure to an Alaskan winter, the nose was peeling from frost-bite. Harcourt's grave face brightened.

"Tubby! Back so soon? Boy, but I'm glad to see you!"

Theodore Grant Junior's green eyes responded to the affection in the greeting. His face was rough from lack of a shave, but his teeth showed beautifully white as he grinned.

"I've got him, ba-gosh!"

"Got who?"

"Got who? Has your memory frozen up? The secretary. An assistant for myself, Theodore Grant Junior, accountant extraordinary for this branch of the Alaskan Expeditionary Force to crack a way through the great Northwest."

"How did you get him?"

"From an agency in Seattle. They sent him on the first boat. I'll bet the old tub had to plow and crush its way through ice."

"Did he know what he was coming to? Did that dumb agent explain that the job was no coast cinch?"

"Is there a coast cinch in this outfit?"

Harcourt laughed. "Relatively. Everything's relative, Tubby. Did you bring him along?"

"Did I! Do you think I'd give him a chance to sneak back on the next boat? I brought him. He — he wasn't all I brought."

"What do you mean?"

29

"Keep your shirt on, Bruce. I brought the Samp girls."

"The Samp girls! Tubby! Have you gone plumb crazy?"

"Now listen!"

"Listen! Look here, does Hale know?"

"Hale! What's he got to say about it?"

"Considering that he's chief of this outfit, considerable."

"Chief! Who's had to take his place most of the time this winter? You. He opened up high, wide and handsome while you were away. He got the Indians on their ears, driving them like slaves when he was sober and chucking their squaws under the chin when he was plastered. He's a bad hombre and we're in for trouble if the Crowned Heads of this enterprise, back home, don't get busy. If anyone's got anything to say, it's you."

"I'll say it pronto. I'd send the Samp sisters out if I could spare a man. But I can't, the break-up's due any minute. Why the dickens did those two women leave the Waffle Shop at headquarters, which is remote enough, to come out here to this wilderness of snow and ice?"

"That's what I asked them. Martha Samp, a little leaner, a little gaunter, a little grayer than when we left in the fall, asked to come. I went into the air at the suggestion, just as you did. I growled:

" 'Take you out to that wilderness! Nothing doing!'

"She inveigled me into the shop to talk it over.

Heaped my plate with the hottest, crispest waffles, dripping with melting brown sugar and butter, Bruce — *butter;* filled my cup with honest-to-goodness coffee and reminded:

" 'Mary and I can't do missionary work with books, but we can with food. One of the biggest forces which prods men on to deviltry is the trash they put into their stomachs. That bridge you're building is a big thing for the country. I've been talking with the men who worked on it. They claim that 'twill stand or fall in the spring break-up.' "

"She's right."

"She argued that we wouldn't be here long, that she and Mary would like to see the interior, and on and on *ad lib., ad infinitum.* That she wanted to keep our courage up with good food. She had the missionary spirit, all right."

"Did Miss Mary come?"

"Of course; she's only a plump echo of Miss Martha. You should have heard the men cheer when I appeared with them. They are busy now clearing out the shack which was the cookhouse. We brought in a sledgeload of their equipment. They'll be ready for business at supper time."

Waffles and brown sugar! Real coffee! Harcourt's opposition oozed. He knew the appetizing quality of the Samp sister's productions.

"Now that they are here, they will have to stay. I can't spare a man to take them out. Got your secretary located?"

"He brought a tent with his outfit. Wish you could see the amount of truck put off the boat for him. Made me think of Archie Harper's pearl-handled revolvers. I asked him where he found out what to bring, and he said from a book in the Public Library. From the amount of stuff dumped from the boat I'd say he'd chucked in the library itself for full measure. Made him park it at headquarters. The Samp girls have taken him under their wings. He's no cave-man. Even in his parka and mukluks he's as slim as a fishing-rod. He's got a little mustache like the down on a yellow chicken's back, black curly hair — big crimson spots on his cheeks."

"I get you. T.B. That's why he was willing to leave the land of lights and movies."

"Said he'd been ordered to live out-of-doors. By the expression of that part of his face left visible by the hood of his parka, as we came over the pass, I reckoned that he hadn't expected quite so much in one dose. I tried to see our surroundings as he saw them and ba-gosh, accustomed to them as I am, it gave me the heebe-jeebes. Miles of untrodden snow. Peaks, spires and ridges of ice, their glittering surfaces crossed by thousands of crevasses and fissures. Overhead an eagle hovered, somewhere, far off, a wolf howled, sinister as the dickens. Mountains thrust jagged fangs through thin vapors. The weather-demon shook out his whole bag of tricks with sound effects. It sleeted, it rained, it hailed. Lightning did its stuff and the thunder was deafening. Then it snowed, so thick and fast that the dogs lost the trail. Suddenly, almost under our feet, a cliff dropped straight down to the gun-metal river. Through it all, neither the Samp girls, nor the secretary, crabbed or whimpered once. They might have been tooling along in a Rolls Royce in sunny Spain. Only the boy's eyes played traitor. Poor little fella, it would be terrible to die in this wilderness."

"Die! Good grief, Tubby, you haven't brought a boy up here to die?"

"No, of course not. I'll bet with the Samp girls' cooking and this air he'll be O.K. Now that's all washed up — what's bust now?" he demanded as one of the workmen raced toward them. As the man struggled for breath which whistled through his porcelain teeth, Harcourt encouraged:

"Take it easy, Gallagher. What's up?"

"Sure" — gulp — "Chester sent me to tell you the false works has suddenly moved!"

Harcourt's face whitened. The false works! The two thousand piles which had been driven forty feet into the bottom of the river!

"How much! Quick!"

"Fifteen inches! Sudden as the crack of doom!"

"Where's Hale?"

"Gone back to headquarters with his dog-team. Said everything was O.K. Didn't need him; he'd take the boat out to Seattle to get Mrs. Hale. Said you'd had your leave, he'd take his."

"Gone! Gone to Seattle! Without letting me know! Get every man out, Tubby!" Harcourt started on a run. A pier supervisor was charging toward him, his eyes like glassies too big for their sockets. The man answered his unspoken question.

"Ice-cap lifted twenty feet. Moving. False works fifteen inches out of plumb."

"We must get it back."

"Back!"

"We must. Otherwise the whole span, supports and all, will be carried away."

In the prolonged nightmare which followed, Bruce Harcourt felt as though he were his own double looking at a great motion picture. Steam from every available engine was turned into every available feedpipe. Men chopped seven-foot thick ice away from the piles. A stinging needle-pointed Arctic night settled down. The river rose. The forest quiet was broken by the chop, chop of picks. The piles must be kept free. Hundreds of cross pieces were unbolted. The shifting into place began. No man relaxed his vigilance until another stood ready to go on with his job.

If he thought of anything but the bringing back of the bridge into place, Harcourt thanked God for the Samp sisters. They were indefatigable. They made the men stop for hot coffee and waffles put together sandwich fashion with succulent brown sugar. Once he glimpsed a boy hovering in the background. The new secretary?

Not that he cared a picayune who he was, but the speculation served to take his thoughts for a moment off the problem of that moving bridge. Hale's had been the master mind in construction, but he had to step in so often when the chief was incapacitated that the responsibility of the result would fall heavily upon his shoulders. The authorities whom he had seen back home had intimated that they were thoroughly informed as to the situation.

Melting. Chopping. Coaxing. Melting. Chopping. Coaxing. The hours dragged on. Harcourt couldn't close his eyes. With every muscle, every nerve in his body, he was holding back the torrent which at any moment might be loosed in the river. Once, hurrying to his office for a plan, he saw a dim face in the purple dusk between spruce trees. He stopped short in his stride. The face of the girl who had dined with him that last night in New York? Behind the absorption in his work, since his return, like the brilliant lining of a cloud, had glowed the memory of those hours with Janice Trent. He could see her as distinctly as he saw her then, the soft waves of hair, the ardent lips, ruby eyes winking in the long, swaying earrings; he could hear the swing and fire of the Polish dance; he could feel her pulsing fingers against his lips. But of course it wasn't Jan! Had the memory of her become an obsession? His heart stopped for a terrified instant.

"Am I going dippy under the strain?" he muttered, and plunged on through the trail.

Inch by slow inch the span settled back on its concrete bed. Haggard, exhausted, with a two days' growth of beard on their faces the engineers watched the last bolt driven in. From the distance came a faint rumble. It increased in volume.

Grant clutched Harcourt's arm. "It's coming!" he whispered through stiff lips.

The rumble increased to a roar. The river had broken loose. Carrying ice and timber before it, it swept along on its mad rush to the sea.

Rigid, tense, the two men watched the wreckage and ice sweep by. The bridge stood immovable against the onslaught. Grant's eyes were unashamedly full of tears.

"You've done the trick, Bruce. This day will mark a crisis in your life and Hale's."

"The credit belongs to him. I only came in at the end. Tell the division heads to get the men off duty as fast as possible. Put them on shifts to watch. I'll turn in. I haven't been off my feet for forty-eight hours. Now that the strain is eased every nerve in them is throbbing protest."

"You'd better, ba-gosh. You're the only one of the outfit who hasn't caught a cat-nap, at least. The boys will be all right now. The Waffle Shop's going at full blast. I'll say that the Samp girls helped mightily in keeping the men fit for their job."

"I'll say they did. When the history of this bridge-building is written, their part ought to appear in the records."

A great wave of heat from the Yukon stove swept out as Harcourt opened the door of his shack. Firelight glowed through the one window, tipped with flame the icicles which fringed the roof, threw eerie shadows on the cache opposite, raised on tall posts, in which supplies were stored against marauding porcupines and dogs. Smoke from the chimney ascended in a column as straight as a near-by spruce. He paused on the threshold.

"What's the name of that secretary of yours, Tubby?"

"Jimmy Delevan."

"Delevan? Did he help during the late excitement?"

"Sure he did. He was everywhere. Perhaps not so helpful in some spots as in others. One of the men found him freeing a snowshoe rabbit which had been snared. When he explained that the rabbits were the chief source of feed for the dogteams, Jimmy Delevan went quite white, walked off without answering, but with the rabbit clutched tight in his arms like a baby."

"Delevan? I think I saw him once and thought he was — Delevan —"

He felt himself swaying. The heat from the red-hot stove was overpowering after the cold. Lord, how his feet throbbed! He must — Delevan — He must — From a great distance came Tubby Grant's strident plea:

"Hold on, Bruce! Don't go to sleep till I can get you over to that bunk."

3

Three shrieks of a small steamer's titanic siren echoed and re-echoed among the snow-tipped mountain tops.

"B-o-a-t! B-o-a-t!"

The cry set in motion Eskimos and Indians, countless uncanny echoes. Dogs responded with wolfish wails. One of a group of white men, against a background splotched with the brilliant blankets of the Yakutats, Bruce Harcourt stood on the shingle at headquarters watching a launch put-putting from the ship which had dropped anchor. Behind him the tableland, fifteen feet above the shore, was littered with piles of lumber, stacks of steel rails, tents, shacks, iron drums in which gasoline had been shipped, locomotives and steamshovels. In front of the Company store an Alaskan bear paced back and forth, back and forth, the length of the chain riveted to a post. Smoke spiraled from the chimneys of long dormitories. Men were pounding, digging, riveting. Huskies were yelping in the kennel yards behind the building labeled OFFICE. The place teemed with industry. Section heads directed the dragging of stumps, the burning of Arctic moss. Engineers, blueprints in hand, were in earnest conference. Broad roads, hacked out of the forest of alders, cottonwoods and spruces, stretched inland. Beyond the office cowered a group of storm-bleached cabins, glinting with one or more tin patches. Each roof had its copper-wire antenna, like strands of a mammoth spider-web, which picked up currents of music, thought, to hold and bind these pioneers to the world they had left behind. A crude hangar occupied the one side of a cleared field which was encircled with sheds. A little world in itself.

Harcourt looked beyond the boat with its armor-plated hull, designed for ice-bucking, out to sea. On the horizon loomed a volcano. The front of the crater had broken away, the back rose in a jagged peak. The effect was that of a caldron with one side gone, spurting and belching gases which took on the glory of sunset coloring as they spread, till the horizon streaked with torn veils of malines, in rose and amethyst, gold and amber, crimson and purple. Far oft, sportive whales sent sparkling jets of water high in air. Great bergs of green ice, surmounted by flocks of lavender and white gulls, floated oceanward. Quite near were snow-crowned mountains whose sides, striped in vivid and dull green, reminded him of the slashed sleeve of a troubadour.

"I never watch that boat come in but I wonder

what turn old Fortune will give her wheel," observed Grant at his elbow.

"Its arrival is packed with significance, Tubby. So many on this last frontier have pasts. The mail the steamer brings is sure to jolt some one of them into activity. You only have to watch the men's eyes to know what it means. Some are feverishly bright with apprehension, some are dull with apathy, many of them are fearlessly gay, thank heaven."

"And thanks to you I have nothing to dread. I'll bet the wheel turns for Hale this time. He and the Mrs. are coming in on this boat. It's six weeks since we fought to save that bridge. He went off to Seattle before he knew that it would stand the break-up. I'm mighty sorry for his wife, but — our reports went by air, must have reached the authorities weeks ago."

"I made mine as charitable as possible, considering the fact that a flaw in construction imperils hundreds of lives and wastes thousands of dollars."

"I'll bet you put on the soft pedal, Bruce. In the interest of cool and impartial accuracy, Jimmy Chester — ba-gosh, how he hates Joe Hale, if he is his brother-in-law — and I didn't. In my capacity as accountant for the outfit I reported unvarnished facts. Here come the mail-bags and Stephen Mallory. It's good to see the Dominie again. I'm glad we're back on the coast, even if we are hundreds of miles from civilization. I wonder how long we'll have to stay in this raw place?"

"Until we have developed a railroad terminal. The authorities have decided not only to extend the tracks north but to connect the Alaskan system with Seattle, San Francisco and Los Angeles. That's what I've been doing these last six weeks. Even got a piece of track laid as an object lesson. Left Jimmy Chester in charge. He's a human dynamo, in spite of the fact that he looks like a stage Romeo. Part of this outfit is to scout by plane and report bridge possibilities. That means that next winter we'll begin pier-setting again."

"Br-r-r! If summer comes can winter be far behind! What price railroads! There goes the mail to the office. I'll hustle along and distribute it."

"How's the new secretary working out?"

"Quick and accurate as a sharpshooter."

"Never see him round."

"He isn't. Sticks close to the Samp girls. I'll bet they baby him. Women have to have something to mother."

"Red spots still in evidence?"

"Yep. They wouldn't admit it, but I suspect the men steer clear of him."

"Poor boy! It's a tough break. Curious I've never seen him."

"Not so queer when you think of it. My office was moved back here the day after the break-up — the King of France and his forty thousand men — I marched the Samp girls and Delevan

41

up and marched them down again. You only arrived a few hours ago. I'll send your mail to the H house. Will you eat there or at the Waffle Shop?"

"The Waffle Shop. Now that I'm back in the metropolis I want to plunge into the gay night life of the cafés."

"Feeling coltish, aren't you? Kind of dropped the load of that bridge off your shoulders. I'll save a seat for you."

Logs were blazing in the roughly built stone fireplaces when Harcourt entered his cabin. The middle portion served as a living- and work-room. A door at the back opened into a kitchenette. The stone chimneys at each end did double duty: they provided fireplaces for the bedrooms which corresponded in position to the uprights of the H. as well as for the living-room. The log walls were hung with blueprints and gay Indian blankets. Laden book-shelves covered one end from rafters to floor; a pair of holsters hung from pegs. A priceless Russian samovar on the shelf of a crude dresser reflected the firelight in wavering, coppery tints: a tea service of old Chinese pewter would have set a connoisseur to smashing the tenth Commandment. A drafting table across one corner was flanked by tall rolls of paper. A broad desk, a radio, a few chairs, one a fan-back of incredible fineness from the Philippines, a couch, a table with a lamp, whose juice was supplied by the company dynamo, completed the furnishings. Pelts of richness and value lay on the rough floor.

A tawny husky, stretched at length on the couch, lifted his head from the pillows and whacked a welcoming tail. His master laughed as he rubbed his wide-apart ears.

"I suspect there's something wrong with this picture, Tong. If we had a missus you wouldn't be allowed to sleep on that couch, old fella." The dog concurred with a guttural rumble.

Returned from a shower and a change of clothes, Harcourt gathered up the mail heaped on the table. Newspapers, letters, magazines. He looked longingly at the big bundle of books which he had ordered while browsing through bookstores in New York. Those would have to wait. He lighted his pipe, settled deep in a comfortable Morris chair and opened a long official envelope. What had the authorities to say to him, he wondered? Dark color rose to this face as he read the letter. The authorities had to say that he had been made chief of the outfit, in place of Hale, demoted and recalled.

Tong laid his nose on his knee and closed his eyes in blissful content. One hand absentmindedly rubbing the dog's tawny head, Harcourt stared thoughtfully into the fire. He had made good. He had come to this northern country after having been honorably discharged from the Engineers Corps of the army six years before. He had believed that Alaska, the last frontier of the United States, offered the greatest, swiftest opportunities for progress in his profession. And he meant to get to the top of it if it were humanly possible. He had no money except what he had saved and a small inheritance. This promotion meant the doubling of his salary. It meant that he could provide certain luxuries for a wife — a wife in this wilderness! Not so good. He had indulged in all sorts of wild visions since his return from the States, had pictured Janice in the fan-back chair which had been designed for a lovely woman. The next time he went he would keep away from attractive girls with eyes like bronze pansies and ardent lips. He might write to Jan about his promotion, she would be interested. Had she married Paxton, Paxton of the golden tongue and purse? With difficulty he switched his train of thought. Hale was out of it. Would he be a good sport and make things easy for his successor or would he fight?

Fight. Harcourt answered his own question as he entered the candle-lighted Waffle Shop and met the malevolent glare of the demoted chief. The rustic tables in the log cabin room were full. Each occupant, with hair carefully slicked down was redolent of soap and water. Cigarette smoke rose in spirals, matching coins clicked. From the room behind came the sizzle of batter on hot iron, the aroma of coffee, the appetizing smell of bacon.

Tatima, the Indian waitress, moved from table to table, a savage from the tips of her beaded moccasins to the top of her superb head. Her face was darkly, tragically beautiful. Her black hair, parted in the middle, was drawn with satin smoothness over her ears, the blood flowed redly under her olive skin. An immaculate white apron partially covered her gay cotton gown, from her neck hung a string of evenly cut, sapphire-blue beads. She might have been stone deaf for all the consciousness she showed of her customers' badinage.

Harcourt took the chair which Grant had reserved for him. He sensed the lull in talk as he entered. Did the men already know of his change of status? Opposite him sat Stephen Mallory, the coast missionary, white-haired, lean, Alaska-seasoned. There was a merry twinkle in the blue eyes which looked with sympathetic understanding upon the struggles and temptations of this northern outpost of civilization.

Mary, the mild partner of the Samp sisters, hovered about the three men. Her round face had the wrinkled effect of a quite elderly, if still plump winter apple; her short upper lip quivered like a rabbit's; her false teeth clicked when she talked. Harcourt nodded a friendly greeting, gave his order, supplemented with the plea:

"Make sure of mine first, Miss Mary. These two men are the world's champion eaters."

The sense of humor had been mislaid when Mary Samp's characteristics were assembled. Her big, innocent blue eyes widened guilelessly.

"Well now, Mr. Mallory don't eat enough to keep a bird a-goin'. Don't know's I can say as much for Mr. Tubby," she added with an unwonted tinge of badinage in her voice.

Grant protested in his best spoiled-child manner. "Oh, I say, Miss Mary. You —"

The sentence thinned into air as a blond giant, with the regular features of a Greek deity, thickened and coarsened by over-exposure to self-indulgence, loomed above the table. He dropped a hand on Harcourt's shoulder.

"So — that was your business in the States. To turn informer! You think you've supplanted me in this — as in another quarter? Perhaps you stopped in Seattle on your way back to report too! Let's see you try the Big Chief business! As the Russians used to say, 'God and the Tsar are far away!' "

Harcourt shook off the heavy hand. Clean cut, well groomed, lean, virile, head high, he was the antithesis of the man glaring down upon him. His gray eyes were like black coals.

"Don't waste theatrical clap-trap on me, Hale. You have your orders. I have mine. I'll see that they are carried out."

"I get you! Wait until I turn in my report, you — you home-breaker!"

Grant sprang to his feet. "Skunk!"

Hale lunged at him. The men in the room rose as in a body. Harcourt seized his erstwhile superior in a grip of steel. His voice was low.

"Cut this out, Hale. You —"

"Get out of this shop, Hale! An' don't you never step foot in it again! You're not boss no longer," twanged a woman's voice from the door which led to the kitchen. Martha Samp stood in the opening like an avenging fury. Wisps of rusty gray hair stuck through the mesh of her mob cap like hay through the interstices of a feed box. The blaze of her print dress, a bewildering riot of color in the modern manner, was only partially eclipsed by a large white apron. Under one arm was a massive yellow bowl. She emphasized her ultimatum with the wave of a batter-coated spoon. Hale met her steady eyes. With a snarled imprecation he stalked from the shop.

A sigh of relief like the passing of a vague wraith soughed through the room as he banged out. Men resumed their seats and their attacks on the waffles heaped on their plates. As the atmosphere cleared Harcourt demanded in a low tone:

"Why the dickens did you fly at Hale, Tubby? Keep out of this mess. Disappointment plus his habits has crazed him. The very absurdity of his accusation should have held you."

"Ba-gosh, I saw vermilion when he insinuated —"

"Forget it! Once get a suggestion like that in the air and the Lord only knows what it will spread into. He is savage, naturally, because he has been demoted, poor devil."

"He wouldn't have been demoted had he behaved himself."

"He knows that. That's the tragedy of it. He has dug his own professional grave and realizes it. He's a wizard of an engineer when he's himself. I've learned so much from him that I shall be everlastingly grateful."

"Mebbe so, mebbe so. He's going, praise be to Allah! There's no room here for a bad boy. Every communication I receive from the authorities reiterates the order that this camp shall set an example of discipline and decency to the Indians and Eskimos — Hale —" the earnestness of his voice shifted magically to lightness. "Well, Tatima, made up your mind to sell me those beads?"

The girl who had stopped at the table, clutched her brilliant blue necklace with a bronzed hand.

"Who, me? Bead used as money by ancestors. Tatima never sell."

"If you pull at them like that some day the string will break and you'll wish you'd taken money for them."

"Huh!" She shrugged disdain, spoke to Harcourt, "Miss Martha she say for you to go to her cabin, soon's waffles eat. Walk in, she say. She come soon."

"Tell her I'll be there. Everything going right with you, Tatima?" Harcourt asked with friendly interest.

"Who, me? Fine." She padded away in her moccasins.

Stephen Mallory looked after her thoughtfully. Shook his head. "Tatima's a puzzle to me. The Christianity she professes is a veneer, and a thin veneer at that. In a crisis she'd revert to the

48

pagan creed of her ancestors, which was to end a quarrel by the surest and easiest method, getting one's opponent out of the way by fair means or foul. Self-preservation was the first and strongest law."

"Ba-gosh, then she'll get Hale sometime."

"Cheerio, Tubby, Hale will be off before she realizes that he's going. Get the engineers together in our office. We need to confer about the new instructions. They will move everybody up. Bring your secretary to take the minutes of the meeting, unless you're afraid to allow him out in the night air. He is as careful of that boy as if he were a drop of radium in a glass tube. Have you seen him, Mallory?"

"No. I came in on the boat, you know."

"Tubby keeps him under lock and key."

Grant's defense was spirited. "Afraid of losing him? I'll say I am! Hard enough to get him. Independent little cuss. Says he was hired to work for me. Threatened to leave if I loaned him."

"You're welcome to him, Tubby. Mr. Mallory, there are two bedrooms in my cabin. One of them is yours while you are here."

"Thank you, Harcourt. The section men have made me welcome in their dormitory. I am happy that they want me. I will make that my headquarters. I'll talk with Hale."

Little lines appeared between Harcourt's brows. "Better let him alone at present, Dominie. He's bitter over his demotion. One can't blame him. That bridge is his triumph."

"Now listen! You know you carried the whole contract on your shoulders, Bruce."

"Forget it, Tubby. Don't let Hale hear you or he will drag you into this mess. One of us at a time is enough. After I find out what Miss Martha wants I'll join you at the office. See that every man in the outfit is there."

"Hale included?"

"Hale included, if he will come. If possible we will play this game with all the cards on the table."

Easier said than done, he thought, as he made his way to the living quarters of the Samp sisters. That had been a vicious thrust of Hale's. Homebreaker! Evidently he intended to twist friendly sympathy for his wife into a sordid liaison. Tubby and he had been sorry for Millicent Hale. Dainty as a figurine, the woman, little more than a girl, had taken her marriage vow, "And leaving all others cleave only unto him," literally. She had followed her husband into the wilderness. Once or twice when her brother had been away from headquarters, she had turned to him or to Grant in an extremity. They had done what they could to help. If Hale pushed that charge —

"Oh, forget it! Forget it!" he admonished himself. There were more imminent problems to be considered. He drew a long breath of the clear air, threw his shoulders back as though to rid them of an intolerable burden. Why did strife and jealousy and their ugly triplet, malice, have to taint this glorious northern world? He remembered Janice Trent's request.

"Tell me of Alaska. It sounds so crisp and bracing — and clean."

Where was she now, he wondered, as he had wondered a hundred times since he had left her standing in the dim light of the vestibule. The color burned in his face as he remembered his almost uncontrollable urge to pick her up and carry her off. Young Lochinvar stuff. Somehow it didn't suit this twentieth century. Had she married Paxton? No, she had too much spirit. Quite plainly he felt the pressure of her hand against his lips, heard her voice with its boyish note protesting:

"Don't say it! Then you'll never be sorry!"

He would always be sorry he hadn't said it, he thought, as he thought in moments like this, when cold reason took an hour or two off duty. She would have loved the beauty of this northern world. The sky above the serrated crater-top of the volcano glowed rose-color. Scarfs of violet and green serpentined from the interior. The afterglow tinted the scattered drift-ice which he could see far out. Gulls, lavender-white wings outspread, dove and floated above the blue waves which rolled in to ruffle into whiteness on the shingle. From the distance came the yelp of dogs. A few stars flamed and faded like prowling fireflies in the darkening dome of the sky.

He obeyed instructions and walked into the Samp cabin without knocking. The room was characteristically New Englandish, furnished as it was with the *Lares* and *Penates* the sisters had brought. It had an atmosphere of homey charm. An old-time melodeon stood in one corner, a radio kept it company. Curious samplers, quaint silhouette portraits brightened the moss-chinked walls. Magazines and a heaped-up work-basket, which gave out a faint scent of lavender, were on the drop-leaf mahogany table, where lay an open Bible. A cathedral clock on the slab of stone which made the mantel was flanked by ancient brass candlesticks. A pair of Hessians in scarlet coats and yellow waistcoats, gold sabres drawn, stood ankle-deep in red-hot embers. From the warm security of the hearth rug a coal-black cat regarded him unblinkingly with slightly disdainful green eyes. Over one arm of a wing chair drawn near the fire dangled a pair of legs and feet encased in leather leggings above heavy shoes. From its depths came the sound of soft, regular breathing.

Harcourt smiled broadly. Grant's secretary asleep, he'd bet a hat. The Alaskan air was getting in its remedial work. The Samp sisters certainly were coddling him. Probably they had had to work their fingers to the bone on their Maine farm. Just like them to spoil the boy. Women of their type had to mother something if it was only a black cat.

He tiptoed across the room. He noted the boots, small for a boy even. His eyes traveled over the curled-up body in its rough brown tweed to the face. His heart suspended action.

His glance flew from the vivid mouth with the faint red line of irritation above the upper lip to the tapering fingers from which dangled a small golden mustache. A wavy lock of black hair had fallen over one eye. Long lashes, golden-tipped, lay on the crimson cheeks.

The world crashed about his ears. The boy asleep in the chair wasn't a boy! It was the girl to whom he had said goodbye in New York. It was Janice Trent.

4

Harcourt never knew how long he stood staring incredulously at the girl's face. Janice Trent! Impossible! What had brought her into this wilderness? Had she married Paxton and found the marriage unendurable? No, had she gone so far as that she would have stuck it out. Had she run away before the ceremony to escape the publicity attendant upon a last-minute broken engagement? He remembered the frozen voice he had heard at the telephone the night he had returned the slipper. The black slipper. He could see the buckle of it now winking and blinking at him in the middle of that stretch of blanched asphalt. To come here disguised as a boy! Reckless child! What should he do? Let her know at once that he had found her out? Send her back on the next boat?

A slight cough at the door drew his eyes as steel to magnet. Lean, gaunt Martha Samp, with admonitory finger at her lips beckoned with the hand which clutched a newspaper. A little edge of red flannel was visible at her wrists below her sleeves. Harcourt's grim lips relaxed. Miss Samp was taking no chances with the northern weather. A heavy crimson sweater, pulled up almost to her ears, was drawn down over the print dress which reached to her thick ankles. Her boots were as clumsy as a man's. Her agate eyes were set in sunbursts of fine lines. She beckoned again.

Without another glance at the sleeping-girl, Harcourt crossed the room. Martha Samp hooked one bony finger into the pocket of his coat and drew him outside the cabin. She soundlessly closed the door. Still holding him she led the way to a rude woodshed. Put her lips close to his ear.

"You've found out?"

He nodded.

"The Lord be thanked! I won't have to take the responsibility. What you goin' to do?"

Towers of purple dusk were rising against the afterglow. Far off snow caps, like white islands, dotted a rose-streaked indigo horizon; hot blue and white stars, cool red stars spangled the sky. Harcourt's eyes came back to the lined, gaunt face of the woman beside him.

"Send her home on the first boat. This is no place for a girl."

"Sakes alive, I'd like to see any harm come to her with Mary an' me here!"

"But, Miss Martha! You don't think she should stay here masquerading as a boy!"

"Course not, now that you know. But, she hadn't oughter go back. Read this. It came in today's mail. Weeks old, I suppose." She opened the newspaper, pointed with a knobby finger.

Bruce Harcourt stared down at the pictured faces on the sheet. Janice Trent! Paxton! The letters of the caption under them danced impishly.

BRIDE DISAPPEARS FOUR DAYS
BEFORE WEDDING.

Janice had run away to escape Paxton. Would he try to find her? She was here, in disguise, asleep in the cabin behind him. What should he do? What could he do but stand between her and a heart-breaking future? He looked at the paper again, tried to say lightly:

"It's absurd to think this has any connection with — with Grant's secretary."

The woman sniffed. "Sakes alive, let's you and me not play at cross-purposes. We're the only ones that child has to help her. I know that's her because she told me that she'd run away from marryin'. When I saw this paper I guessed that she was the girl 'twas all about. Lucky she had spunk to throw him over. You kin tell from his face, handsome as a picture, easy-goin', that, where women's concerned, he's as false as Mary's teeth."

In spite of his anxiety Harcourt laughed as he visualized the glittering uppers and lowers of the younger Samp sister. There could be nothing more blatantly false in the world than those.

"Does Miss Mary know?"

"Of course, but she won't tell no one. We've lived long enough to've learned that if you don't want a thing known you mustn't take anyone into your confidence. When I stepped into the cabin, I knew you'd found out by the look on your face. I'm glad. The girl — Jimmy Delevan, she calls herself — told me that she'd known you back in the States an' then she kinder half laffed an' half sobbed an' said,

" 'Tagging him as I useter.'

"An' I says to her, 'Child, there's a gate in every wall if you'll keep huntin' for it. I guess you found the right one when you came here.' "

"Does she think that I suspect her identity?"

"Sakes alive, no! She's sure you don't. First time she laughed since she arrived — she's got a laugh like music — was after she came face to face with you up in the woods, the time the bridge was movin', an' you didn't recognize her. She's safe with Martha an' me. We're tickled to death to have someone besides a black cat to make fools of ourselves over. The men haven't come near Jimmy Delevan. They don't like the red spots on his cheeks."

Harcourt's throat contracted unbearably. He had forgotten. That lovely girl threatened — he demanded unsteadily:

"You don't think it's serious?"

Martha Samp grunted derision. "Serious! Don't you know paint when you see it? She's as sound as I am, an' there ain't nothin' sounder between here and India's coral strands. She thought the red cheeks would be an explanation as to why she came up into this country."

"Has she seen that paper?"

"No."

"That helps. Be sure that no one else sees it. Burn it. A useless precaution. Others like it, doubtless, have come in this mail. I must go to the office. You haven't told me yet why you sent for me, Miss Martha."

"I want another room built on the cabin for her. She's brought all her handsome wedding things, sheets and pillow slips made of pink crêpe. There's no truer sayin' than that one half the world don't know nothin' about how the other half lives. If anyone'd told me some folks slept under such beddin' I'd have thought them plumb crazy. Mary's near gone out of her mind over it all. She loves pretties. If the girl is goin' to stay she ought to have a cabin hitched on to ours."

"I'll talk with you about that later. I'm due now at the office. So is — is Jimmy Delevan, but tell him not to come. Grant must take the notes."

His mind was in a turmoil. Should he let Janice stay? Suppose Hale found out that she had come to headquarters disguised as a boy? Fuse to dynamite. What wouldn't he do with the knowledge! But Hale was ordered out on the boat which would stop on its return trip. He would have no time to discover anything. Besides, he would be drowning his anger and disappointment. The readjustment of his own status and that of the other engineers would be difficult enough without having this Janice Trent complication. He must get in touch with her brother. Billy couldn't have known that she was coming. With the remembrance of the feel of her soft hand upon his lips, could he let her go? Most of the men in the outfit were a fine lot, he wasn't afraid of them.

Pasca, his part Indian, part Eskimo servant, who filled the dual rôle of house-boy and mechanic, was shuffling about the cabin living-room when he entered for his papers. His coarse, jet-black hair, above his flat-nosed Mongolian face, was carefully parted and slicked down. His arched brows were heavy and sleek, his dark sharpshooter eyes were set aslant, far apart, his lips were as thick as a negro's. His plaid shirt, blocked with clear red and green, his heavy trousers, had been designed in a New England mill for the Arctic trade.

"Office lighted?"

"Yes sirree!" The stolid face warmed into a smile. "Make heap quick work after Meester Grant tole me. Whole darn outfit come, he say."

"You needn't wait round, Pasca. I will attend to putting out the lights."

The man shuffled about with a typical Indian tread. He looked up under heavy brows, as he dropped an immense log on the fire.

"We all mighty glad you big boss now, yes sirree."

"Thank you. Don't put on any more wood. You'll have me roasted alive."

"Cold later. I know these country. Much number cold nights. But I do what you say." He lingered.

"What is it? Got something on your mind?"

The man's confirmatory grunt deepened the two little lines between Harcourt's brows.

"I got Kadyama on mind."

"What's the matter with him? Doesn't he like helping at the Waffle Shop after his regular work? Want more money?"

Pasca's dark eyes narrowed to glinting slits in his heavy face. "No sirree. He lak helpin' Mees Samp seesters, much good eats. He t'ink he marry on Tatima. He big chief's son. One day Meester Hale tell her she fine gal — Mees Hale off in Seattle — pay her plenty money to keep hees cabin clean. Tatima lak money. She lak beads an' gold nuggets. Now she tell Kadyama, 'Who, me marry on Indian! No sirree! I lak gol'-hair men.' An he say, he get Hale some day. You big boss now. You do somet'ing to mak Tatima lak heem. Save much trouble."

Harcourt's lips tightened as he looked up into the earnest face. Another complication. If he had his way he wouldn't have a woman within a hundred miles of camp, but the Indians and Eskimos wouldn't work unless they could have their families with them. He didn't like that threat to Hale.

"Tell Kadyama to take it easy, Pasca. Hale goes out on the boat day after tomorrow. He'll never come back. Tell him to buy one of Ossa's silver chains for Tatima. It won't take her long to forget that she likes gol'-hair men."

The man's expression lightened. "He go day after tomorrer you say? I tell Kadyama, yes sirree. He t'ink Tatima under spell. Says black cat — black debbil. T'ings happen after he come. Bad! Bad! Bad! He keel him, sometam, p'raps."

He shuffled out. Harcourt looked after him in consternation. He had known that the native laborers regarded the black cat askance, but he hadn't realized that Blot was looked upon with superstition. Better suggest to the Samp sisters that they keep their pet under guard at present.

He wondered if he were as colorless as he felt, as later he faced the men of the outfit, the consulting engineers, the heads of divisions. It happened that they were all at headquarters making preparations for going into the interior. Hale was not present, he noticed with relief.

"What the dickens has Janice done to her hair? I thought it was brown," he caught himself wondering before he directed curtly:

"Take the minutes of the meeting, Grant."

"But, my secretary —"

"Isn't coming." He was conscious of Tubby's grunt of surprise before he called the meeting to order.

As in a haze he read instructions and outlined plans from the data furnished by the authorities. At the close of the meeting while he received the congratulations and commendations of the men, his mind split and ran on two tracks. Even while he laughed and talked, he wondered if Hale suspected, if Grant knew the truth about his secretary.

Later, in the living-room of his cabin, he slipped into a brocaded lounging-robe, crimson as a Harvard banner, girdled like a monk's frock. His taut nerves relaxed as he felt its softness. He had seen it in a shop-window in New York. In a sudden surge of longing to carry a bit of luxurious civilization back with him, he had paid a whacking price for it. It had been money well spent. With the slipping of the garment over his shoulders, steam-shovels, washouts, ditchers and riveters faded into the background. He regarded himself in a small mirror. His head with its clipped dark hair, his bronzed skin with the touch of red at the cheek bones, the fine crinkles at the corners of his eyes, the stern set of his lips seemed strangely incongruous above the rich brocade.

"You should see the fighting line of your mouth," Janice had said that night in New York.

"The present complication won't soften it any, Jan," he thought, as he crossed to the desk which held his mail.

Tubby Grant slammed in. Stopped to stare with open mouth. "Our Hero as the lead in a Broadway comedy! Where'd you get that ritzy outfit, Bruce? Better not let the Indian guides see it or they'll lose you in the wilderness, and come back to fight over your garment." He slouched in an easy chair before the fire.

"What's the big idea cutting out my secretary, Jimmy Delevan, tonight?" His greenish eyes were indignant, his voice aggrieved.

"Delevan! Do you know who Delevan is?"

For an instant the guarded eyes of the two men met. Grant grinned sheepishly.

"I'm not dumb if I am fat."

"Do you know who she is? She's a New York girl."

"How do you know so much about her?"

"I visited her home in college days. Her brother was my best friend."

Grant's whistle was prolonged. "Movie-stuff. Childhood sweethearts reunited in the frozen North. Zowie!"

"Cut out the comedy. This isn't a joke. We met by accident my last evening in New York. In an effort to entertain her I told her what a job I was having to find a secretary for you, described Alaska."

"Sold it to her! I'll bet you soft-pedaled the crude stuff. Didn't mention the fact that occasionally we have a shooting party, that a tidal wave has been known to pick up headquarters in lovin' arms and carry it off to sea, that Kodiak bears have a way of sliding down hill on their haunches to land in a track-laying camp, did you?"

"No. Neither did I relate our experience of three days on an ice-floe, when we lived on walrus meat. But, you may bet your bottom dollar, had I suspected what she had in mind I'd have told those things and a few more."

"You're a spell-binder when you get started with words, Bruce. Well, now after the first repercussion, what are you going to do about it?"

"No use bristling like a turkey-cock, Tubby. My mind's made up. I'll send her back to Seattle."

"Ba-gosh! Don't." The plea was a wail. "Think of the time we had finding a secretary. We've got to get those reports ready. Now that the Crowned Heads back home have gone thrifty, have decided that the situation here as it now exists is one of economic waste, they have called on me to forward the engineers' reports on where savings may be made by the rip-rapping of banks and the raising of grades; the cost of temporary repairing due to floods; a hundred other things. They must have burned the midnight watts thinking up subjects. It isn't humanly possible for me to do more clerical work than I've been doing. She — Jimmy Delevan's a wiz at it. She — he's perfectly safe here with the Samp girls."

"Suppose the men — suppose Hale finds out?"

"The men won't. Those who aren't good fellas are too dumb. Hale is the only one to fear and he is ordered out on the next boat. Did Martha Samp show you that paper?"

"She did."

"It's up to us to shield the girl. Why send her back to the man she ran away from?"

"Shield her? Of course — but how? It's a tricky situation."

"Sleep on it. Shall I talk it over with the Dominie?"

"No! Every person who knows adds to the risk. Tell her — tell Delevan to stay in the Samp cabin till I see — her — him tomorrow. Good-night."

Harcourt stood at the open door watching Grant's stubby figure till it melted into the dusk. What ought he to do? The fact that he wanted Janice to stay, added another complication to the problem. The authorities had O.K.'d a secretary for Grant, but a girl secretary, who had secured the job by masquerading as a boy, might hit them wrong. In that case what wouldn't they do to the chief of the outfit? And he was now the chief, responsible for everything. Some smarty in camp would see that paper, would be keen enough to detect the likeness in the two faces, might notify Paxton in hope of a reward. Paxton would come after her, and then — well, he shouldn't get her. Neither should he find her living a lie. There were two alternatives. Send her back, or acknowledge to the men that she had been sent under false pretenses and have her appear as a girl. She and Tubby could take their choice. That was his decision. He didn't need to sleep on it.

Before he closed the door, he looked off to sea.

The water was as calm as a gigantic mirror. Thin veils of clouds threw fantastic shadows on the snow-capped mountain tops. The light from the high-hung moon transmuted prosaic steam-shovels into silver coaches, sooty engines into magic steeds, every pebble on the beach into a shining nugget. From one of the dormitories drifted the music of a song. Evidently the men were trying out new records which had come in on the boat. New to them, but doubtless already supplanted by later favorites back in that country which they thought of longingly as home. A caressing baritone sang:

" 'Once in a lifetime
Someone comes along
Bringing happiness for two.' "

The song flung wide the door of memory. From it trooped visions of the gay restaurant where he and Janice had dined; the palms and flowers; her lovely wistful face across the table; her eyes, her voice as she had bade him good-night.

" 'Once in a lifetime
Someone comes to you,
Making idle dreams come true.' "

With the last note the light in the dormitory blinked out. From the Indian camp rolled the muffled beat of drums. From the Samp cabin drifted the notes of the melodeon. Harcourt listened. That was not Miss Mary's thrummed out style. Janice must be playing. Janice! She was real. He was not dreaming. The girl was here. On the roof of the world — with him.

5

"Good morning, Bruce!"

With a barely repressed exclamation of annoyance, Harcourt returned the greeting of the woman who smiled at him from the office door. She was small and slender. A stupid-faced little Pekinese peered with beady eyes from under her arm. Her rouged mouth was a trifle pinched, her fair hair was almost as yellow as the smart sports frock and felt hat she wore. From under the brim two feverishly bright violet eyes interrogated him. The brilliant morning sunlight cruelly accentuated the grayish shadows in the cheeks which should have been round, shadows at the base of the slender throat. Pity succeeded his annoyance. He crossed the room, hand extended, his height and leanness emphasized by his khaki shirt and breeches and leather puttees. Tong padded at his heels. His fox-like head was high, his brush curled like a plume over his back. Wide-apart ears pricked, he regarded the snub-nosed Pekinese with brilliant slant eyes. The yelping and yipping of dogs in the kennel yard behind the office drifted in through the open window.

"It's great to see you back again, Mrs. Hale."

Color flooded the thin face. "Mrs. Hale! Why this sudden assumption of ceremony, Mr. Harcourt?"

He laughed. "Business for business hours. I picked up that slogan when I was in the States."

"Does that mean that you'd rather I didn't come here in business hours?"

Remembering Hale's ugly thrust, "Homebreaker!" uncomfortable, feeling like a cad, Harcourt stuck to his guns. Could he warn the little woman without seeming a conceited fool?

"Come out, Millicent. I want to talk to you." As they stood in the strong, warm sunshine outside the door, he regretted gravely:

"I'm sorry about Hale's demotion. He can't have a very friendly feeling toward me. You'd better —"

She shrugged her understanding. "Better keep away from your office, you mean? Why should you be sorry? The best man wins in the end always, doesn't he? I've felt all that I can feel about Joe. When he reached Seattle, I was refreshed, rested. He was like his old self. I had the courage to go on, but since he heard of his demotion he has been unbearable. I suppose I shouldn't have left him alone last winter — they tell me that he was worse than ever — but, I had reached the stage where I couldn't endure my life here another moment. However, I shan't be on your mind much longer. I came to tell you that we are going out on tomorrow's boat, to ask you to help. If I'd known that he was to be sent home, I wouldn't have come back. I don't dare confide in Jimmy: he goes off like a rocket if he thinks me unhappy. Joe says he won't go, but, he's going. I've ceased being a dumb Dora. He's going." Her voice rose on the last word and broke in a sob.

"Take it easy, Millicent. Grant and I will help you get him off. I'll see that Jimmy keeps on the track-laying job till you get away. Perhaps when Joe is back among his own people he'll straighten out."

"Do you think I fool myself? Do you think I believe that a man who has let himself go so far as he has can ever come back? Why, why couldn't he have seen the inevitability of his habit? Surely there are enough horrible examples in this northern country. Oh well, what's the use talking about it. You've been dear to me, Bruce. If only — if only I could stay with you."

Her reckless suggestion sent the blood surging to Harcourt's forehead. He controlled an impulse to look behind him. Suppose Hale overheard? What wouldn't the man do with that admission? He didn't care for himself, but it meant tragedy for her.

"Millicent, you've heard me say before that an engineers' camp was no place for women. I'm mighty glad that you are going back to civilization."

"But you like having the Samp sisters here."

"They are not women, they're ministering angels. I suspect they are fixtures. Were I to banish them and their waffles, I'd have a strike on my hands. I'm going to the shop now to discuss building another cabin for them."

"They've gone maternal over Tubby Grant's secretary, Jimmy Delevan. Have you seen him? He's an effeminate little fellow."

Harcourt with difficulty swallowed his heart which took-off to furiously run its engine in his throat.

"I haven't spoken to the boy. Tubby tells me that he's a wow at his job." They started along the board walk, Tong at their heels, toward the Waffle Shop, connected by a covered passage with the Samp cabin. Millicent Hale stared at the snow-capped mountain with the faint cloud of smoke hovering above it.

"I — hate to leave you here with — with no one to look after you. Sure you don't want me to stay, Bruce?"

"Sure, Millicent."

Color stole over her thin face. With a quick drawn breath she turned away. Harcourt pulled out his handkerchief and wiped beads of perspiration from his forehead. He felt like a brute. Poor little woman, grasping at any hand which would hold her from going on with the man who had failed her. Thank heaven there were situations where the law could rightfully step in and set a wife free — but, would she take advantage of it? She hadn't meant that about staying here with him. It was only that she was crazed with despair. She wouldn't leave Joe Hale to shift for himself, now that he'd lost his job, any more than she would desert a sick child. Hale must go on the boat tomorrow. Tubby and Mallory would help get him off. It wouldn't do for him to appear interested. Life seemed one pitched battle after another. He had a fight on his hands now. His knock on the door of the Samp cabin was grimly imperative.

"Come in."

"Stay outside, Tong." The husky dropped to the ground and regarded him with reproachful eyes.

A slim figure in brown tweed and leather puttees wheeled from a window as Harcourt crossed the threshold of the homey room. From the top of the wing chair the black cat watched his every move with enigmatic emerald gaze.

He closed the door behind him, backed against it as he regarded Janice Trent, alias Jimmy Delevan. The soft yellow mustache had been discarded. Eyes like velvety bronze pansies met his defiantly as the girl demanded in a voice forced to bravado pitch:

"What — what are you going to do with me?"

In the wall mirror he caught a glimpse of his face. It was white, his eyes were blazing. It was no part of his plan to terrify her to death. His attempt at a laugh was a grim failure.

"Why did you come?"

"Suspended sentence? Prisoner to be allowed to be heard in her own defense?"

He took a quick step forward. "Cut out the sarcasm, Jan. Sit down and listen to me." As she snuggled into the enfolding wings of the big chair the black cat touched her hair with a velvet paw.

"Let's not start out as though we were about to fight and die over this. Why did you come here in disguise?"

The girl locked and interlocked her fingers. "Now that your voice and eyes are human, not like those of a tiger about to spring, I'll tell you. Remember the evening you returned my slipper? I had already broken my engagement to Ned Paxton. Early that morning, when he was taking me home from a prenuptial celebration, I demanded the truth of a story which Billy had heard — that two nights before he had wined and dined some notorious show-women in a near-by city. He was insufferably flippant in his answer. Insultingly sure of me. I pushed open the roadster door to jump. He pulled me back, but not my slipper. Then he tried to cajole me into a forgiving mood."

"You didn't forgive him?"

"No. I returned his ring. He laughed. Said that with the marriage but a few days ahead I wouldn't have the nerve to break it off. Assured me in his caressing voice that I was the only girl he had ever asked to marry him. He tried to

73

make me understand that the man who played round with other women was an entirely different self from the one who loved me, that his pursuit of the good and beautiful in me was to his credit. He was almost convincing, but not quite. I told him that not being Reno-minded the double personality argument left me cold. That I would cancel my part of the wedding preparations, he must take care of his. That night, just after you entered the house, he called me on the phone to inform me that he hadn't given me up, that he was sorry that he had pulled rough stuff in the roadster — Ned can be appealingly sorry; it's one of his charms — that he would see me later in the evening, he had pearls for me."

"And then?"

"I saw you. I clutched at your suggestion that we go out for dinner. Suppose my resentment proved but a wooden sword of defense against Ned Paxton's persuasive smile, suppose it broke, I asked myself. If I were out of the house when he came, its strength wouldn't be tested. And then as we talked all my old liking for you, my trust in you, came sweeping back. You sold me Alaska. When you spoke of the secretary you couldn't get I had an inspiration. After my first year in Society with a large S, feeling as futile as a goldfish in a crystal bowl, bored to tears by the ceaseless round of teas and dinners and dances, of ushering here, selling something there, I plunged into a secretarial course and made good, rather exceptionally good. Father lost his money before he died. I had the choice of three alternatives: marriage, living on my brother, or getting a job. The first was no longer to be considered, the second was an impossible situation. Why should I not take that Alaskan position? Remember that I observed that there would be dozens of girls ready to go?"

"I do."

"Don't bite my head off. That was a test question, to get your reaction to the idea of a girl secretary. I got it. It was like water flung on the spark in my mind. I thought it sizzled out. Later in that sleepless night I began to wonder why, if it meant nothing in my life, you should have been the man out of all the hundreds astir in the city to appear at the dramatic moment to pick up my slipper. You had acknowledged that you believed that there was an unknown force in the world which no one as yet understood. That force wouldn't bother with me the second time, I argued, if I were dumb enough to ignore its attempt to help. Was this my chance to earn a living, to escape the publicity which my cancelled wedding would broadcast? Remember that you said that young trees grow more sturdy after transplanting?"

"They don't bring plants from a hothouse to this wilderness and expect them to grow."

"Perhaps they don't, Bruce, but I'll take a chance that I'll flourish. I've seen so many of my friends lose their fineness, crack-up under the strain of the sort of life I've been leading. You said that you would advise any youngster in quest of a career to hop on the Alaskan band-wagon. I'm not a youngster, but I hopped. I reasoned that transplanting might be as beneficial to me as to you, that it might mean the road to happiness and achievement."

Harcourt steeled himself against her charm. "Go on! Explain Jimmy Delevan."

"Mussolini! Holding my nose down to the grindstone of facts, aren't you? I devoted two days to thinking the situation through, while at the same time I superintended the return of wedding presents. I knew that so far as the work went I could do it. I decided to try for the position, to put thousands of miles between myself and Ned Paxton."

"Do you still love him so much?"

"I wonder now if it was love. This northern country has done things to my sense of values. To proceed with the story of my young life — I left New York stealthily — to evade reporters — with my trousseau — almost all of it — I remembered what you said about the chic women — and a few cherished possessions. I had told Billy that I had broken with Paxton. He was white with relief. Then one day I slipped away leaving a note, telling him not to try to find me, that I was going away to stay until after the excitement had blown over, to be near an old friend — that's you."

"And you didn't see Paxton again?"

"See Ned? Not once."

"Go on."

"That was what I did. I went on to Seattle. It had seemed delightfully easy when I planned it. Imagine my amazed consternation when I found that the agency at which I applied would not send a girl to an engineers' camp in Alaska. A man had been demanded and a man would be sent. The agent glared at me with such suspicion that I scrunched like a gypsy worm beneath the heavy heel of his disapproval."

"At least there is one man in the business with sense."

"Don't growl; you cramp my narrative style." She disciplined a nervous laugh. "Because my imagination began to project all sorts of hazardous risks I determined to crash through or perish in the attempt. I won't give in to a fear complex — ever again. I settled down to constructive thinking. I remembered a newspaper story of an English woman who for years had passed herself off as a man, remembered that because of the husky note in my voice I had taken men's parts in dramatics. Good old subconscious had done the trick. I would apply as a boy. A dye for my hair, a low drawn hat, Prince of Wales style, tweed suit, a hectic, a super hectic flush on my cheeks to suggest a reason for my exile, and lo, Jimmy Delevan evolved."

"You need a guardian!"

"From what Tubby Grant confided this morning I suspect that I am about to acquire one. Don't growl, Bruce."

Harcourt passed his hand over his face as though by the gesture he could smooth the perplexities from his mind.

"And one darnfool agent fell for you?"

"With a groan of relief he swallowed me, bait, hook and sinker, signed me on the dotted line."

"Did you come up on the boat as a boy?"

"Don't roar. Of course I didn't. I'm not quite a dumbbell. I had two days to wait before the boat sailed. I invested some of my ancestral gold in a movie-camera — I'm planning to tour the country as a lecturer when I get back to civilization — packed the disguise carefully in a steamer trunk and engaged a reservation in the name of J. Delevan. That was noncommittal. When the ship was in sight of headquarters I dressed as a boy again, and with the agent's letter clutched in my hand prepared to give you the grand surprise of your life."

"You succeeded."

"But not as I had planned. The agent had said that he would cable you when I sailed. I expected you to meet me. Instead Mr. Grant appeared. I couldn't tell him. What would he think? He tried to be kind, but he couldn't conceal his disappointment as he looked at me. He said that he had orders to join you at the bridge, did I think I was strong enough for the trip? Before I could answer he told me that the Samp sisters were also going. My spirits mounted like a balloon. I assured him that I was rarin' to go, or words to that effect."

"I have no words in which to express my opinion of your infernal recklessness in coming to this wilderness!"

"You are doing fairly well. Stop pacing the floor as though you were an Alaskan bear and listen. I'll acknowledge that for a moment the silence, the wildness, the terrific expanse of land, sea and sky got me by the throat. I hadn't had the slightest conception of what the word Alaska stood for, this part of it. When later I thought of the clothes I had brought — trunks of them — ordered and designed for the prospective wife of a millionaire, the table linen and bedding I had selected from my bountiful supply, for the first time in my life I touched the borderland of hysterics. I laughed till I cried. But I licked the fear-complex. I'm here."

She rose laughing, exultant, lovely. "And I have made good, yes? Haven't I, Mr. Grant?" she demanded of the man who entered the cabin with the husky at his heels. The dog thrust his nose into the girl's hand. Every hair of Blot, the black cat, bristled as though electrified.

"I'll say you have. What's he going to do?"

Harcourt looked from Grant's round, smooth face, with its belligerent green eyes, to Janice's. A man like Paxton wouldn't let such a lovely girl slip away. She was safe here. The outfit needed her.

"Sentence!" she demanded impatiently. "I

hate to be kept in suspense. Sentence!"

"Jimmy Delevan goes."

At Grant's sharp protest and an indignant exclamation from Janice he held up his hand.

"Wait a minute! Your secretary stays, Tubby, but only as Miss Trent. And if she stays she will do exactly as I say." Ignoring her indignant protest, he went on: "Make up your mind to it — otherwise there is a boat going out tomorrow — and you go with it."

Color stained her face as she looked down at her tweed suit.

"What's the matter now? Haven't you other clothes?" Harcourt demanded with excusable impatience.

"My entire trousseau from soup to savory. I — I was only wondering what explanation you could make to the men."

"Late to think of that. However, I'll undertake to straighten out the tangle. Fortunately, Hale goes back on the boat tomorrow."

"Mrs. too, of course?"

"Yes, Tubby."

Harcourt felt himself redden as he met the question in Grant's eyes. Did he think there was truth in that malicious accusation of Joe Hale's? His jaw set grimly. How a feminine invasion could mess up a situation! His turmoil of mind was reflected in his voice.

"Does Jimmy Delevan go or does Miss Trent stay?"

"Miss Trent stays," the girl assured promptly.

"Then she is not to report for work until after the boat goes out tomorrow." Without waiting for an answer Harcourt crossed to the door. Tong lingered on the threshold to cast a biding-my-time glance over his shoulder at the bristling black cat before he followed his master.

Had he been a weak fool to allow her to stay? Harcourt asked himself as he followed a winding path through a well cleared field to the hangar. At the open door he stopped to give directions to Pasca and Kadyama who were fueling and cleaning the amphibian within. His perplexity was submerged in a glow of satisfaction as he regarded it. The authorities had provided a flock of planes of different makes and sizes, but this great winged thing was in a class of its own. In order to permit of operation in very rough water and to minimize injury from driftwood, an exceptionally strong and thick metal bottom had been provided. A touch on a control, and landing gear dropped, enabling it to taxi up a pebbly beach, or across a flying field. This was an especially desirable feature for surveying in the northern country. The landing wheels tucked away into the sides when alighting or taking off from the sea. The body was a bright yellow with the name of the outfit in huge black letters. It was equipped to carry a pilot and three passengers and enough fuel for a twenty-four-hour cruise.

As he walked toward his office Harcourt's thoughts returned to Janice Trent. A lovely girl would raise the dickens with the men's attention to work. Tubby argued that she was needed. She was, but he turned his motives inside out for inspection. He had wanted her to stay. No intangible presence seemed to stand between him and her. Had it been the memory of little Jan Trent which had guarded the entrance to his heart all these years? Every time she had moved her hand he had felt its satin softness against his lips. And she had run away from her prospective bridegroom because she didn't trust him, yet loved him so much she didn't dare stay. His lips tightened. He paraphrased the creed of the rollicking Russians in the time of Baranof:

"God's in his heaven and Paxton is far away."

The Hales would be off tomorrow. Millicent was sweet and much to be pitied, but she had claws, and he had a conviction that she would scratch deep and raggedly where other women were concerned. She had reigned as queen in this outpost camp. She would not abdicate gracefully. These very human men would quickly transfer their allegiance from a married woman to a charming girl. Well, she was going, Hale was going, two of his problems would sail out with the tide when the boat weighed anchor at dawn.

At the door of his office he collided with a man coming out. His red face registered relief.

"Been looking for you everywhere, Chief."

"What's wrong'?"

"Hale! Had a slight shock. We radioed to

82

Fairbarks to ask if we should take him to the hospital by plane. Answer came, 'No! Keep him there.' "

"We can't keep him here."

"Search me. Mrs. Hale says he'll go tomorrow if he goes on a stretcher — but the Doc will have the say."

6

"Where were we, Miss Trent?" Theodore Grant Junior tilted back in a chair beside the typewriter desk in the administration office he and Bruce Harcourt shared at headquarters.

Janice read from her note-book. " 'Re: Ditching gang No. 2 —' "

"O.K. Get this: Ditching gang No. 2, operating ditcher No. 25 loaded approximately 3500 cubic yards of gravel at pit at mile 207.8 and about 1500 cubic yards at mile 265 for ballast in the vicinity of the pits."

His voice went on and on till steam-shovel gangs and ditching gangs filed in endless procession through the girl's mind. She stopped for an instant to flex her fingers. Grant noted the surreptitious action.

"I'm sorry. You're such a bird at it I forget that you're not a machine. That will do for the present. Get those reports ready. I'll be in later to give them the once-over and my signature."

He picked up his papers. As he rose, Tong, who had been dozing in a pool of sunlight, sprang to his feet, thrust a cold nose into his hand, looked up at him with hooded slant eyes. Grant patted the tawny head absentmindedly as he glanced out of the window. The businesslike crispness of his voice changed to companionable friendliness.

"Ba-gosh! There's Millicent Hale. I wish she'd stop hanging round here. She's after Bruce, I'll bet my hat. She's getting on his nerves. He's pretty edgy. My mistake. She's gone on, to the Waffle Shop probably, praise be to Allah!"

"Is Mr. Harcourt — are they —"

"They are not. But, Joe Hale is sore. If he could find the least flaw in the character of his successor, our villain without portfolio would laugh his head off. His own career has ended in disgrace. There have been some fierce rows among the Crowned Heads because through influence he has been kept on the job; some of them are seeing red. One breath of scandal about Harcourt and they'd chop his professional head off with a blow. Our Hero's got a big career before him if he has half a chance. Sometimes I get the heebe-jeebes, feel as though we were all walking on the thin crust above a volcano which, sooner or later, is bound to erupt with a bang. I've been uneasy as the dickens since Jimmy Chester came back to headquarters. It's because Hale is still hanging on. Sometimes I wonder if he's faking helplessness. People have recovered from slight shocks quickly. I don't know why I'm blowing off steam to you. Forget it. Get those reports ready as soon as possible."

He departed. Tong bestowed a moist doggy kiss upon Janice's hand before he followed at his heels. She thoughtfully watched the man and dog out of sight. The usually ebullient Tubby was troubled about his chief. Unnecessarily troubled, she decided. How could any sane person look at Bruce Harcourt and believe for an instant that he would be dishonorable? But, Hale probably wasn't sane when he thought of his successor. After all, it wouldn't be surprising if Bruce had fallen in love with the only attractive white woman on location or she with him when one realized the sort of man to whom she was tied. He had said the night they had dined together in New York:

"Life — human life in Alaska — is no different from life in other places. People are born, die, marry and divorce, love and hate, the last two a little harder, perhaps, than when nearer civilization."

She clasped her hands behind her head, tipped back in her chair, regarded the moss-chinked walls, the old-time Yukon stove, which made the modern filing cabinets seem blatantly *nouveau riche*, the high desk at which the chief of the outfit worked when he was in the office. Through the open window she could see the kennels and the huskies in the yard, some rollicking, some soaking in sunshine, some yelping. Beyond them a ditcher was lumbering inland like a prehistoric monster trailing its prey. Her eyes traveled on to the sun and shadow sectored world. Fair weather after a week of gray mist, of the sound of a sullen surf pounding on the shore. Inexplicably the trickily bland blue sea chilled her; the snow-capped mountains oppressed her; the clamor of steam-shovels and rivets seemed sordid and unbearable. The land breeze blew in from the natives' quarters laden with the smell of drying tom-cod, of simmering seal-blubber. The innumerable stakes which indicated prospective boulevards and imposing municipal buildings — now on paper — which sanguine promoters declared would make this remote spot on an Alaskan inlet a railroad terminal which would revolutionize the great white north — seemed a grisly joke. One day passed after another as monotonously alike as sardines packed in a tin. For an instant she was devastatingly homesick for the glittering show of Fifth Avenue, for the purr of luxurious automobiles, the music and laughter of tea-time, the flash of jewels.

A plane droned far overhead. She could see it, a gigantic bird against the blue dome. Bruce? Her mood changed. Silly to think for an instant that he would be interested in another man's wife. What a glorious world! How purple the cloud shadows were upon the mountains! Did that smoky smooch mean that old Katmal was erupting again?

Months had passed since the night Bruce Harcourt had returned her slipper, had brought vividly to mind her childish adoration of him. When he had stepped out upon the stage of her life again he had seemed a divine answer to her prayer to know what was right to do. Their paths crossed. Immediately the pattern of her life was changed. Her trust, her belief in him, in his power to surmount obstacles, surged up from her subconscious where it had lain quiescent through the years. He knew what he wanted and went after it. Why shouldn't she do the same? He had made Alaska seem a paradise where men and women lived full, clean, purposeful lives. Through a labyrinth of picturesque sounds and straits, by glaciers and totempoled villages, she had sailed north thrilled, eager, happy, that she would be financially independent of her brother, that she had burst the chains of fascination which had shackled her, to crash into this enterprise. Had she realized the immensity of the wilderness, the rawness of this camp with its mixture of educated men, life-licked derelicts, oily Eskimos, furtive slit-eyed Indians, would she have come?

The way which had threatened to be rough with complications had smoothed out like a trotting-park when she had seen the Samp sisters. She had told them the truth at once. Gaunt Miss Martha's agate eyes had disappeared in a network of fine lines.

"If you're bent on keeping this job, tell Harcourt the truth, quick, or he'll send you back hummin'. Keep clear of Hale; he might — well, just keep clear of him, that's all."

Three weeks had passed since she had discarded her disguise and gone to the office in one of the sports suits of her trousseau. The engineers had greeted her with smiling courtesy, the workmen with sheepish grins. What explanation had Bruce Harcourt made to them? As usual the brunt of the burden had fallen on him. She had her own log house now, connected by a covered passage with the Samp cabin. It had gone up as by magic after Bruce had decided that she might stay. Sometimes at night when she couldn't sleep because of the long, long twilight, of strange rustlings in the chinked walls, the frenzied barking of huskies, the sombre muffled beat of Indian drums, the far faint howl of a wolf, perhaps the sharp yelp of a coyote on the trail of game, the memory of the manner in which she had forced herself into the outfit set her aching with mortification. Bruce had been right. It was no place for a girl — even a modern of the moderns. It was a primitive world and values were different. Then she would stoutly justify her presence to herself.

"I do help. I do. They couldn't get anyone else!"

However, those moments of depression came only in the night. Why was it, when one couldn't sleep, one thought of all the pesky little misfortunes which might occur, instead of radiant possibilities? With the day's activities returned a Monte Cristo, the world-is-mine, assurance.

Bruce had commanded her to keep out of sight till Hale had sailed and then — Hale hadn't sailed. The physician from Fairbanks had decided that it would be a risk to move him, that he would be better where he was, had warned him against excitement, letting his temper get the best of him. Was his wife in love with Bruce Harcourt? Was he in love with her? Had Millicent Hale been one of the lures which kept him in this northern wilderness? Did she resent the presence in camp of another woman of his class? Even light-hearted Tubby Grant was troubled by the situation.

"But to every man there openeth
 A high way and a low;
And every man decideth
 The way his soul shall go."

Memory broadcast the verse. There was no doubt which way Bruce had chosen. Faint color mounted to her hair as she remembered the fascination that Ned Paxton, a man who had not chosen the high way, had had for her. Who was she to condemn another woman for a poor choice? She herself had broken away before it was too late. Had she? Suppose Ned were to come into her life again? She had tried time and again to visualize his face. It just wouldn't materialize. She couldn't conjure up his voice. Had change of scene, like a piece of blotting-paper, soaked up all her memories of him? She forced her thoughts back to her distrust of Mrs. Hale. Aside from the fact that she, Janice Trent,

90

had procured the position she wanted under false pretenses — a position in which she was making royally good, she flung that sop to her uneasy conscience — what could the wife of the demoted chief say about her? Suppose she were to hear of her engagement, broken at the last minute? What capital could she make of that? What was a broken engagement in this divorced-while-you-wait era.

What did Bruce Harcourt think of it all? He was rarely in the office. One day he would be up the inlet in the launch to inspect the damage done by the rise of a stream, next he would be off with a section-gang and a steam-shovel; perhaps before forty-eight hours had elapsed he would be miles away inspecting the work of a ditcher. Not once had he entered the Samp cabin which had become the evening rendezvous for the engineers. Why didn't he join them? Why did he treat Tubby Grant's secretary with distant courtesy? Her leisure time was full. Jimmy Chester was teaching her to shoot; Tubby was patiently training her to be a fairly efficient photographer; the geologist of the outfit provided her with a hammer and showed her how to get at the secrets pebbles and rocks had concealed within them. What fun she and Bruce might have together.

The ring of the telephone brought her iridescent day-dream and the front legs of her chair down in a simultaneous crash. She answered the call.

"Office."

"Hale speaking. Is this Miss Trent?"

"Yes."

"Will you take pity on a poor duffer who's been forbidden to write and take a letter or two for me?"

"Certainly, Mr. Hale. When?"

"At once if you will. I want it ready to go in the first plane that takes off."

"I will come."

As she removed protecting shields from the piqué cuffs of her beige jersey frock — Miss Martha had views as to her tax on laundry facilities — and picked up her note-book, she wondered what Tubby and Bruce would say about her going. What could she have done but consent? She had a great curiosity to see the deposed chief.

She had a sense of breathlessness as she pushed open the door of the Hale cabin. Joe Hale was seated in a wheel-chair near a window. A shaft of sunlight brought out gold and copper glints in his fair hair, etched deeper the lines in his face, ravaged by dissipation and depression. A brilliant Yakutat blanket was over his knees, an immaculate white shirt and an impeccable tie showed between the revers of a dark green lounging-robe. He would have been good-looking had he lived decently, Janice told herself in that first glance. She didn't quite care for the little flames which leaped in his eyes as they met hers. She had seen that blaze in the eyes of men before and had hurriedly crossed to the other

92

side of the street in spirit.

"Good of you to come, Miss Trent, particularly as I now have no claim on your time. Feel like a boob not to bring up a chair for you, but the doctors won't let me take a step. Tyrants! Mrs. Hale ran over to see the Samp girls fifteen minutes ago. Seized this chance to get an outline made for a codicil to my will. Not that I have the least intention of passing out, but, I've had a tap on the shoulder." He opened a brief case on a stand beside him and pulled out some papers.

Curious that his explanation left her with the same sense of uneasiness which had seized her as she entered the cabin, Janice thought. Of course it was nothing but her hectic imagination taking the bit in its teeth again. As she turned for a chair, she looked about the room. It was attractive, homelike, with no sense of over-crowding. She could care for that gorgeous screen before the door leading, she presumed, to another cabin; it must have come straight from the Orient. The stone fireplace was good too. That single massive blue jar filled with stalks of golden berries, on one end of the mantel picked up the groundwork in the cretonne hangings. Was smoke coming from that pipe laid on the mantel? Had Mrs. Hale been gone fifteen minutes? Would tobacco keep hot that long? If she were away and Hale himself couldn't move, who had put it there?

It seemed as though she stared at the betraying smoke ages, but it couldn't have been more than

93

an instant as the man in the sunshine still rattled his papers. She looked at him as she placed the chair. Tubby had said: "Sometimes I wonder if he's faking helplessness." Was he faking? Was he? she asked herself. If so, why? Was he scheming against Bruce?

He selected a paper. "Here is the memorandum of what I want to dictate. You look as though you could keep a secret, Miss Trent. Beautiful women as a rule are dumb; I'll bet my gold nuggets you're an exception. I kiss your hands — in spirit."

She had heard that caressing inflection before too, she told herself, with a bitter little twist of her lips. If he wanted to impress her with a sense of friendliness, not in the manner of Ned Paxton should he approach her. She responded in her crispest voice.

"A secretary is supposed to be a machine, not a person when taking dictation, Mr. Hale. Ready."

She tried to remain indifferent to the meaning of the codicil she was transcribing, but it was startling. He interpolated remarks into his dictation, as to his longing for a home, his intention to settle down and become a solid citizen, his private fortune. He paid her several fulsome compliments. She sensed a chuckle behind the words as though he were in possession of a secret. Trying to make her realize that he knew from whence she had come and why she had come? Whatever he was insinuating he was boring.

Once she stopped him.

"Please keep to the dictation, Mr. Hale; you confuse me."

"My mistake, Miss Trent. I've been shut up here so long that it's a temptation to be garrulous. Where were we? Oh yes — close with, 'This is —'"

Plop! Plop! Plop! Plop! Plop! Plop! The sounds came from behind the screen. Small revelatory crashes that meant but one thing. A broken string of beads. So, Mrs. Hale was at home. Listening. What was the big idea? By a supreme effort of will Janice kept her voice indifferent.

"What was that?"

Was it imagination or did Hale relax?

"Buttons. That nitwit dog of Millicent's has upset her work-basket again."

A brilliant blue bead rolled soundlessly across the rug and stopped behind his chair. Janice brought her teeth sharply into her lip to keep back an exclamation. Tatima! Tatima was behind the screen.

Hale's suave voice broke into her reflections. "So, you ran away from marriage. Kiss and run type, yes?"

Janice's blood sang in her ears from fury. She managed to keep her voice steady.

"Go on with your dictation, Mr. Hale. I have left important work at the office."

"Where were we? I remember. That's all." He pulled a thick roll from his coat pocket. Peeled off a ten-dollar bin. "Take this. I've no right to your time."

Janice rose. "Thank you, no. I will type the material at once and send it for you to look over."

"Efficient, aren't you? I'd thought of letting the deserted bridegroom know where you were, but, we need you here."

She looked steadily back at him as she snapped the rubber band on her note-book.

"May I suggest that you mind your own business?"

The force with which she closed the door behind her relieved her overcharged spirit. In her dash from the cabin she collided with Jimmy Chester. His thin, worn face was white, his gloomy dark eyes were smoldering coals as he caught her by the shoulder.

"Someone told me that you were here. What do you mean by coming when Millicent is at the Samps'?"

For an instant Janice stared incredulously. Then she twisted herself free. She vented the remainder of her fury on him.

"What business is it of yours why I went there?"

"I'll make it my business," he answered savagely and pulled open the cabin door.

Her breath was still coming raggedly when she reached the office. She gazed unseeingly out of the window. Why had Hale sent for her when his wife was out? Was that codicil the real thing or had he used it as an excuse? How did he dare carry such a wad of money in this camp? Who had told Jimmy Chester where she was? Bruce would better send him off laying tracks again or there would be trouble. His brother-in-law was getting on his nerves. Why had Tatima been behind the screen? Had the Indian girl laid the lighted pipe on the mantel or had Hale been standing there when she had rapped on the door? What would be his object in pretending invalidism. Should she tell Bruce and Tubby her suspicions?

Harcourt loomed in the doorway. "Good morning." He crossed to his desk. Two little lines deepened between his brows as he opened letters. Had he even heard her reply to his greeting, Janice wondered. A shadow fell across the floor. He looked up from his papers. Smiled.

"Good morning, Mrs. Hale. How's Joe?"

Millicent Hale stood in the doorway. Under one arm was her toy Pekinese. Her haunted eyes were smooched with shadows as violet as her frock. Her lips drooped. Her slim body sagged. Her laugh was as unsteady as her hands, yet her voice held the assurance of a woman confident of her welcome, secure in her charm.

"I know that I'm breaking rules, your rules, coming to the office, Bruce, but I'm desperate. I — I —" she bit her lips, clenched her frail hands as though with all her being she were holding back a flood of emotion. "Tubby Grant told me that you and he were to air-trot tomorrow, were to scout out a place on the river from which to start the road toward the new bridge. That after that you would fly to the city. Take me. I'm fed-up on myself, on everything in this terrible wilderness. I haven't left our cabin for more than an hour since Joe's break-down, my nerves are on edge. If I go I can get some things he needs. Mary Samp promised to look after him. Why not take Miss Trent, that is if Argus of the Hundred Eyes will let her go."

Whom had she meant by that jibe? Including her in the party was an after-thought, Janice deduced, even as she answered:

"Nice of you to think of me, Mrs. Hale, but — wouldn't two women be frightfully in the way on an exploring expedition?"

"It's not an exploring expedition, it's a scouting party." Millicent Hale slipped her hand under Harcourt's arm. "Please take me — us, Bruce."

Her voice, her wistful lips, her misty eyes set off fiery pinwheels of anger in Janice's mind. Harcourt smiled indulgently. Men were pulp, mere pulp, in the hands of a soft, purry, "little woman" like that, the girl told herself furiously.

"Do you realize that we start at sun-up? That we won't land till we get to the city at breakfast time?"

Hooey! His voice hadn't been so smooth as that when he had spoken to her a moment ago. He was stooping to parley. Millicent Hale sensed her advantage, pressed it eagerly.

"All the more fun. You will take me — us, won't you?"

"If Miss Trent will come. Care to go air-trotting, Miss Trent?"

Fly! Janice throttled her imagination, attested fervently:

"I'd love it."

"Then it's a date. Be sure you're ready on time. The plane starts the minute the sun pokes its rim above the horizon, passengers or no passengers."

With eager assurance of a prompt appearance Millicent Hale departed. As Bruce Harcourt returned to his desk, Janice inquired:

"What did she mean by 'If Argus of the Hundred Eyes will let her go'?"

His grave face broke into laughter. "Forgotten your mythology? Argus was the watch-dog of Olympus, the favored mountain of the greater gods and goddesses. The engineers have dubbed Martha Samp Argus of the Hundred Eyes. Get the connection?"

"Do they mean — that she's guarding me?"

His jaw tightened, the smile left his eyes. "I mean that Martha Samp — Argus of the Hundred Eyes — is all that stands between you and a quick return to civilization. You know you shouldn't be here. I know it. While we're on this subject I'll suggest that you go slow with Jimmy Chester."

A little demon of contrariness took possession of Janice. She thoughtfully nibbled the end of her fountain pen, as she looked up with ingenuous eyes.

"I'm surprised that you don't include Tubby Grant in the taboo."

"Tubby's immune. He's working to prove to a girl back home that he can make good. Jimmy's different."

Janice indulged in a delicately regretful sigh. "He is fascinating even if his eyes are tragically old."

Harcourt left his desk, loomed over her. "Attractive! Jimmy's a corking engineer, but he's pulp where girls are concerned. The war left his eyes old and his temperament slightly twisted. You might as safely play with high explosives. He's the type who would do something desperate if he got the wrong slant."

Her laughing voice challenged. "You wouldn't, would you?"

His eyes darkened. "We were talking about Chester. Watch your step."

"Is that a threat or a warning?"

"Neither. It's a reminder."

7

Squatted cobbler-fashion on the cot bed in her cabin Janice regarded herself in the roughly framed mirror above a dressing-table fashioned from a packing-box. Even the gay chintz cover couldn't disguise its strictly humble, if useful, beginnings. The looking-glass faithfully reflected the sheen of her dahlia satin pajama coat, the orchid of blouse and trousers, the soft rose of the brocade bedspread. As though brushed in with living colors, caught there, held there, her figure stood out, clean-cut against an impressionistic background of log walls.

She barely breathed as she met the mirrored eyes. Who was that girl really? What was she? Did she herself know what lay deep in her mind? What profundities of passion and sorrow, love and hate smoldered within her visible body? She had come north in quest of a different self, a fearless self. Had she found it? At least she had exposed her mind to new ideas to a drastic reversal of her mode of luxurious living. Where was it taking her? Bruce had warned her to watch her step. Should she have told him that she had been to Hale's cabin? No. He might resent it and the feeling between the two men was sufficiently bitter as it was. Why had Jimmy Chester been so furious? She wouldn't admit it to Bruce but he had been waxing uncomfortably sentimental of late. She had treated him with the same friendliness she had bestowed on the other engineers, he was beginning to resent their presence in the Samp living-room in the evening. She was conscious that Millicent Hale was warily watching their friendship. She had had her Pekinese under her arm when she had stopped at the office door. A basket overturned by the little dog, Hale had explained the scatter of beads. Buttons! He hadn't seen that straying bit of blue glass. Why had Tatima been behind the screen?

Her glance dropped to the profusion of silver and rose enameled appointments on the dressing-table. Over the room it traveled, past the rough wall to the wash-stand, with its elaborately monogrammed towels, came back to the mirror.

"Bruce was right; you shouldn't be here with this absurd paraphernalia — absurd for this camp. You ought to have the sense to wear a flannel bath coat when you rest after work, but these gay things pep you up and help keep up your morale, don't they? They put color and romance into quiet Miss Mary's life too; they're making her style-conscious, they and the fashion magazines for which you subscribed when you knew that you were coming into the wilderness — not that you had the slightest conception of what it really was, Miss Trent. No matter what anyone says or thinks, my dear, keep on changing for evening as you would at home. It might grow easy to be careless and sloppy in this wilderness, and a sloppy woman's the meanest work of God."

Through the open window drifted the notes of a bugle. Retreat! She jumped from the bed to watch the slowly lowered Stars and Stripes gathered in by outstretched hands. She blinked her long lashes, swallowed hard. The sight of the Colors in this northern frontier tightened her throat.

Light as day. Thin clouds like torn veils streaked the sky. No sign of rain. All indications pointed to a perfect day for tomorrow's flight. Bruce hadn't appeared madly enthusiastic at the prospect of taking women passengers. Why worry? He had consented to their going, that was enough. It would be the first time she had been far from headquarters since her arrival. She had been up the inlet a way in the motorboat, had taken long tramps with Jimmy Chester and the geologist over the rough roads, but tomorrow she would fly hundreds of miles. It seemed unbelievable.

Dishes were rattling in the Waffle Shop. That meant that supper preparations were going forward. She'd better slip into her gown. Miss Martha would be sending a tray into the living-room shortly. The Samp sisters would not permit her to step foot in the Shop when the men were eating there. She was guarded with nine-teenth-century standards of propriety. They were dears. Could she ever repay them for their kindness?

Kadyama was filling the wood-box in the living-room, she could hear him shuffling back and forth. Regular as clockwork. One could tell the time by his coming and going. A curious character. Sardonic. Taciturn. She avoided him when she could.

What was that sound? Coat half off, she listened. Something running round and round like mad. Blot having a fit?

She thrust her arm back into the satin sleeve, dashed through the passage, stopped on the threshold of the livingroom. Overturned chairs waved legs in air as though in exercise of their Daily Dozen. Spools rolled on the floor from the overturned work-basket. A slammed door cut a terrified "Meow!" in half.

Blot! Blot had been kidnapped! By Kadyama? Hadn't Bruce said that the natives feared the cat as they did the Evil Spirit? It would break the Samp girls' hearts if anything happened to their pet. Could she rescue it?

She jerked open the door, ran in pursuit of a bent, scurrying figure hooded in a brilliant Yakutat blanket. The tip of a lashing black tail hung below it. Where was the Indian taking the cat?

Janice's breath came unevenly, the wide, full trousers swished about her feet, the strap of one parchment-kid sandal snapped. "Darn!" She was neither shod nor costumed for a rescue stunt, she told herself with an hysterical giggle. Silly, just as though clothes mattered if she could save Blot from harm. Not that she liked the cat. To her mind he was the last word in treachery. But she couldn't stand by and see the Samp girls hurt. Where was the man going? Was she the only person on location who saw him? He had passed the Waffle Shop without being noticed. To the kennels? They were back of the office. Surely someone there would see him. What was the kidnapper's idea? He didn't intend — he did! He did!

Her shout of protest cracked in her dry throat — for all the world as though she were shrieking for help in a nightmare — as a struggling, kicking, spitting black ball was flung with terrific force into the yard where a dozen or more slant-eyed, ruby-tongued huskies were yipping and yelping and rollicking. They stiffened to rigidity as they regarded the motionless black heap. A trimly built Siberian broke the spell with a joyous yelp. He nosed the stunned cat, tossed it. A husky with baleful yellow eyes caught it, sent it whirling back. Like a shuttlecock it flew from dog to dog to an accompaniment of barks and growls.

For a split second Janice hesitated as imagination projected a picture of herself being torn to ribbons. The kidnapper has vanished. Then she fumbled frantically at the gate. They would kill

Blot. Where was the trick latch? She had it. She dashed into the midst of the excited tormentors, caught the black cat in the air, held it high as the dogs sprang for her. Gleeful yelps deepened to menacing growls. She backed toward the gate. Two or three huskies, she couldn't tell how many, sneaked behind her. Her heart pounded in her throat. She didn't know much about dog psychology, but she knew enough not to run.

Claws ripped at her dahlia jacket, at her satin trousers. She lost a parchment sandal. The slim gray Siberian carried it off, worrying it as he went. She backed cautiously, saying over and over, soothingly:

"Nice boys! Down! Down!"

Her lips were too stiff to voice command. The husky with the baleful glare stalked toward her in a sullen wolf-walk, lips lifting in spasmodic snarls. Suddenly he reared. His goldflecked eyes were on a level with hers, his wrinkled nose bared yellowed fangs. Sneering at her, was he? Would she ever get outside that fence? Miss Martha would say, "There's a gate in every wall, my dear." There was in this one if she could only make it. The wolf-dog was leaping —

"Drop the cat! Good God! Drop the cat! At him, Tong!"

Janice was conscious of a tawny shape flashing by her, of the impact of bodies, of a yelp of pain before an arm was flung about her shoulders. She looked up into eyes blazing in a face, livid, lined. Bruce! Of course. Hadn't he appeared at the exact psychical moment to pick up her black slipper? She still clutched the cat as he drew her outside the gate.

She looked over her shoulder. Tong, his brush hanging straight, fangs bared, beautiful head lowered, glared at the dogs cringing away from him. She controlled a shiver.

"Come on."

She looked up at Bruce Harcourt whose fingers bit into her arm.

"I'm going as fast as I can with one sandal. This ground isn't a trotting-park."

She glanced down at her silk-stockinged foot, regarded incredulously her shredded pajamas. She laughed, sobbed, laughed again.

"Stop it! You'll have hysterics in a moment."

Her voice caught treacherously in the midst of indignant denial. Without warning, Harcourt picked her up in his arms. She tried to free herself.

"Stop wriggling. You're heavy enough as it is."

"I can walk. It's absurd to carry me."

His look burned her voice to a thread. She thought "My word, but he's furious! Will this escapade mean the next boat out for Tubby's secretary?"

Breathing hard, he set her on her feet in the living room of the Samp cabin. He closed the door and backed up against it. His face was darkly red as he demanded:

"Don't you know better than to run round this

camp dressed in those things? I saw you from the office window. Couldn't believe my eyes. Look at yourself."

Still clutching the black cat who was stirring in her arms, Janice looked. The dahlia sleeves were ripped from shoulders to wrists. Through slashes in the orchid satin of the trousers, her flesh showed ivory smooth. Lucky that the dogs hadn't dug into her skin with their claws. Of course Bruce hadn't thought of that, he was too concerned with her costume. She blinked furiously to keep back nervous tears. She knew from experience that fright did things to a man's temper, but this was the limit. Wasn't it sufficiently maddening to have one's clothes ruined without being bawled out for it? Her eyes flashed to his.

"What's the matter with the sartorial effect? There's a classic simplicity about it which intrigues me. If I had on a bathing suit you wouldn't be shocked to see my skin. Think I was running out to the kennels for exercise? Someone came into this room and kidnapped Blot. I heard the scuffle. Doubtless you would have stopped to change your tie and brush your hair. My one thought was to rescue the Samp girls' pet. Those dogs nearly ate me up and you stand there glowering at me because I'm not properly dressed! Now you'll threaten to send me out on the next boat. It's the best thing you do. Well, I won't go. I'll stay —"

With a furious lunge for freedom Blot flung up

a spiked paw, clawed her cheek from brow to chin. With a cry of pain Janice dropped him.

"Demon! You ungrateful —"

Harcourt flung an arm about her half-bare shoulders. "Jan! Jan, dear! That infernal cat!" His voice broke. He pulled forward a chair. "Sit here. Don't touch it, dear, don't touch it. I'll bring something to ease the pain."

His voice was shaken, his face taut, colorless. He was no longer furious, that was something to the good, the girl told herself. She gently touched her cheek. Bleeding, of course. Smarting unbearably. From under the couch Blot peered at her with inscrutable emerald eyes. It eased the ache to pick up a spool, a large spool, and fling it at him.

"The next time you're kidnapped, little one, you'd meow your black head off before you'll get help from me." Harcourt entered with a bowl in one hand, scissors and gauze in the other. "Don't bother with me, Bruce. I was so stunned by Blot's ingratitude that my mind stopped clicking. I'll take care of the scratch myself."

"Sit still." He drew up a chair, set the bowl on it, dipped a piece of gauze in the liquid it contained, bent over her. "This will make it smart like the dickens at first."

"Like the dickens" was expressing it mildly. Janice shut her eyes tight to keep back tears as he gently swabbed her cheek. His touch was gentle, steady. She might have known it would be. Even as a child she had loved the feel of his strong, finely kept hands.

"Hurting unbearably, Jan?"

She opened her eyes, managed a twisted smile. "Can't say that I would choose it for an indoor sport. My face is getting stiffer and stiffer. Will the scratch leave a scar? I hadn't thought of that before."

"Not if you take care of it. Miss Martha will tell you what to do. That's all. I won't touch it again."

He seemed extraordinarily tall and stern in his old shirt, corduroy breeches and polished puttees as he loomed over her. If only he would be friendly, stay and talk it over, she thought wistfully. Whenever they were together, which was seldom, she sensed that he was straining at the leash, eager to escape. In an effort to hold him now — for which strategy she despised herself — she confided:

"I'm sure that Kadyama was the kidnapper." She put her hand to her cheek and winced. "Perhaps Blot has clawed him."

"I doubt it. The natives regard the black cat with malevolent superstition. Kadyama may have been acting for them. Forgive me for lashing at you about your clothes, Jan. They were an excuse to blow off steam. Looking out of the office window I saw you in the kennel yard. I thought I'd never get to you." He cleared his voice. His turbulent eyes met hers. "You were wrong. I'll not threaten again to send you home.

I'll try another plan. Take care of that scratch. See you later."

He closed the door behind him. She listened to the diminishing sound of his footsteps. What had he meant? It didn't sound too good.

"I'll try another plan." The words ran like an undertone through her mind as, after the Waffle Shop had closed, she sat at the secretary in the Samp living-room making out orders from a catalogue. A pile of sealed, addressed envelopes attested to work accomplished for the engineers.

What could Bruce have meant? Nibbling the ornamental end of her fountain pen, she examined her reflection in the mirror. Two red, angry scratches streaked her cheek from brow to chin. They showed up in startling contrast to the delicate blue of her frock. She was a sight, and the black cat snoozed as peacefully in the firelight as though he never had done anything more harmful than lick cream from a saucer. Her anger cooled as she looked at Miss Martha in the wing chair beside the table with the open Bible. Her gnarled, big-knuckled hands gripped a newspaper. She seemed tired. She was absorbed in a murder case, of course.

Crime accounts were meat and drink to her. Her white-stockinged feet were stretched at ease, her heavy shoes were beside her chair. Rosy, benign, Miss Mary was absorbed in a copy of *Vogue*. She looked up to ask in a thrilled voice:

"Janice, did you notice this dress the Princess — I can't pronounce her name — is wearing?"

111

Janice blinked a mist from her eyes. Dear little Miss Mary, starved for what gaunt Miss Martha called the "pretties" of life. She said gaily:

"Gorgeous and then some, isn't it? You and I simply eat up the fashion magazines, don't we, Miss Mary? We've just got to know how many inches below our knees to wear our frocks and whether the languorous lady is in, or the sporty female."

"And just how to fling our sable coat over the back of our chair when lunching at Pierre's," the younger Miss Samp added with unwonted humor.

"Sakes alive. Janice and her fashion magazines have started a clothes epidemic in this camp. Caught Mary sending for a free week-end sample of tissue cream and face powder. Tatima spends every spare minute with her nose in a mail-order catalogue. Even that Indian Ossa, who carves silver, begged for the jewelry advertisement pages. Wanted ideas for next summer's trade, he said." With a sniff of disdain Miss Martha returned to her paper.

Chair tipped back against the chinked walls, Tubby Grant strummed a ukulele, crooned softly to its accompaniment. Black-haired, tired-eyed Jimmy Chester, lounging on the couch, pulled at his short mustache, with a hand which looked surprisingly white in contrast to the dark seal ring on the little finger. The musician stopped playing to inquire:

"What's the matter, Lady? Struck a snag?

112

We've got to send these orders out in the plane tomorrow or the goods won't come on the last boat in October. Got any *hors d'oeuvres?*"

Janice turned the pages. "Gelatine — Ginger —"

Jimmy Chester sat up. "Hi! Stop there. Put ginger on my list. Choy Fong. You know the kind comes in painted jars. Mother —" he coughed to camouflage the traitorous break in his voice — "Mother used to have pots of it to put in icecream, and Milly and I snitched it whenever we found it not under lock and key."

What sports these men were! Home must seem heartbreakingly far away as the days shortened and the long, dark winter stole relentlessly forward, Janice thought. Now that Bruce had said that he wouldn't send her out, she would make Christmas the happiest that this outfit ever had spent in Alaska. Already she had written to New York for an sorts of holiday trimmings. She turned another page.

"Here you are, Tubby. '*Hors d'oeuvres.* Varied combinations, besides lending a cheerful aspect to the table, beguile the guests' attention from the moment of entering the diningroom.' I call that literature. What will you have? Antipasto, seven-ounce jars, $1.10."

"Order a dozen."

"You don't care what you do, do you? Expecting to entertain royalty?"

"Mebbe so, mebbe so. Mebbe I'll eat every scrap myself. If you're good I may give you a taste, but you'd have to watch your step. You'll serve it for me, won't you, Miss Martha?"

Martha Samp peered at him over the tops of her spectacles. "I don't know what new-fangled dish you're talking about, but if it's baked, fried or boiled, I can do it."

An authoritative knock was followed by the opening of the door. Bruce Harcourt entered. "What's the matter? You look as though you had seen a ghost."

Miss Martha rose stiffly, pattered forward in her stockinged feet. Her voice was warm with affection.

"It just does my old eyes good to see you here, Mr. Bruce. You haven't dropped in for the evening for weeks an' weeks; now I come to think of it, since Janice came. Mary, bring out the bowl an' cracker with the nuts we've been savin' for him."

Mary Samp fluttered forward to take his cap. Miss Martha patted a chair invitingly.

"Sit here, Mr. Bruce. My, I'm all flustered havin' you back again."

Tubby Grant drew his hand across the strings of his uke. Struck into "Hail to the Chief." Reminded crisply:

"When you get through staring at the Samp sisters' whitehaired boy, Miss Trent, I'll complete my order."

"Come over here and make out your check, then I'm through."

Janice turned her back on Harcourt and bent

over her papers. Why had he appeared tonight for the first time, as Miss Martha had reminded him, since she had come? Anything to do with that "plan" of which he had spoken? Tubby Grant, his order completed, straddled a chair beside his chief. Jimmy Chester took his place at the desk. With Bruce's warning prickling in her mind, she welcomed him with gay enthusiasm. Above his low, confidential voice, she could near the tap of a hammer, the crack of nutshells, the give and take of badinage. In the mirror she could see Miss Mary beaming on the two men; from time to time Miss Martha looked around her newspaper at them.

"Give these to the lady who turned her back on us, Tubby." There was laughter in Harcourt's voice. Beginning to be friendly, was he? A trifle late in the day, Janice resented indignantly.

"Thank you, I don't eat nuts."

Grant paused in the act of setting down a saucer full of meats. "Says you! Who gobbled all that walnut fudge Miss Mary made for me? All right. We'll keep these for them as likes 'em, eh, Chief? Anything new in crime circles, Miss Martha?"

Martha Samp frowned at the date-line of the sheet she held. "This paper's four weeks old, so it's not very new, but here's something about a man who shot his wife 'cause she looked at his hand while he was playin' Contract. Claimed that he just naturally got sick of her tellin' him how to play."

115

"I've never shot a woman," observed Grant reflectively, "but I think I might under those circumstances."

"There are some men who'd be better for a little shooting," attested Chester gloomily.

Martha Samp reproved affectionately: "You boys make a joke of everything, but it's no joke to be married to a naggin' wife. I've seen it work out."

"How's a man going to know he's picked a nagger? Girls are all sweetness and light when you're stepping out with them."

"Our romantic Jimmy's speaking from the depths of his young and bitter experience." Grant dodged a nut-shell before he went on. "What's the remedy, Miss Martha?"

Martha Samp pushed back her spectacles. "Do you know what I'd do about it? I'd have a law that no two young folks should marry till the girl'd spent a month with his folks, an' he livin' there, an' he'd spent a month in the bosom of her family. They'd see each other as they really were, day in an' day out. She'd know if he came down to breakfast fit to bite, an' he'd find out if she appeared lookin' like she was goin' to take the sunshine out of the day for the rest of the folks. They'd know each other's faults. If they still wanted to marry they'd be wise to just what they'd have to put up with."

"I'll bet there'd be a slump in the marriage market after that acid test."

"Oh, I don't know. Young people are great for

takin' chances, Mr. Jimmy."

Harcourt laid down his hammer and rose. He patted Miss Martha's angular shoulder.

"When I'm President I'll have you in my Cabinet as minister of matrimony." He crossed to the desk, gently lifted Janice's chin.

"How's the scratch, dear?"

The color flamed to the girl's hair. Her heart seemed to stop. What did he mean by speaking to her in that possessive voice, touching her with fingers that sent a tingling warmth from feet to head. The room was so still she could hear furtive rustling in the moss chinking. Were they all as paralyzed with surprise as she? Chester, face white, took an impetuous step toward her.

Grant caught his arm, laughed, an embarrassed, shaky laugh. "Come on, Jimmy. We're *de trop*. Nightie-night, Miss Martha, Miss Mary."

The door closed. With an inarticulate word or two about lights in the Waffle Shop, the Samp sisters hurriedly departed. Janice roused from her stupefaction. Hands gripping the back of the chair behind her, she faced Harcourt's indomitable eyes.

"What did you mean, speaking to me like that, before — before everyone. I felt as though I'd been tagged or — or posted 'No Trespassing.' "

She stopped for breath.

"Glad I got the idea across. Good night, Jan. We start at sun-up, remember."

Speechless with amazement, she stared at the door he had closed behind him.

8

A faint pink glow was brightening the east as Janice stepped from her cabin attired in a one-piece flying suit of weatherproof gabardine over her blue wool sports suit. The close cap fastened tight about her neck. There were deep pockets above the knees of the trousers, which tightened into ankle cuffs. It had been considered as necessary a part of her trousseau as riding-clothes. New York and its environs had gone aviation mad long before she left. Flips and zooms, solos and licenses, tri-motored ships, single-motored wasps, amphibians, great and small, had been the absorbing subjects of conversation among her friends. New York! It seemed worlds away as she looked down upon the quiet water, broken frequently by a flash of silver as a fish leaped high in air only to fall back with a splash and sparkle of spray. The air was chilly, that curious chill which comes from the proximity of snow and ice. A light breeze stirred gigantic fern fronds, a cratertop on the horizon shone pure gold.

What an atom she was in the vastness of this

northern world! A world wonderful beyond human imagining. She felt its beauty like a tangible thing, drew a long breath of sheer delight. There were no dark places in her soul this morning. Gone was the sense of monotony. The possibility of adventure waiting round the corner thrilled her, not a doubt lurked in her consciousness. Something might happen on this expedition, something big, the atmosphere tingled with possibilities. She had been wise to follow her hunch. Transplanting had broken up the old design of her life. It had developed a determination to make an art of living, to conquer her fear complex, to meet problems and disappointments with gay courage. It had set her mind pulsing with new ideas, new ambitions, new plans. Suppose she had lacked the nerve to hang on till she had secured the position of secretary to the outfit? Devastating thought.

"If at first you don't succeed, try, try again," she intoned softly, as she gripped the handle of the gay Indian basket which the Samp sisters, always mindful of the paramount importance of provisioning an expedition, had packed to the brim. In the other hand she carried her camera. Under one arm she had tucked a soft felt hat, to wear when she reached the city. City. The mere word had her all excited.

As she followed the trail to the hangar, the sudden remembrance of Bruce Harcourt's eyes, his voice as he had inquired, "How's the scratch,

119

dear?" sent her blood flaming through her veins. What had he meant? What was the plan of which he had hinted? Whatever it was, it was not to send her home as though she were a bad child. A disturbing thought pricked at her complacence. Somewhere she had heard emphasized: "Persistence is a virtue, but — be sure that it is intelligent persistence." Could hers in this case be classified as intelligent? Had she selfishly added to Bruce's cares by coming to Alaska? He had warned:

"I mean that Martha Samp — Argus of the Hundred Eyes — is all that stands between you and a quick return to civilization. Better watch your step."

Miss Martha was a dear, even if she did fuss over her. She had superintended the building of the new cabin for the outfit's secretary, had insisted that it be connected with the Samp living-room by a covered passage. Evidently she was a care and anxiety to them all but — she did help. Tubby Grant would have had no secretary if she had not come. As for Jimmy Chester, if his friends were to be believed, he couldn't get within sentimental earshot of a girl without imagining himself in love with her. His present too-fervid interest in her would pass. She drew a long breath of the sparkling air. Aloud she chanted:

" 'God's in his heaven and the Tsar is far away.' "

A head-in-the-sand philosophy, she would

grant, but — why worry?

Harcourt nodded and called a greeting as she approached the plane, which looked like nothing so much as a mammoth darning-needle observing her approach with two calculating, sinister eyes. He seemed taller and sterner in his flying-clothes. There was no hint of his manner of last night. The lapels of his helmet flapped with every motion of his head. Pasca, in a big coat with shaggy white fur collar, was squirting gasoline into the exhaust. Kadyama, one eyebrow, one corner of his mouth lifted in a sardonic twist, was leaning against the great propeller, awaiting the signal to pull out a block. Did he know that she had snatched Blot from under the very noses of the savage dogs? Grant came puffing up. His beatific expression proclaimed a holiday mood.

"Good morning, little Bright-eyes. It's a wow of a day. Ba-gosh, he's taking the new Tanager. It's a humdinger. Jump in. Done much flying?"

"No. This is my positively first experience. My friends happened to prefer boats and cars." Janice's heart was beating uncomfortably hard as she swung a leg over the side.

"You hop in like a veteran."

"I've seen it done on the screen."

"Score one for the educational value of the movies. She's never been up before," Grant explained to Harcourt as he approached, eyes on his wrist-watch. He glanced at the girl.

"Sure you want to go?"

Janice nodded assent. Her voice wouldn't come.

"You will be perfectly safe and comfortable. Almost no bumps or air-pockets in the early morning. I'll see to her straps, Tubby. Toddle over to the Hale cabin and hurry up Millicent. She's always late."

He appeared as cool and impersonal as might a hired pilot, as he explained the mechanism of the plane. Janice's mind was a jumble of cockpit, rudder bars, clips and control-sticks. Grant returned.

"She was watching for me. Can't come. If you ask me, that woman has about reached the limit of endurance. Joe made a row last night, somehow he'd heard of her plan, she didn't dare cross him for fear of consequences. The sooner a man like that is kissed good-bye the better. She gave me a list of things to get for her in the big city."

"Will you go, Jan?"

Janice sternly controlled a frantic desire to jump out. Assented breathlessly:

"Yes! If I won't be in the way."

Grant dropped into the seat beside her. Harcourt adjusted his goggles, secured the flaps of his helmet, fastened his sheepie coat, climbed into the cockpit.

"Turn her over."

A broad band of static electricity shot from the whirling propeller-tips. The motor roared. The pilot throttled it to warming speed. With a sudden rush the plane raced along the field and leaped into the air. No trees, no projections to prevent a clear get-away to the sky.

"Bruce is feeling perky," Grant shouted.

Janice caught her breath in an unsteady gasp, shut her eyes tight, opened them, cautiously looked down. The plane wasn't moving. The earth, all blurry patches of color, was falling away. Ground mists were pelting after one another like a flock of white sheep in a Gargantuan pasture. Toward the horizon, the sun, a disc of flame, tipped mountain-tops with scarlet, gold or blinding white. Heaps of cumulus clouds were piled against the hazy skyline like mounds of whipped cream. Far away green glaciers glinted through shimmering mist. She tried to speak. Grant grinned and advised through the ear.

"Better talk in this till you get your air-lungs."

The sun rose clear and ruddy. Colors of sea and sky shifted in ever changing values: claret to pink; ultramarine to turquoise; purple to amethyst; burnt umber to topaz. The clouds retreated like white courtiers with crimson-tipped helmets backing from the presence of their king. Lakes and streams which had seemed opalescent silver warmed to molten gold. Harcourt throttled to a speed to maintain altitude. Grant prepared his camera.

Breathless with interest, Janice watched him as he made an exposure every twenty-two seconds. After a while she looked down upon a panorama of forests, spruce and cottonwoods; lakes and rivers; barren uplands; plateaus connecting mountains, like jade links in a mammoth necklace; fields of seed grass cut by bear-trails, like lines of experience worn deep in the face of an elderly giant. No sign of habitation save an occasional shack of a wood-chopper or fish-wheels set in a river. A sluggish, meandering stream issued from a narrow gap. Far off to the west, across the waters of a deep, jagged inlet, towered a vast, serrated range of snow-clad mountains, the highest peaks of which were slumbering volcanoes. Between them timbered and mysterious valleys lured to exploration. She could see miles of glaciers, gulleys, rounded knolls, iridescent flashes of color, wagon roads, like threads crossing and crisscrossing. Precipices, their ragged sides the nesting-places of eagles and gulls, dropped sheer to the beds of turbulent streams. The plane passed high over craggy ravines, a green pasture where animals were grazing. Variety, color, movement everywhere, yet the predominating impression was that of order — beautiful order. Lakes like huge sapphires seemed to have been dropped into green enamel settings. A railroad, looking in the vast stretch of world like a toy abandoned by a boy called away from play, twisted and turned like a glittering serpent, sometimes by caverns which were abandoned gold mines on gold-producing creeks.

Far below, ethereal as a spider's web, unreal in

that wilderness as a castle in the air, a trestle spanned a frothing river. Janice pointed eagerly, a question in her eyes. Grant nodded. Said through the phone:

"That's it. Our Hero's bridge."

Skimming, racing, scudding, the plane flew on. Grant took innumerable pictures at the direction of the pilot. They left the wilderness. Houses and farms increased in number. They hovered over a city, a city laid out like one half of a wheel, its spokes converging toward a lovely sweep of river.

Harcourt thrust out an arm to indicate a left curve. Pointed earthward. Made an easy turn.

"Going to land," Tubby Grant interpreted.

Janice looked down upon a field dotted with lethargic flies. The plane circled, losing altitude. The flies swelled to bumble-bee proportions. People? People moving. The ground rose. In one corner lay a twisted, smoking mass of framework. A little bounce, another. The plane taxied to a stop.

The two men stood up and stretched, pushed back their goggles, peeled off their jumpers. Harcourt was on the ground first. He held out his arms.

"Come."

As Janice stole a surreptitious glance at the smoking embers he pressed her face against his shoulder.

"Don't look at that. Someone trying a crazy stunt, probably. Wonders have been achieved in plane building, but no genius has yet designed one warranted foolproof. Better leave your flying-suit in the bus. Get a taxi, Tubby, while I see if I can help."

Grant deposited Janice in a cab and disappeared. It seemed as though she waited hours before they joined her. Their lips were compressed, the blood seemed to have been drained away from under their bronzed skin. Harcourt gave a curt direction to the driver and the automobile shot along the street.

Was she really thousands of miles from New York, Janice asked herself, as she passed modern buildings, a college, homes with gardens, riotous garden borders, with clumps of pale yellow day lilies, spikes of larkspur in every known shade of blue, patches of early pink phlox, mists of Gypsophila. She was amazed at the size of the flowers and fruits forced to tropical luxuriance by the constant dew and mist baths. As in a crystal she saw the weather-beaten cabins at the outfit's headquarters, the clutter of steam-shovels, rails and gas drums below. Would it be possible to make a garden there? She might take some plants back with her.

She was mentally tabulating the varieties of flowers she had noticed as they entered the lounge of an hotel, set in the midst of several acres of ground. It was thronged with tourists who had arrived by the railroad. She pulled her blue felt hat lower over her eyes, wished feverishly for an invisible cap. She would hate to meet anyone she knew. There would be a flood of questions. Some officious person would radio her whereabouts back to New York. The mere name brought a sickening memory of her tumult of mind and soul during those last weeks before she had determined to break with Ned Paxton. Life had been a prolonged nightmare of conflict. What a coward she had been. How she had agonized over what now she felt tempted to laugh at. Was life like that? Making a tragedy of what in retrospect seemed rather amusing? She would try to remember the next time she was worried, that there was a gate in every wall, that nothing hurts forever, that problems have a marvelous, unbelievable way of straightening out.

Refreshed, with her skin wind-burned to a dusky pink, cooled by a dust of powder, she met Grant in the foyer.

"The main dining-room is swarming with tourists. Harcourt has ordered eats in a private room. There are a lot of newspaper men about and he's dodging being interviewed about the bridge."

"Interviewed!" Janice remembered the trying weeks before her prospective wedding, when a reporter had lurked round every corner and a camera had snapped whenever she left her door. "Let's escape this crowd, lead me to the private room."

From a broad window she booked out upon lawns, gay flower beds. Yellows, blues, greens, pinks, reds, and purples seemed richer, more brilliant in coloring than any blossoms she ever before had seen. Everything in this northern country was on a mammoth scale. Beyond glittered a lake, encircled by low-lying shadow-splotched mountains, blue as the dome above it. A river meandered seaward, dotted with picture-book islands connected by rustic bridges to the banks. She turned as Harcourt entered.

"Hope you don't mind the cramped quarters. The place is jammed. The tourists will be off after breakfast."

"Breakfast!"

"What time did you think it was? We started at sun-up."

"I can't believe it. How far have we traveled?"

"Hundreds of miles. Unless you want to shop extravagantly, we'll be back at the Waffle Shop in time for the mid-day meal."

Indian boys, in native costume, entered with trays. Amber coffee, pots of it; rolls, crisp and delicate; raspberries, crimson, gigantic — for raspberries — cream clotted; bacon in crisp curls; a thick bear steak which oozed delectably red at touch of a knife; potatoes baked to bursting flakiness. Janice purred content as she tasted the fruit.

"So this is Alaska!"

Grant grunted skeptically. "A part of it. Wait till we take you bridge-building next winter out into a country where nothing ever happens, where the mail is as temperamental in its appearance as a movie-headliner, and the nights are twenty hours long."

"Why think of a frozen future, Mr. Tubby Grant?"

"She won't be taken bridge-building next winter," corrected Harcourt curtly, as he cut the steak into juicy slices.

"Ugh! Big Chief! Heap bossy!" Janice let her protest go at that.

Grant chuckled. "Says you. With that point nicely washed up, what shall we do next?"

"Show Miss Trent the town, Tubby. Don't let her buy any fake furs. There was an unusually heavy catch of everything this last winter. And don't let her go tourist over the baskets. We'll see that she gets the real thing when she buys."

Later he asked, "Need any money, Janice?"

"No thanks, I brought all my pay." She lingered on the threshold. "Aren't you coming with us?"

"Can't. Business. I will walk as far as the bank with you and Tubby, then I'll meet you at the field in an hour."

A depression which seemed mysteriously involved with the word "business" settled over the girl's spirit. She struggled to shake it off as she waited for the two men in a secluded nook of the veranda of the hotel. The streets were thronged with tourists, with automobiles, luxurious imported models, smart town cars, shabby out-at-the-elbow flivvers whose only possible excuse for existing was that they kept moving. Fat oily Eskimos with square flat faces, fat little

129

noses; bronzed Indians in lurid blankets; squaws selling baskets and beads; brazen women, their chains of gold nuggets their fortunes; sourdoughs with heavily lined faces, humor sparkling in their faded eyes; officers in o.d.; a Jesuit father in his black robe, threaded the crowd like strands of color in the loom of a master weaver. A team of malamutes trotted by, foxlike heads high, brushes curled over their backs, proudly indifferent to the attention they attracted. Over all a sapphire sky, the horizon rimmed by mountains, their bases darkly green, their white crowns glinting.

A hand touched Janice's shoulder. She had been too engrossed in the panorama to hear footsteps. She smiled radiantly.

"Tubby, this is a wonder —" She looked. The world went into a tailspin. Ned Paxton? She must be dreaming. No, those were his intensely blue eyes; that was his ash-blond hair with the girlish wave in it; no other lips were like his, full, red, under his slight mustache. His hand tightened. She was conscious of mounting anger under his caressing smile.

"So here you are!"

At his touch the memory of her past unhappiness set her nerves a-quiver. Maddening. And she had thought she had conquered fear. Did he realize it? She twisted free.

"So here you are! What are you doing so far from the Great White Way?"

His eyes held hers. "I came for you."

"For me! How did you know where I was?" She could cheerfully have bitten out her tongue for gratifying him with the question.

"Oh, an interested party, who had seen our pictures in the paper, and recognized you, radioed your whereabouts, and I started. I expected to find you, but not so soon."

An interested party! Hale? Was that the explanation of the demoted chief's sinister chuckle yesterday? He had said that he had contemplated sending information to the deserted bridegroom when already he had sent it. She must get rid of her ex-fiancé before Bruce and Grant came. Could she infuriate him so that he would hate her, leave her?

"Did you buy that radio information as you have bought everything all your life? You boast that you bribed your way out of college scrapes. You were the youngest captain in your regiment. Why? Not because you were a better soldier, but because your father was a Senator with oodles of money and influence. You've bought friends just as you've bought boats and automobiles and bootleggers, a château in France. You think you've paid for them with money; you've paid for them with the respect of almost every person who knows you."

She stopped for breath. His eyes were dark with amazement, his lips hung open. Of a sudden, color surged under his fair skin as though it would burst through, it reddened even his ears. Had she at last pierced his complacency, touched the quick? He smiled. She had flattered herself.

"If I buy, you'll admit I pay the highest market price." He took a step nearer. "Like you all the better for that flare, Jan. Crazy about you. Now I'll never let you go. You know that you love me. I'll forgive you this school-girl trick. We'll be married here."

"Oh, no, we won't." Who was speaking? Janice listened to the voice which seemed like her own, yet not her own, which came from a long way off. "It would be awkward — because — well, because I'm already married."

"Married!" His grip on her shoulder tightened till it hurt. "Married!" He turned her toward him. "What's the matter with your face? Does friend husband beat you up? To whom are you married?"

The strange voice so like her own yet not her own answered promptly.

"To Bruce Harcourt. I —"

She turned at a curious sound. Behind Tubby Grant, whose green eyes bulged, whose boyish mouth sagged in surprise, stood Bruce Harcourt.

9

His eyes steadily compelling her eyes, it seemed
hours to Janice before he spoke. Then he said
evenly:

"Met an acquaintance, Jan?"

Paxton laughed. Anticipated the girl's answer.

"An acquaintance! I am the man she was to
marry. Is to marry. Just who are you?"

"Bruce Harcourt. Janice told you that she was
already married to me. After that, your boast is
an insult to her and to me."

Janice stepped between the two men as he
took a step forward. His face was dark with
color, his hands were thrust hard into his
pockets. Tubby Grant moved the fraction of a
foot nearer him. Janice clutched at his coat. She
was rapidly emerging from the senseless panic
which had shaken her when she had looked up at
Ned Paxton. What evil spirit had prompted her
to drag Bruce into the mix-up? The least she
could do was to get him out as soon as possible.
She would flippantly confess that she had been
joking — a silly enough excuse, but it would
serve. She opened her lips. Harcourt laid a

silencing hand on her shoulder. He ignored the blond man regarding them with skeptical amusement.

"We must be off, Janice. Found orders here which will take us back at once."

Paxton laughed indulgently. "Don't linger on my account, Jan. I know where to find you. Sent my boat up the coast; I am to join it by plane. Life may be real, life may be earnest in this wilderness, but I'll bet by the time I arrive you'll be fed up on it, be Reno-minded and raring to get back to the Great White Way."

Harcourt reached for him. Janice blocked his advance with all her strength.

"Bruce! Bruce! Don't make a scene here — please."

With a laugh and a mocking bow Paxton backed away. The girl and the two men watched him until he was lost in the passing crowd. Harcourt gently loosened the fingers gripping his coat sleeve. Janice's throat contracted unbearably as she met his eyes. She admitted unsteadily:

"I'm sorry. I'm terribly sorry. I don't know why I said it."

"Said what?"

"That you — that I — oh, don't make me repeat it. You know."

"Come."

He slipped his arm within hers and led her to the sunny room in which they had breakfasted. She crossed to the window from which she had

134

looked out upon gardens and river such a little while, such a very little while before. She could hear the murmur of voices behind her. Bruce and Tubby conferring about the return trip doubtless. It wouldn't be surprising if after her brainstorm they abandoned her on someone's doorstep. She deserved it. What had possessed her? Fear. Would she ever conquer it? Fear of Ned Paxton's fascination for her. When he had said: "I'll forgive you this school-girl trick. We'll be married here," some outside force seemed to take possession of her. She had spoken as though in a dream. Who had closed the door? Had Bruce left in anger? She turned. No, he was standing by the table. Tubby Grant had gone. Her heart thumped maddeningly. Why, why was she letting a stupid little lie upset her? His face was colorless. Was he troubled about it too? He pushed a chair toward her.

"Sit down, Janice. I want to talk to you."

She sat forward on the edge of the chair, hands clenched in her lap, as she acknowledged breathlessly: "I'm sorry. I'm terribly sorry. I don't know why I said it." In a burst of angry impatience she added: "Why am I making a mountain out of such a little molehill! One would think that I was the only girl in the world who had barricaded herself behind a silly lie."

Harcourt leaned against the table, arms crossed on his chest.

"Although his name wasn't mentioned I gathered that the man was Paxton?" She nodded assent. "Why did you barricade yourself behind a lie?"

"Someone touched me on the shoulder. I looked up expecting to see Mr. Grant. When I saw Ned, a sense of unreasoning terror, panic, stampeded me. The world went into a tailspin. My one thought — if you can call my mental process thinking — was to put an unscalable wall between us. I had been so happy all morning —"

"You had been happy?"

"Gorgeously. When I looked up and saw that man it was like — like a plunge back into the nightmare of those weeks before you found my slipper. When he said that someone who had seen my picture in the paper had radioed him my whereabouts —"

"Did he say who?"

"No. When he said, 'We'll be married here,' I heard a voice which didn't seem to be mine, retort: 'That would be awkward because — well, because I am already married,' and then he said —"

"I heard the rest." Harcourt walked to the window and looked out.

"Ever seen anyone else, Jan, for whom you cared enough to marry?"

"Marry! I! Never! I'll never allow myself to love anyone again. I'm through with sentiment forever. I intend to be one of those secretaries you read about in novels, who becomes more and more efficient until finally the boss doesn't dare make a decision until he has consulted her.

That's how good I mean to be."

Harcourt laughed. "That being the case there is only one thing to be done now. Remember that yesterday I told you I had a plan? It won't interfere in the least with your onward, upward business career. I tried to prepare you for it last evening when I hoisted that 'No Trespassing' sign. I want you to marry me."

"No! No! No!"

"It is the only way out. If he finds that you were bluffing, Paxton will use your admission to injure you, to bring pressure to bear to make you marry him. This is the twentieth century, but Mrs. Grundy still carries poison gumdrops in her envelope purse. You have hurt his self-love, and easygoing as he appears — I know his type — he won't admit himself beaten. I suspect that Hale was the informer. There isn't another man in the outfit who would do it. If you are coming back to headquarters —"

"Of course I'm coming back!"

"Don't be so breathless. Let's work the situation out dispassionately. Because of his enmity to me, Hale will aid and abet Paxton, he will start a whispering campaign which will hurt you. It will give his malevolent self something to do while he sits bolstered in his chair cursing me for his demotion."

Into the girl's mind flashed Grant's troubled confidence.

"Joe Hale is sore. If he could find the least flaw in the character of his successor, our villain without portfolio would laugh his darn head off. His own career has ended in disgrace — because of him the Crowned Heads are seeing red. One breath of scandal about Harcourt and they'd chop his professional head off with a blow."

What had she started? If her selfish defense were to injure Bruce — it couldn't, it mustn't. She admitted eagerly:

"I don't care about myself, really I don't. Whatever Ned Paxton says I can live down, but I realize that I may have injured your professional chances by my fool statement. I'll marry you, do anything to help."

"Cut that out! Think I would save myself at your expense?"

"You are suggesting that for me."

"That's different. You can't go back to head-quarters except as Mrs. Bruce Harcourt. Tubby's gone for a notary public — luckily there is no five-day marriage law in the northern wilderness — when we get back we'll announce that we set off this morning with every intention of being married, wanted to avoid fuss, etc., etc., Lindbergh tactics. One good lie deserves another. Now for the alternative. We will get you to the coast in the plane. You can take passage on the tourists' steamer which is en route to the States. You have plenty of friends to whom you can go till you can talk things over with Billy, haven't you?"

"But Ned Paxton said that he was going to

headquarters. What will he say when he finds I'm not there?"

"Don't worry about that. He will follow you at once. He may use your admission today as a lever to force you into marriage with him. I advise the civil ceremony here. Let's try Miss Martha's test. We will live in the same house for two months before the marriage decree becomes final. Get me? It won't be any different from living with your brother Billy. If you discover at the end of that time that I appear at breakfast ready to bite, annulment is easy. We'll be modern — call it trial companionship. Understand me? I will give you ten minutes in which to think it over."

He opened the door, closed it behind him. Alone, Janice turned to the window. Hands clenched behind her back, she stared at the blindingly white snow on the highest mountain. It seemed no colder than Bruce Harcourt's voice when he had suggested annulment. Of course she understood him. What modern girl, age twenty-six, didn't understand the difference in the meaning of that word and divorce? He had meant that he didn't want a wife. How he must hate her! He was probably saying to himself now as he had said to Billy when she was a little girl tagging at his heels: "Let her come along. What's the difference?"

She tried to weigh the situation dispassionately. Suppose she went back to New York? Never again would she see the Samp sisters, whom she had grown to love, the homey log cabin, the wonders of sea and sky and earth of this northern world. She never would see Bruce or Tubby again, they would have no use for her. Would Ned Paxton — she shivered. She must not let thought of him influence her decision. If she hadn't been a coward she wouldn't have landed in this mixup. Was life everlastingly messed up by crossroads? Continually pulling one up short and saying:

"Here's a parting of the ways. Which road will you take?"

Suppose she consented to the plan Bruce advised? She would still be secretary to the outfit, do her share in opening up the great north country. Why shouldn't she help as well as the Samp sisters, who were making history with their Waffle Shop? Life here thrilled her. Occasionally — less and less as the days went on — a wave of homesickness swept over her, a frenzied desire to crash through the monotony seized her, a longing for something, she didn't know what — but the mood vanished as quickly as the thin filament of cloud which was drifting above the highest crater-top. The civil ceremony would hardly make a dent in her life. She would be called Mrs. Harcourt — nice name — instead of Miss Trent and —

A knock at the door. Had ten minutes passed already! Her heart shot to her throat and fanned its wings. She steadied her lips.

"Come in."

Bruce Harcourt closed the door behind him. He kept the knob in his hand.

"Well?"

Janice swallowed hard. "Don't stand there like a judge about to announce a life-sentence. I — I've decided. I'm going — back."

"To New York?"

"No. To — to headquarters."

"You understand that you go only as Mrs. Harcourt?"

Something in Janice's heart snapped. How could he be so cool, so steady, when she was shaken, quivering inside? Her emotion boiled up and over.

"Of course I understand. You made it plain enough that you wouldn't take Janice Trent back with you. I know that you don't really want me — I know that I'm tagging again — that I'm utterly selfish — but — I want to stay in Alaska. I can't really hurt you by marrying you — temporarily, can I?"

The tense gravity of his face broke in a smile. It widened his clean-cut mouth, revealed his perfect teeth, touched his eyes with brilliance, deepened his voice richly.

"No. You can't really hurt me by marrying me." He picked up the telephone.

"Office? Harcourt speaking. Tell Mr. Grant that I am waiting for him."

He hung up the receiver. To Janice the room seemed as chill, as still as a tomb. The only sound came from the clock on the mantel ticking off the seconds with muted importance. It seemed to take on the tone of Miss Mary's soft voice deprecating:

"Well, *now!* Well, *now!* Well, *now!*"

Janice caught her breath as she noted the hour. Was it possible that so little time had elapsed since she had entered the room for breakfast? It seemed years since sun-up. She remembered her heady assurance as she had followed the path to the hangar, her thrill as she had thought of the possibility of adventure lurking round the corner. It had lurked, all right, it had stalked out into the open, if one considered trial companionship — which after all meant nothing — an adventure. The silence was growing unbearable. Why didn't Bruce say something — anything. Perhaps she would wake up and find herself in her cabin. She moved her hand experimentally. She was awake.

The sense of unreality persisted through the civil ceremony, performed by a short, fat little man who intoned through a nose pinched to compression by tortoise-shell eyeglasses. The cord which attached them to his rotund person, puffed forward, shrank back as he breathed. The rhythm fascinated Janice. Once as he paused to turn a page a vision of the last wedding she had attended as bridesmaid flashed upon the screen of her mind in colorful detail. A breeze from the open window stirred the masses of flowers. She could see the aisle at St. Thomas's bordered by smiling faces, curious faces. It seemed miles to the candle-lighted altar with the exquisite reredos behind it. Her feet dragged in time to the music with which all good and true wedding processions keep step; she could see the green hats of the bridesmaids in front of her — they were wearing them small with sheer nose-veils that season — could hear the swish of the harmonizing moiré frocks, could even smell the talisman roses — could feel the hushed silence — was it the bride saying "I do" — or was she —

The glow, the beauty, vanished like a fairy-ring as a hand touched hers, slipped something on her finger. She met Bruce Harcourt's eyes. Asked breathlessly:

"Is it over?"

He looked at her without answering. Grant and the notary said a few words of felicitation and departed. Harcourt released her hand.

"Quite over. Now, Tubby will take you shopping. We haven't much time. I must get back to headquarters."

Resentment at the lightness of his tone, at the fact that he was eager to turn her over to his henchman, pricked at Janice's not too steady nerves. How could he take the situation so lightly?

"You speak as though you were in the habit of being married every day."

"Not every day. Never before to a girl who was miles away during the ceremony, who didn't sense the fact that I existed."

Janice's heart was twisted by contrition. He

had sacrificed himself to help her and she had repaid by being hateful. Impulsively she held out her hands.

"Bruce! Bruce! Forgive me. I was beastly. I was dazed, that was all, dazed. It came so suddenly. Let's not start out as though we were going to fight and die over this. Remember when you said that to me? Oh, my dear, we mustn't begin by being bitter with one another. I'm not sorry I did it, really I'm not. I'd do it again this minute."

The smile she loved flashed in his eyes, his hands tightened on hers. "That makes it unanimous." He raised her hands, dropped them quickly, said lightly:

"What will you do with your half hour? What do you want most? Beauty parlor?"

His friendly matter-of-fact tone wiped the last ten minutes from her mind. She answered eagerly.

"No, much as I longed to come to the wilderness I wouldn't have dared had I not been born with a permanent wave. I want plants. Dozens of plants. Any color, any kind that the florist thinks might grow in front of the Samp cabin."

He caught her lightly by the shoulders, held her till she looked up.

"Why the Samp cabin? Why not in front of mine?"

10

"Why the Samp cabin? Why not in front of mine?"

The question tap-danced round and round in Janice's mind as she kept pace with Tubby Grant along the concrete walk. He was abnormally silent, his green eyes were clouded, his boyish lips were clamped to repression. Two girls in a smart roadster passed.

"Glad that I wore my swankiest sports-clothes under my flying-suit," Janice confided irrelevantly. Grant's eyes appraised the perfection of her blue wool costume.

"Look like a million."

"One would better here. I am as amazed at the up-to-the-minuteness of this place as I was at the expanse of wilderness when I landed at headquarters."

"This city is like any city. The gold kings, and their satellites, are as ritzy, make whoopee like the leisure class anywhere. Then there are the families of solid citizens, business men, educators, clergymen, clean-living, law-abiding. Of course there's the lower strata, deeply, tragically

145

wise to all the tricks and illegal traffic of a metropolis."

"Does Bruce know any of these people?"

"Yes. He is asked everywhere. Before he was chief, when Hale and headquarters got on his nerves, he would fly over here for a day."

They stood for a moment looking in at a fur sale. Skins of fox, polar bear, seal, wolverine were spread on tables. An old chief, dressed in furs, his face crackling with wrinkles, huddled in the midst smoking a pipe, as he listened stoically to offers.

Janice watched the bargaining without a quickening of her pulses, only to stop with an ecstatic "Oh!" before the window of a Japanese shop in which was seductively draped a sumptuous mandarin coat of turquoise blue, lavishly embroidered with iris which ran the gamut of shades from pale orchid to deep amethyst.

"Want it?" inquired Grant sympathetically.

"Want it! I would want a potato sack if it had that divine coloring."

"Get it. We have time."

"Just like that! You don't realize, Tubby, that my total principal is fifty dollars I had left from the family estate after buying a trousseau. I had to plunge. One can't marry a Croesus and go to him with clothes like a beggar-maid's."

"Was that bozo at the hotel the millionaire?"

"Yes. You knew it, didn't you, knew that I broke the engagement a few days before the ceremony? Didn't Bruce tell you?"

"Nope. Only said he'd known you when you were a little girl. So your total invested capital is fifty dollars?"

"That was what I had left after paying my traveling expenses to Alaska and for excess baggage. I nearly lost my reason over that last charge. Do you wonder that I almost had heart failure when upon my arrival I saw: 'Ba-gosh! He won't do!' writ large on your open countenance? I am hoarding my present salary to be sure I have enough for a return ticket in case I lose my job."

"Lose your job! Fat chance now that you've married the chief." His green eyes became ludicrously terrified. "You won't stop work, will you?"

"Don't be absurd! As though those few words spoken by that wheezy little notary meant anything. You know and I know that Bruce only pulled me out of a silly shell-hole I had dug for myself."

Grant's usually cherubic expression hardened. "Says you. No one must know that it wasn't a carefully planned flight — object matrimony. And if you ask me, I'll add, at the risk of being thought a butter-in, that you're in luck to have Bruce step up. That millionaire boy I'll bet is a bad loser."

Janice, indifferent to the crowd milling by, slipped her arm within his as they stood before the shop-window.

"Will Ned Paxton follow me, Tubby, when he thinks it over? The dread of his appearance will hang over me like the sword of Damocles."

He patted her hand. "Lady, pull yourself together. Just remember that the sword of that old sport never fell — that is, it didn't get into the news if it did. Suppose he does follow you? We're not living in the dark ages, when a girl can be dragged off captive. Yours truly can land a telling left to the jaw even if he is a bit over-weight, and you have a perfectly good husband to look after you, haven't you?"

"A hus—" The word broke and rattled in her throat. Her fingers tightened on Grant's arm. "That word makes the ceremony we went through this morning seem horribly real."

"Looked like the real thing to me. If you've decided not to buy that mandarin coat, let's go. Perhaps sometime you'll strike pay-dirt. Then you can come back for it."

It was fifteen minutes after the hour set, when they rattled up to the flying-field in a taxi spilling over with huge pink and red geranium blooms.

Would Bruce be annoyed at the delay, Janice wondered. Anything but — she told herself caus-tically as she saw him standing beside a smart roadster. A girl was leaning toward him. He was laughing as he held a lighter to her cigarette. So, that had been the "business" which had pre-vented him from joining the shopping expedi-tion. She shrank back among the plants.

"To whom is Bruce talking, Tubby?"

He poked his head forward with the motion of a short-necked bird reconnoitering. "That girl in the snappy roadster? Peggy Casson, a gold king's daughter. She's forever running Our Hero down. Lucky she doesn't pilot her own plane or we'd have her dropping in on us at headquarters. Want to meet her?"

"No. Not with this scratched face."

"Your face scratched has hers beaten a mile. She's going anyway. Hi, Bruce."

Janice watched Harcourt as he approached. He was in his jumpers, his helmet swung from his hand. She never had thought of him as having social contacts in this wilderness. Her mind went back to the days when he and Billy had stepped out with girls before the war. She had flamingly resented his popularity then. Was that what pricked like a burr against her heart now? Hadn't she grown up? Apparently he was not annoyed at the delay. Why should he be? Doubtless he had been well entertained.

"Why didn't you bring the greenhouse?" he teased. As he and Grant helped extricate her from among the mass of plants, a radio broadcast over the field:

"Weather report. Few broken clouds. Ceiling three thousand feet. Visibility eight miles. Northwest winds."

"That's all right. Leave the plants where they are for a minute, Tubby. I want to talk with you while Janice gets into her flying-suit."

He drew Grant to one side. Janice heard the murmur of his voice, punctuated by an occasional eager assent from Tubby, "Sure!" "Great idea!" "Ba-gosh! I get you." "I'm all excited."

As Harcourt turned away with a final word he caught his sleeve. "Hold on, Bruce, I forgot something." He held his chief by a strap on the sheepie coat.

"Of course, get it. Look for us at five o'clock."

She watched in amazed unbelief as Grant returned to the plant-laden taxi, stepped in, gave an order to the driver who wheeled the cab and started townward.

"Is Tubby returning the plants, Bruce?"

"No. Come on."

The plane had more the look of a sinister-eyed creature than before, as Janice approached it.

"Hop in!" He fastened the straps. "Decided that I would stop on the way back and inspect a gang which is repairing a stretch of track not far from the shore of a beautiful lake. The camp has a good landing-field — we keep in touch with the various outfits by plane — and this bus was designed to take-off and stop in a small area. We'll fly over hidden reservoirs of oil more extensive than any yet discovered, above gold deposits richer than the Yukon. They are so far from the railroads and shipping facilities that it would cost more to develop them than they are worth. No telling what magic aviation will work. It may prove the 'Open Sesame!' to fabulous wealth. It's a grizzly and Kodiak belt. Might see a bear!" His laughing eyes met hers. "No danger at this time of day or I wouldn't take you. Thought you would like to see the country.

Seemed a pity not to use the contents of that bulging basket the Samp girls provided. We will lunch on land and take-off in time to reach head-quarters in the late afternoon. You said you liked parties."

"Adore them."

"Can't have our wedding day all business."

This time she was quite sure that her heart had parked in her throat for keeps. "Our wedding day! Bruce. You are not taking this crazy mix-up seriously, are you?"

He lowered his goggles, climbed into the seat beside her, adjusted the earphone. "Your voice sounds terrified. Afraid to fly with me alone? I'm a reliable pilot."

He had deliberately misunderstood her. What had she started by her cowardly lie? He should find that she could be a good sport some of the time.

"Of course I am not afraid. Tubby says that you're a wow of an aviator. Aren't we to wait for him?"

"No. He will charter a small plane which will take him — and those million or two plants, directly to headquarters. He has things to do for me. Pull down your goggles." As her fingers fumbled, he stripped off his gloves, gently pushed aside her hand, adjusted the glasses.

"Remember the fishing trips, Jan? You trusted me then. Can't you now?"

At his smile, the friendliness of his voice, her heart folded contented wings. Her spirit stood

151

a-tiptoe with eagerness.

"I do trust you. I would rather be tagging along with you, Bruce, than be doing anything else in the world."

He opened his lips, closed them in a grim line. She remembered that she had called it a fighting line the night they had dined together in New York. What had he been about to say? He leaned over, nodded to the man at the tie-chain. The dusky breed called:

"All set?"

"All set."

"Give her the gas."

The mechanic snapped the chain-catch free. Harcourt opened the throttle. The plane taxied along the field gathering headway, soared.

On and on, through thin cloud, out again. Janice's thoughts were a chaotic jumble of past, present and future. What had she done to the life of the man sitting as still as a bronze pilot beside her? Was that a torch of flame spouting from the serrated mountain-top? What had she done to her own life? Shut the door of it in Ned Paxton's face. She had that satisfaction. She hadn't been fair to him about the army. Even if influence had boosted him into a captaincy, he had been decorated for extraordinary bravery. He had many good qualities to offset those she hated. Was that why he had held her so long? How dense the forests were. What would Billy think when he heard of her marriage? Was the silver ribbon clinging to the rocky cliffs a railroad? Would Ned follow her into the wilderness? That sinister gorge with precipices on both sides dropped sheer to the turbulent bed of a mountain torrent. She could hear the ceaseless roar, the hollow boom of the cataract. Flying gave one too much time to think. Suppose Ned Paxton did appear at head-quarters?

"Cold?" Harcourt asked through the phone. Had he felt her shiver at thought of her late fiancé? She shook her head.

"Coming down on that shore."

Problems and doubts vanished as she watched the twin lakes below. One was as blue as a sapphire, one as green as a chrysoprase. Through the narrow, rocky gorge which connected them plunged and frothed a noisy cataract. As the plane lost altitude forests and fields and glinting water came up to meet it. From among the trees back of a field three tiny columns of smoke rose and spread like the violet gauze skirts of a danseuse.

The wheels lighted like a butterfly. The plane staggered a little, shuddered a little, stopped. Harcourt cut the switch, pushed up his goggles, smiled.

"Like it?"

Janice released the breath she had been holding during the landing.

"Love it! It's marvelous! How still the world seems!"

The lake stretched smooth as a mirror, with a mirror's sheen. The shrubs and trees and tall seed-grass which bordered it plunged their reflected tops down into its deep-lying shadows. A man with several days' growth of beard grinned a welcome as he approached.

"Glad to see you, Chief. We've been hoping you'd get around."

"Janice, this is Johnson, the section boss here. I wanted Mrs. Harcourt to see this lake. Know of a good spot beside the stream where we can have luncheon?"

So easily and casually he announced his marriage. Janice felt her color mount as she met the man's astonished eyes. He pulled himself together with obvious effort.

"If you can call any place in this God-awful country good. As though we hadn't trouble enough fighting flies and mosquitoes, a couple of hunters have been stirring up the bears. Better take some cushions. I'll carry them. This way."

He crashed into what seemed an unbroken wilderness. Gray-bearded trees stood like spectral sentinels on guard. Weathered branches held great beds of moss, like mammoth hanging gardens, from which sprouted and dripped ferns and vines. Under them the ground was a maze of fallen branches and tree trunks, some of them brilliantly green. The air was stirred by the murmur of running water, perfumed with the scent of flowering shrubs, the spicy fragrance of spruce, the smell of rich leaf mold. Janice tripped in a net-work of trailing vines. Harcourt caught her arm.

"Watch your step!"

He kept his hold as they dodged overhanging boughs which reached out clutching tendrils, stumbled over the rough ground, crossed crushed and broken underbrush, where some huge creature had left the story of its passing. They emerged into a clearing through which the brook flowed swiftly, singing to itself, now softly, now loudly, as it tumbled and rippled its way to the lake. Mammoth ferns with drooping fronds clustered along its banks. The devil's club spread wide tropical leaves. Bushes of berries splashed a tangled mass of vines with yellow gold. The swift water was white as snow, the deep pools black, the shallows clear amber. Part way up the stream a fall, a few feet high, plunged into a sombre, bush-rimmed pool. The pagan beauty of the spot was awe inspiring.

Harcourt arranged the cushions on a comparatively smooth stretch of ground. "Sit here while I get a fire started."

In a few moments twigs and small logs crackled cheerily. Johnson, having accumulated a pile of wood, departed. Janice laid a white cloth the Samp sisters had provided, bordered it with feathery ferns. She spread out the tempting lunch. Gulls' eggs stuffed with anchovy; sandwiches so wafer thin you could taste the knife, as the English say. Little balls of minced salmon, coated with tomato jelly. A jar of mayonnaise to accompany them. Dates stuffed with orange marmalade or marshmallows. Coffee, hot, pungent. From the distance came the sound of men's voices, the ring of steel on steel.

"We seem very near the workmen." She passed sandwiches to Harcourt seated on the ground across the cloth.

"Their camp is just beyond here. Later I will talk business with Johnson, after which we'll take-off again. This harmless appearing brook did its darndest during the spring thaw and flooded our tracks. We are raising them to a new grade line."

His voice ran off her mind like rain from a slanting roof. Not a word soaked in. She felt his hand on hers.

"You haven't been listening, have you?"

She shook her head. Her eyes met his steadily, directly. "No, Bruce, I haven't. I was thinking that it was a pity I hadn't been dropped from the plane before I messed your life up as I have done."

He clasped his brown, muscular hands about one knee. "You haven't messed up my life, Jan. Today merely precipitated what had to be done if you are to stay here. When I've been away from headquarters my mind has been half on you, half on my work. When I saw you in the kennel yard — it stops my heart now to think of it — I swore to myself that either you would go back to Billy, or you would give me the right to look after you here. I intended to fight it out with you tonight. Paxton's appearance merely precipitated the crisis."

"Crisis! I'd call it a climax."

"Not a climax, only the end of a chapter. I had thought we would talk things over when we reached the H house, but I believe you'll be happier if we get it behind us now. Let's begin at the moment Paxton touched you on the shoulder at the hotel. You set me up between you as a barrier, didn't you?"

She nodded. "I'm soggy with remorse every time I think of it."

"Stop thinking of it. It will be weeks before the last boat goes out. I told you that one acquired the habit of thinking things through in the wilderness. You will know by the time you leave just what you want."

"I know now that I don't want Ned Paxton."

"You think you don't. Wait till he appears at the mouth of the inlet in his palatial yacht. Meanwhile, get this straight, except that you will take up residence in my cabin and be called Mrs. Harcourt, life for you will go on as usual. You will have your secretarial work to help make time fly. I shall be away days at a time. I shan't bother you."

"You wouldn't bother me if you stayed, Bruce."

He stood up. He looked immensely tall, his face bronzely immobile.

"Thanks. I will interview the section boss, then we'll takeoff."

"Why not give these eats to the men? Miss Martha provided for an able-bodied army." As she re-packed the basket he frowned down upon her.

"Didn't you eat anything?"

"I'm not hungry. I ate an enormous break-fast."

He caught her hands in his. Held them. "Don't let this marriage spoil our friendship, Jan."

She smiled at him valiantly. "I won't. My mind will settle down after a time. At present it still rocks. Don't worry about me. Go interview your section boss."

"I'll be back in fifteen minutes. Don't mind what Johnson said about bears. They are not feeding at this time of day. You are perfectly safe here, I can hear you if you call. Exercise all you can, we have a long flight ahead of us, but don't wander away from the brook."

Janice watched till his tall, lean figure was lost in the underbrush. She poked about humming, "If a great big bear should come along down, what would I do, what would I do?" Having collected a dozen varieties of ferns, she perched on a huge boulder beside the chattering stream. She rearranged her hair with the aid of the small mirror in her compact. Rays of sunlight filtered through the trees, dappled it with gold. A dry leaf floated down, settled on a patch of emerald moss like a broken butterfly.

Heavenly peaceful. Not that she would want to spend her life in this back-water — she would much rather live where she had to do some hard, muscle-straining swimming — but the quiet gave her a chance to think things through, made her realize again what an atom she was in the scheme of things. It couldn't be mere chance that Bruce should have appeared at the exact psychical moment. She could see his eyes, his clear, direct eyes. Hear his clipped voice.

"Met an acquaintance, Jan?"

Having blundered into this situation, was she big enough to meet it staunchly, without self-consciousness, confusion? Trial companionship, Bruce had called it. Not such a bad idea. She looked at the narrow band on the third finger of her left hand, saw it for the first time. Platinum and diamonds! He must have bought it during the ten minutes he had given her to decide. Could he afford a ring so choice? She knew so little about him. He was taking it for granted that she would go out on the last boat. Would she? Millicent Hale had remained at headquarters through a winter. Millicent Hale! How much had Bruce cared for her?

Brows knit, color coming and going, she sat motionless so long that two martens in a drift-wood dam down stream resumed their interrupted house building. Their stealthy motions brought Janice's attention back to her surroundings. What a picture! For the first time she thought of her camera safely reposing in the cockpit. In the excitement of landing she had forgotten it. Tubby would be exasperated when he heard of her forgetfulness. She watched the little animals thoughtfully. How the instinct of home-making persisted everywhere. Those two furry creatures laboring, Bruce Harcourt and the sick boy planning and building a cabin in this wilderness. Bruce mushing back to headquarters through the snow, sensing home behind the lighted windows of the H house.

How still the forest was. The fire had died down to blinking red coals and flaky gray ashes. Violet haze hung above it like a brooding spirit. A bluejay as large as a New York State crow, which had perched on a swaying branch across the stream, regarded her from beady eyes in a pert, tip-tilted head. A humming bird flashed and stabbed into the hearts of pink blossoms on a tall spike. Bees hummed. Long festoons of moss swung like flitting gray wraiths. The shadows were turning to amethyst dusk. She could hear men's voices, the crashing of branches.

Squawking protest, the curious bluejay took wing. The martens vanished. She jumped to her feet, her heart pounding. The sound of snapping branches wasn't coming from the direction in which Bruce had gone. The alders across the stream shook violently. A bear! Darn her imagination! Hadn't Bruce said that they weren't feeding at this time of day? Just the same —

Her eyes dilated in terror. Across the brook a great Kodiak crashed through a clump of alders. It stopped. Regarded her, its head swaying from side to side as though in pain. Two bloody marks on a shoulder were alive with flies. To the girl's excited fancy the creature looked as big as a house. With an infuriated growl it splashed one great foot into the brook. Coming for her? She kept her eyes on it as she backed cautiously away. She tried to call. Her voice wouldn't come. Nightmare, that was what it was, nightmare. What red eyes! Terrible eyes! An ear-splitting roar. That ought to bring the men. They were coming. She could hear their yells. Branches crashing. The bear stopped in the middle of the brook.

"Jan! Jan!"

She tried to answer the anxious call. Her voice cracked.

"Don't shoot, Johnson. You might hit her. Jan! Jan!"

"Here!" The word was a mere whisper. Nightmare. If she couldn't call she could move, couldn't she, not stand as though she were hypnotized. With all the force of her will she dragged her fascinated stare from the red eyes, coming nearer and nearer. She ran in the direction of the voices, stepped into a hole filled with water. Fell heavily. The shock freed her voice. Pulling herself up she called. She stumbled over a hummock. Harcourt caught her before she reached the ground.

"Jan! Jan! You're not hurt?"

She rested against him as she struggled for breath. Laughed shakily.

"Hurt! No. At last — I've — I've seen a bear, Bruce."

"For the love of Pete! What a target!"

A rifle shot followed Johnson's shout of exultation. Another. Then a crash, splashing water. A yell of triumph.

"Sure you're all right, Jan?" Harcourt was feeling of her arms, her shoulders.

She stood erect, pushed back her hair. "Quite sure. Let's see the bear."

He drew a revolver from its holster before he went on. Johnson and two section hands were bending over a huge brown body, measuring it. A group of natives, awed, terrified, ready to run if the animal moved, skulked under cover of a thicket. Johnson stood up grinning.

"Eight feet long, if it's a foot, and four feet high at the shoulders. I'll bet it weighs fourteen hundred pounds, Chief."

Harcourt bent over the head lying on the pebbles. "How do you account for its being out at this time of day, Johnson?"

"Hunters. See the two marks on the shoulder? The bullets didn't kill the old fella and he hid in the bushes. I bet they gave him a pain." He grinned at Janice. "We'll send you the pelt for a wedding present, M'arm."

"Thank you, Mr. Johnson, I should love it." She looked curiously at the revolver in Harcourt's hand. Its mother-of-pearl butt gleamed rainbow colored. "I had no idea that a six-shooter could be so beautiful."

He thrust it back into the holster. "That isn't a six-shooter. That's a Colt 38. You've been reading wild and woolly west stories. It was Archie Harper's. I shouldn't select anything so dressy, but he wanted me to carry it, so I do. It is just as deadly as a plainer weapon. Let's go."

He kept Janice's hand tight in his as they stumbled and broke their way back to the field. She looked up at him as he followed her into the plane. Her voice shook with thrilled laughter.

"My word, what a day! Since yesterday noon life has been just one excitement after another."

His tense face relaxed. "Doing our prettiest to entertain you, Jan."

How one could love him for his smile, the girl thought, as she met his laughing eyes; how deeply and achingly one could love him for his smile — if one hadn't determined never to love any man.

Johnson watched their take-off. As the plane climbed Janice waved to him. The wind flung her arm back across her breast.

Could it have been only this morning that she had left the Samp cabin tingling with a desire for adventure, she asked herself, as hours later they came down in the field at headquarters. Pasca, his bronze face split by gleaming rows of white teeth, charged from the hangar.

"We all mighty glad you and Mees get marry. Yes sirree."

Harcourt swung Janice to the ground. "Thank you, Pasca. We are mighty glad, too. Has Mr. Grant arrived?"

"He come two — tree hour ago. Much flowers.

Much bundle. Mees Samp seesters, they cry. They make for beeg party. Yes sirree."

Harcourt smiled at Janice. "I'm afraid that we're in for a celebration."

She looked at the grinning, expectant Eskimo. A flicker of amused comprehension in Harcourt's eyes was reflected in hers as she echoed debonairly:

"Afraid! I should hope that there would be a celebration. One — one doesn't get married every day."

11

Harcourt thoughtfully bowed his black tie before
the mirror in his room at the H house. What a day!
Little he had thought as he had shaved in front of
the same glass this morning before sun-up, that he
would return to it a married man. The eyes
looking back at him narrowed. Married! Hardly.
He would have Jan where he had the right to look
after her, that was all. "And that's a whale of a lot,
my friend," he told the man looking back at him.
A leap into the dark. A blood-tingling leap. Not
unlike stepping out of a plane in the air, only one
was reasonably sure that one's chute would bring
one safely down. So many marriages cracked-up.
If it were possible to prevent it, this one should
not. He would send Janice out on the last boat —
no winter for her here — he would join her as soon
as he could get leave. Then — if she cared — they
would have a glorious honeymoon. He nodded to
the man looking back at him with blazing eyes.

"You are traveling fast and far. Paxton is still
in the running."

He buttoned his silk waistcoat, slipped into his
dinner-jacket. The other engineers and he had

agreed to dress for the Samp girls' party. Why not? They kept evening-clothes here that they might appear in civilized garb when they dined and danced at Fairbanks or Nome. Miss Martha and Miss Mary were entitled to their finest courtesy.

He glanced at the clock in the living-room as he entered. Too early to go to the Waffle Shop. Janice would be dressing. Tong descended from the couch, stretched lazily, before he thrust a cold nose into his hand. Had she had time to rest? What a day for her! He lighted his pipe. One arm on the mantel he looked about. Green boughs outlined doorways and windows. A great jar of golden berries and their leaves beautified a corner. Someone with taste must have superintended the decorations. Had Tubby executed his commissions? He bent over the bowl of red roses on the desk to inhale their fragrance. Not such a wilderness when a florist could produce blooms like that within flying distance. Would Janice think the H house unbearably raw? He spoke to the dog. "Come on, boy, let's see how it looks to us." He opened the door at the end of the room opposite his bedroom, snapped on the light. Miss Mary must have worked like a beaver. Crystal and enamel appointments covered the top of a dressing-table. Two perfect pink roses, in a slender vase behind a photograph of Billy Trent in a silver frame, perfumed the room. He lifted the chintz which covered one of the log walls. Frocks. The colors made him think of an old-time perennial border with the blues of lark-spur predominating. A battalion of shoes, slippers and sandals stood in close formation on a shelf below. He dropped the curtain as though it burned him. His eyes traveled on to the cot-bed with its soft rose brocade spread. He spoke to Tong watchfully waiting on the threshold.

"Together we ought to keep her safe and happy, old fella."

The dog responded with a promissory lick of his rough red tongue. With a last glance about, Harcourt snapped out the light. A crude place for a girl like Jan! Not much like her surroundings had she married Paxton. But — she had turned Paxton down. She had come to him. She had trusted him enough for that. God help him to keep her faith and confidence.

He picked up the belt and holster which he had dropped to the desk when he came in. As he hung it on a peg on the log wall the lines between his brows deepened. The shoulder holster which held its twin was empty. The missing revolver had been there this morning — he had debated for an instant as to which one he would wear. He opened the kitchen door.

"Pasca."

No answer to his call. The boy was doubtless helping the Samp girls in their preparations. He would look him up at the Waffle Shop. Perhaps one of the engineers had borrowed it.

Plump Miss Mary in a dove-gray taffeta, its balloon sleeves proclaiming it of the vintage of

'94, its rosepoint bertha suggesting a grandmother of parts, greeted him as he entered the Samp living-room. Obviously she was flustered.

"Well, *now!* Well, *now!* Janice is dressing, Mr. Bruce. Mary and I begged her to wear one of her lovely evening dresses for our party. She let us choose it from a trunk in the storehouse." She patted his sleeve. "Don't you look nice."

"That goes for you too, Miss Mary. You almost knocked my eyes out with your pretty dress." He bent his head and kissed her rosy, wrinkled cheek. "Thank you for arranging Jan's room. When did you hear the news?"

"You're the most heart-warming person, Mr. Bruce. I feel as though I'd been sitting in the sun after I've been with you." She smiled through tears, dabbed at her eyes. "Mr. Tubby radioed the news before he left the city. Such a surprise. No one had suspected a love affair between you two — that is, not until last evening here — not but that Janice is sweet and pretty enough to be loved, but you've seemed to think of nothing but your work."

"Never can tell what is going on in a man's mind, Miss Mary."

"That's what I told Martha. After we'd had a good cry over the news — a happy cry, you understand — she said, 'We'll have a party!' If there aren't folks to feed in the next world Martha'll wander round like a lost soul. I guess we baked about a ton of cakes after we got Mr. Tubby's message. M's. Hale wouldn't believe it at first. Said 'twas Mr. Tubby's idea of a joke, that you'd have told her that you were going to get married. She got over being miffed and offered to superintend the placing of the greens in the H house."

"Had we told anyone you and Miss Martha would have been the first to know. Hope you are not hurt that we didn't take you into our confidence?"

"Hurt!" Miss Mary clasped rough-skinned red hands on her dove-gray breast. "Hurt! Well, now! I claim that marryin' an' buryin' is folks' own business. If they can't do those two things without advice or criticism, what can they do? I asked M's. Hale if she was coming to the party an' she said she didn't know, Joe was pretty sick. Here's your bride."

His bride! Harcourt felt the blood burn in his cheek bones, saw Janice's color steal up in response. She was lovelier even than he had thought her. Her pale blue gown, silvery as the edges of a cloud, suggested a fairy loom. Straps of brilliants framed shoulders, white in contrast to a sun-tanned throat. An half dozen glittering bracelets gleamed on her left arm. Slippers which matched her gown had bows of sparkling stones which were repeated in the clasp of a bag of antique brocade. She laid a mandarin coat, heavily embroidered with mauve and purple iris, carefully over the back of a chair.

For an instant the stillness of the room was stirred only by the snap of the fire, the rhythmic purr of Blot asleep on the rug. Miss Mary broke the spell. She caught the bag, pressed it against her cheek. "How pretty! How pretty! My dear, isn't it absurd for an old woman like me to care for such things? I'll go tell Martha you're ready." She hurried out of the room like a fussy little tug-boat under full steam.

Harcourt smiled. "Is she afraid of playing gooseberry?"

Janice's eyes and voice were wistful. "She thinks it a real marriage, Bruce. But she confessed that everyone was terribly surprised. I feel like such a — such a fake letting them do all this for us."

He laid his hand over the brown, rosy-nailed fingers clutching his sleeve. "Forget it, Jan. Don't look over your shoulder. Look forward. From now on they will have every reason to believe that I'm mad about you." His tone, his eyes sent the color flooding to her face. He laughed, lightened his voice, "You see what a good actor I am, I almost convinced you."

She drew a breath of relief. "I will have to go some to keep up with that. I almost lost my reason when I came in and saw you in dinner-clothes."

"Always pay my hostess the compliment of dressing for her party. We keep evening togs here, now that we can fly to Nome and Fairbanks and the Fort, just so we won't forget how to wear them."

Janice's memory projected a close-up of a girl

170

in a roadster leaning forward for a light. She said hastily:

"I am glad that I dressed the part too. The Samp sisters begged me to wear something bridal —"

"That isn't the wedding gown you had for —"

"Don't look so murderous. It isn't. The woman who made my trousseau took that back, credited it on my account, praise be to Allah, as Tubby would say."

"Have you a lot of bills worrying you? If you have, I —"

"You will pay them? No. This marriage is not real enough for that. I haven't any. I paid every cent I owed, invested the remainder of my — er — fortune, and fared forth into the far North."

He ignored the theatrical exaggeration of the last sentence. "Is that true?"

"Is what true?"

"About investing the fortune — I had heard that you and Billy had lost everything."

"Not everything, Bruce. I am not an heiress — but — I have enough. I have saved my salary. No chance to spend money here. If at any time you require a loan, I may be able to accommodate you."

She was laughing, gay, audacious. He answered in the same spirit.

"Thanks. That's a rash offer. I might sink it in a gold mine. Has all your stuff been taken to my cabin?"

"Almost all that I use. There are an half dozen

trunks in the storehouse. Miss Mary spent every minute she could snitch from cooking to move my belongings. You — you still think it necessary for me to live there?"

"Answer that question for yourself. We have set out on the road of deception. It will be full enough of shell-holes without our plowing up any. When two persons marry, it is still the custom, at least it was when I left civilization, for them to live in the same house. Be a good sport and see it through, my dear."

"The night we dined together in New York you said: 'Be a sport. Acknowledge that you've made a mistake. Don't go on with this marriage.' I didn't tell you that already I had broken with Ned Paxton."

"That fact will be one of the enduring satisfactions of my life. Come on. I hear the boys tuning up. Ought we to enter arm in arm?"

"At the risk of making a frightful social blunder — let's not."

"Taking this?" He picked up the mandarin coat.

"Yes. I'll use it as a wrap. Isn't it gorgeous? I found it in my room here. Tubby must have bought it for a wedding present when he went back to the city. He knew that I was mad about it. I suspect that it was frightfully expensive. It is taking goods under false pretenses for me to accept it. I ought to give it back, but I love it. Can he afford to buy a thing like this?"

"Probably not every day, but weddings do not

occur every day at headquarters. Why hurt the donor by returning his gift? Let's go."

An orchestra, consisting of fiddle, flute and saxophone, agonized into the Wedding March from Lohengrin, as they appeared in the doorway of the Waffle Shop. Each musician had a table all his own. Seated in a chair on top of it, he had the air of an adventurous gull perched on a small berg, floating out to sea. They scraped and puffed and blew till rills of perspiration trickled down their faces, which had been scrubbed till they shone and shaven till the blood came through in spots. The big room had been cleared of chairs and tables; candle shavings had been sprinkled lavishly over the rough floor; the air was spicy with the breath of the spruces which had been used as decoration.

Janice laughed and parried questions, played her part brilliantly. No one could suspect from her manner that she was not the most gorgeously happy bride in the world, Harcourt told himself with a tinge of bitterness. Her radiance vanished like sunshine blotted by a cloud as Millicent Hale approached. Something deep in the woman's fatigue-rimmed eyes gave him the uneasy sense of an animal at bay. They reflected the green of her gown as she purred:

"Dear Mrs. Harcourt, how sweet of you to provide an occasion for civilized clothes. I am consumed with curiosity to know how you accomplished it. I've heard Bruce declare repeatedly that never, while he was in Alaska, would he marry. What brand of coercion did you use?" She shook her head as though in amused admonition. The earrings of brilliants which almost touched her shoulders sent out a myriad colorful sparks.

The malice of the attack rendered Harcourt speechless. Was the little woman whom he had considered pathetically helpless like that? Was Janice as amazed as he? He glanced at her in concern. She was looking straight into the eyes watching her with cat-like intentness.

"It was a method quite my own, Mrs. Hale. You couldn't possibly use it." Harcourt came out of his trance of surprise, laid his hand on her bare arm. She shook it off, turned to extend her hand to Chester. Challenged gaily:

"Why the gloomy brow? Cheerio! This is a party, not a memorial service."

Before he could answer Tubby Grant seized him.

"Want you, Jimmy. Going to stage an old-timer. The Samp girls are stepping out in a quadrille. The wicked Lancers is the only dance they know. Bruce, you take Miss Martha. I'm leading-out the bride — with her permission — you beau Miss Mary, Chester. Mrs. Hale may take her pick from the stagline. That completes the set. Ready. Let's go."

With much shifting and laughter the four couples took their places. Janice and Grant were opposite Harcourt and the elder Samp sister. The leader of the musicians nestled the fiddle under his chin, face beatific, drew the bow with a powerful, flourishing sweep, shouted:

"Salute Partners!" Miss Martha spread her plum-color taffeta skirts with work-worn hands and curtsied to the floor, recovered, made a deep obeisance in response to a shouted, "Salute Corners."

Her beautiful dignity set the keynote for the dance. The others kept watchful eyes on the sisters, who sailed through the figures with the grace of an angular and chubby swan. The engineers and section heads leaning against the log walls beat time softly with hands and feet to the rhythm of the music. The dancers caught fire from their enthusiasm, pranced Forward and Back, wound in and out of Ladies Chain, Balanced Corners, with gay abandon. Someone shouted:

"Change Partners!"

A quartet of engineers took the places of the men in the quadrille and the figures began over again. The Samp sisters puffingly but gallantly carried on. Millicent Hale was the first to give out. Breathless, she retreated to the wall where Harcourt was standing. She slipped a hand within his arm.

"I haven't danced so much nor so hard since the winter I came out. Do take me home, Bruce. Jimmy has disappeared. Joe will be furious if I stay longer."

For the fraction of a second Harcourt hesitated. Why pick on him? Better to humor her.

She might make a scene. Anything was credible after her hateful attack on Janice. He looked across the room. The bride was surrounded by men begging for a dance. He would be back before she knew that he was gone. He followed Millicent Hale out of the Waffle Shop. A faint glow still tinted the serrated mountain-tops.

"How cold the nights are getting!"

She shivered as she drew her heavily fringed, heavily embroidered shawl of silver cloth about her shoulders. She slipped one hand within his arm.

"Of course I didn't need an escort this short distance, Bruce, but I had to consult you about Jimmy."

"Jimmy! What's the matter with Jimmy?"

"That's what I want to know. Today when I entered our cabin, he was threatening Joe with a pistol."

An empty shoulder holster hanging against a log wall flashed on the screen of Harcourt's mind and was gone.

"Millicent! You've been dreaming."

Her laugh was bitter. "I'll admit that my life is one long hideous nightmare, but the part about Jimmy really happened. As I entered he was saying:

" 'Send for her again and I'll shoot you. You've messed up my sister's life, that's enough. Get me?'

"I couldn't believe it was Joe huddled in his chair, livid, afraid. Joe afraid! As I looked at him

I thought what a poor fool I had been all these years, not to stand up to him, not to threaten him. He is a bully and a coward, Bruce, and I've never before found it out."

"If you have lost your fear of him, it is a lot gained, Millicent. For whom did Joe send, do you know?"

"No. Unless — unless Jimmy found out about Tatima. Joe has made a fool of her with flattery. Nothing worse, I'm sure, but she follows him about like a dog."

"I'll speak to Jimmy. He will have to turn over his gun to me, if that is the use he is making of it."

"Talk with him, Bruce. Poor boy, he has never forgotten his experiences overseas. You will have more influence than anyone else." She laid her hand on his arm. "We all dump our worries on your shoulders, don't we? I shan't dare do it now that you are married. I feel as though I had lost you."

Under pretense of producing his cigarette case Harcourt stepped back.

"You can't lose what you never had, Millicent. Goodnight!"

He heard her little gasp as he turned on his heel, too embarrassed to wait until she was inside the cabin. Good Lord, one would have thought from her voice that he had been her lover! How she had changed in this last week. It was the wilderness, the rawness of the camp which was responsible. It was a cruel life for a woman. And he had tied Janice to it. What else could he have done? She had been in a panic of fear. She had turned to him. She was safe married to a man whom she trusted. They had not seen the last of Paxton. He would appear in his luxurious yacht, and make headquarters look like thirty cents. Let him try to get her. She was his. He was hers, heart and soul and body. She must not suspect it yet. She must go out on the last boat — no winter in Alaska for her — then when she had had time to think things through, he would get leave and join her.

His dream castle tumbled about his ears. Meanwhile he had this new problem of Jimmy Chester to meet. What the dickens had started him after his brother-in-law with a gun? What had sent the memory of his own missing revolver slashing through his mind when Millicent had told him of Jimmy's threat? Jimmy Chester wouldn't borrow. He had an arsenal of his own. It couldn't be because of Tatima. He had known that Hale had hired her to take care of his cabin. For whom had Joe sent? He would straighten that situation out quick. Jimmy would be dispatched with a track-laying gang tomorrow. Kadyama had to be watched. One was enough.

What an infernal mix-up! He ought to concentrate with all his intelligence on the problems of construction, instead, he was getting mixed up in a family row. All of which confirmed him in his original contention that an engineers' camp was no place for women. If the Hales would only get out. Tubby had been hinting that the late chief was not so helpless as he appeared. He would do a little sleuthing, and if Joe were shamming, out he would go on the next boat.

As he entered the Waffle Shop Miss Martha and Miss Mary, crimson faced from the exertions of the dance, with mammoth white aprons over their creaking taffetas, were serving the ice-cream which Grant had brought hundreds of miles in a plane. As he approached Janice he heard Jimmy Chester say harshly:

"He'll never send for you again."

Had Joe Hale sent for Janice? The suspicion tightened Harcourt's lips. The girl looked up at him. There was a hint of resentment in her voice.

"Oh, you have come back. Jimmy and I had decided that you didn't like the party, hadn't we, Jimmy?"

It was evident that she had seen him go out with Millicent. He answered evenly.

"I'm crazy about the party. Did you think I would leave before I had danced with my bride? The musicians have finished their gorge and are tuning up. By the way, Chester, be ready with a track-laying gang to go up the inlet at reveille. You have all the specifications. Short notice, but you can make it. Want to push the work while this weather holds." He held out his hand. "My dance — Mrs. Harcourt."

He was conscious of Jimmy Chester's pale, frowning regard as they moved away in rhythmic step to the music. He watched him until he left the room. Janice looked up.

"Sorry I was catty, Bruce."

He held her the fraction of a degree closer. "Were you catty? Millicent was raw to you, Jan, but don't lay it up against her. This last year has set her nerves on edge."

"I wonder if a year here will do that to mine."

"You won't have a chance to find out."

"Won't I? Perhaps you will like having me here so much you'll beg me to stay."

His arm tightened. "Dance well together, don't we?"

There was a hint of strain in her laugh. "The fighting line again. Tubby wants me here if you don't. Yes, we are good. We might make a dancing team, if engineering fails."

"That's a thought. Sorry, but it is time the festivities broke up. All of us must be sons of toil again tomorrow. We, being the guests of honor, should make a move. That correct? I suspect Tubby of a theatrical climax. We will dance round to the door, vanish and escape."

As they stole surreptitiously from the Waffle Shop, the squeak of the fiddle, the quaver of the flute, the blare of the saxophone rose on a triumphant note and ceased. The air was cool and clear as crystal. The green light in the radio tower glowed like an emerald eye in the forehead of a watchful god. The heavens still held a trace of the glory of the sunset. Above the broken crater spread a coppery glow. Seemingly near but in reality miles away, snowy mountaintops glimmered pearl and gray. Suddenly across the sky swept a film of glittering silver. The Northern Lights! They mounted and receded like the tide of the sea, now breaking into ruby waves, now into malachite billows. One shade melted into another, a blending harmony of delicate color. Shafts of red and green, orange and purple shot to the zenith of the indigo heavens. The light shattered into silver stepping-stones which mounted and mounted as though to form a skyway to the Celestial City. Colors streamed into half-tones, faded to amethyst and gold, fused into the dusky horizon, blinked out like pale witch fires. The moon swung clear of a fluff of cloud, the stars leaned low as though to catch the murmur of unseen life in the still night. The Aurora shimmered, faded like a low strain of melody into the illimitable silence of sea and forest.

Janice drew a long uneven breath. "It is more gorgeous than I had imagined." As they turned toward the H house, she said lightly: "Ever since I arrived as Jimmy Delevan, I have been consumed by curiosity to — to see the inside of your cabin."

He answered by throwing open the door. As they crossed the threshold a shower of confetti pelted them. It powdered their hair, lay like colored snow on their shoulders, one adventurous particle clung to Janice's eyelashes. She laughed unsteadily as she brushed it away.

"The trail of the resourceful Mr. Grant.

Doubtless he expected you to carry your bride over the threshold, as big strong men do in the movies and points south."

Harcourt laid his hands lightly on her shoulders. "We will postpone that ceremony. Take off your wrap. The room is hot. Pasca keeps these fires roaring."

She slipped off the heavily embroidered mandarin coat. He laid it on the couch, crossed to the fireplace and lighted a cigarette. Arm on the mantel, he watched her eyes travel from the Indian blankets on the log walls to the Russian samovar, saw them glow with admiration as they rested on the Chinese pewter tea-service, linger on the rich pelts on the floor. They met his.

"Like it?"

"Love it. How did these rare things get into this wilderness?"

"Small trading vessels stop for any one of a dozen reasons. The captain or mate usually has something choice he will dispose of for a consideration."

"I'm mad about that Chinese pewter. We'll have tea every afternoon."

What a gallant child she was! As unselfconscious as though she had dropped in for an evening call. God help him to keep her so. She laughed.

"Perhaps I should have added, 'With your permission.' "

"Everything I have is yours, Jan." The huskiness of his voice sent the color to her face. That wouldn't do. He opened a door, snapped on a light, said grandiloquently, "Behold the kitchenette!"

She stepped to the threshold. "Pale green, and a gray-and-white linoleum on the floor. My word, but you are modern!"

"I told you that I lost my head over the H house. After we had finished the chimneys, they just naturally required bedrooms to utilize their other sides; bedrooms required baths; a house this size needed a kitchen. I have never regretted it. Planning and ordering kept Archie Harper busy and happy. He worked up to almost the last moment of his life, and now I have it for you." He nodded toward a lighted room. "Your things are in there. If you are not too tired I should like to talk a while, Jan."

"Except for the fact that my feet are shredded to ribbons — that wasn't a dance, it was a riot — I am not in the least tired. I will change my slippers and come back."

"I'll get your sandals." He pulled the fan-back chair a bit nearer the fire. "Sit here —" As she hesitated he added, "Please."

As he pulled aside the chintz curtain in her room, the buckle on a black satin slipper winked at him colorfully; he could almost hear it chuckle. It seemed years ago that he had picked it up on Fifth Avenue, had searched the Lost and Found column. Had a crystal-gazer or a palm-reader foretold that its owner would be seated in his cabin tonight, married to him, he would have

183

accused the fortune-teller of a melodrama complex. After all, didn't melodrama hold the stage in real life more often than critics would admit?

Janice was in the fan-back chair when he returned with the sandals. The firelight set every facet of the brilliants on her frock a-twinkle with rainbow colors. She looked up with a laugh.

"I was preparing to wriggle out of my slippers the way Miss Martha sheds her shoes at every opportunity."

He dropped to one knee in front of her. "Stick out your foot." He gently removed the high-heeled blue slipper with its sparkling bow, put on the sandal. "That better?" She nodded. "The other." He held the slender foot in his hand after it was shod. "Jan, you understand, don't you — Who the dickens is pounding like that? Is Tubby trying to be funny?"

"Someone is beating with both fists. Go! Quick!"

Harcourt pulled open the door. Millicent Hale stumbled into the room. "Bruce!" Her terrified eyes widened as Janice took a step toward her. She shut them. Sobbed. With arms outflung she braced herself against the log wall. Brilliants swinging from her ears, on her green frock, quivered with light. She shuddered. Gasped for control. Harcourt caught her shoulder.

"Steady, Millicent. What has happened?"

Her throat contracted. Her voice was a hoarse whisper. "Joe's dead! Shot!" She covered her eyes with one hand. "You're white as death,

Bruce. Don't be sorry for me. I'm free! Free! If you'd only waited."

With a stifled exclamation he withdrew his hand. She crumpled to the floor.

12

Harcourt picked his way through the maze of the Eskimo camp, past rudely constructed shacks, canvas tents, shelters of walrus hide. He cleared a baby that crawled in front of him at a jump, only to land on a dog which slunk away with a howl. The atmosphere was heavy with the odors of simmering seal-blubber, wet fur, drying fish. Bead-like eyes peered at him from cavernous interiors. Malamute pups worried bones, or dug frenziedly at the ground to bury them. Swarthy children pulled at the blankets of women with jet-black braids of hair who slapped them, nursed at the brown breasts of women who cuddled them. Virile youths in high skin boots, mail-order trousers and shirts, stared at him sheepishly; girls with brilliant red lips smiled at him shyly. Shadowy figures scuttled in the background, like supers assembling for a chorus; witch-like old women, with stripes tattooed from lower lip to the point of the chin, stirred the boiling contents of pots over small fires. Outside a tumbledown shack, two men pounded with white rods on stretched-skin drums as big as dishpans. They crooned as they boomed in perfect time.

He stopped before a shack. Silence followed his knock. He opened the door. Under a light which hung from a rafter a little man with a face like a walnut-shell, bone button through the flesh near the edge of his upper lip, worked at a bench littered with tools and pieces of silver. Propped against a crude blower was the advertising page from a magazine. On pegs on the wall hung bracelets and chains beautifully carved. A number of silver dollars were stacked in one corner. His face cracked into a smile of welcome.

"Howdy, Boss! Buy somet'ing?"

"Not this morning, Ossa." Harcourt looked at the design from which the man was working.

"Where did you get this?"

"Mees Secr'tary bring it. Say I might mak' same. Ossa get beeg trade nex' summer she t'ink. She kin'. She help squaws with papooses, teech 'em much."

Harcourt's brows contracted. Janice in the native camp! Why hadn't some one told him? If he got her away from this wilderness safe and sound, he never would worry about anything again in all his life.

He stepped to the table, set near a window hermetically sealed. Kadyama stared at him from above a handful of greasy cards. The eyes of the three other men shifted from one face to another.

"Pasca told you that I wanted to talk with you, Kadyama. Why didn't you come to the office?"

187

"I no work no more. I go huntin'. Much money huntin'."

"You won't go hunting till you have talked with me, get me? No one leaves headquarters for the next three days. The Commissioner and his men are coming." He watched the four faces. "Mr. Hale was shot last night." Stupefaction in three pairs of eyes, into Kadyama's triumph flamed.

"Klosh! Good! The damn black cat go. He go."

Remembrance of the abduction of Blot, which had been submerged in the rush of events, flashed back into Harcourt's mind.

"Did you kidnap that cat?"

The Indian shrugged. "Good-for-nodings, I drop him in kennel yard, play with huskies. He like to fight. He fight 'em fine."

"You'll pay for that, Kadyama, after we get this other business cleared up."

The Indian pulled himself to his feet. "W'y you talk lak dat to me? You t'ink Kadyama shoot Meester Hale? No. Know too much. Make heap bad work to shoot he. Whole pack peoples after. Yes sirree."

"I don't think you shot him. You must answer some questions though. Come to the office at two o'clock. If you don't come I will send for you. Then some other people may think you did it. Understand?"

"Yes sirree. I be there." The man's servility was sardonic.

On his way back to the office Harcourt recaptured the picture of Janice in the fan-back chair last night in the H house. Lovely child. She was not a child; she had been a woman as she sat there, a beautiful, self-possessed woman. Cool. Steady. What had he expected? That the words of that marriage service would set her a-fire with love for him? It had taken iron self-control to keep from catching her in his arms and telling her he adored her. Millicent Hale's entrance had been opportune, but what had Jan thought of her frenzied cry: "I'm free! Free! If you'd only waited!"

He had been furiously angry at the implication, had opened his lips to refute it when Millicent had crumpled. For an instant he and Janice had stared into one another's eyes, then she had pointed to the woman on the floor.

"Better put her on the couch. Looks as though she had been wading. Her skirt is wet."

He had only vaguely noticed that as he lifted her, but now the memory of the bedraggled lace of her frock came back to him. Had she come straight from her cabin to the H house there would have been a board walk all the way. Running round crazed from shock, probably. He had laid her on the couch before he had rushed back to the Waffle Shop for Grant, who was talking with the Samp sisters; even the musicians were gone. Together they had entered the Hale cabin. Joe lay where he had fallen. The wheel-chair was overturned. Death must have been instantaneous; his face showed no distress. If one could imagine it on such a still mask, the expression was contemptuous surprise. The Pekinese was playing with something on the rug. They had searched for a revolver, had found nothing but Hale's own which hung in its holster, unloaded, clean barreled. Even a tenderfoot would know that it hadn't been used for weeks. He had sent Tubby for Jimmy Chester and two engineers. While he was waiting, he had picked up the dog to shut him out of the room. A blue glass bead had rolled from between his paws. Tatima! Incredible.

Hale had flattered her, spoiled her for her own kind. Stephen Mallory had prophesied that her Christianity was a veneer which wouldn't stand a test. Even so, it was unbelievable that she would commit a crime. He put his hand over the breast pocket of his khaki shirt. The bead was safe in case it was needed in evidence. He had not told the other men of his find.

Could it have been Jimmy! He would have a hard row to hoe if his threat to Joe Hale came out at the inquest. Millicent had heard it. Had she confided in anyone but himself? No matter what Jimmy had threatened, he wouldn't shoot Hale. What had he been saying to Janice when he had interrupted their talk at the dance? "He'll never send for you again!" Good Lord, Hale must have been lying on that rug then! Jimmy had been white, jumpy, unlike himself last night but he had charged his mood up to disappointment. He had hung round the Waffle Shop ever since Janice's arrival, had seemed immensely attracted to her. Small wonder.

He forced down memories of her. He must concentrate on unraveling the mystery. A crime had been committed. The authorities back home would rightfully look to him to bring the criminal to justice. He stopped on a rise of ground. The distant mountains whose snowy tops loomed from haze-swathed middles, the sapphire sea whipped into countless sparkles by a crystal breeze, the illimitable stretches of wilderness, the weather-bleached cabins, ugly steamshovels and dredges, the devil-may-care men working them, were brought into spiritual unity by the azure and crimson and white flag which streamed against the clear sky.

Instinctively Harcourt brought his hand up in salute. One couldn't know how that red, white and blue was of the very warp and woof of one's heart and soul, till one saw it floating free in the wilderness. One sensed then as never before what it had meant, what it did mean, what it would mean in the years to come.

Tilted back in a chair against the wall of his cabin, Jimmy Chester was gazing straight ahead, slipping the dark seal-ring back and forth, back and forth on his little finger. As Harcourt entered, he looked up. His expression was that of one whose thoughts suddenly had been dragged back from a far country. His eyes cleared. He jumped to his feet.

"Boy! In the excitement I forgot about that track-laying gang you told me to take out at reveille, Chief. I've been at the H house with Millicent this morning trying to find out what she wants done about — things."

"How is she?"

"Hazy. Can't seem to understand what I ask her."

"Can you wonder? The shock of finding Joe like that must have been terrific."

"Why didn't she come for me instead of you?"

"Because the H house was nearer, I suppose." Harcourt became absorbed in lighting a cigarette. "Heard that you were all excited day before yesterday because Hale had sent for someone. For whom did he send?"

Jimmy Chester stared out of the window. "For Miss Trent."

"Janice! How did you know?"

"Met her coming out of his cabin. Had just been talking with Millicent at the Waffle Shop, so I knew she wasn't responsible. She wouldn't tell why she had been there, I went at her wrong, I guess, so I just walked in and read the riot act to Joe Hale. Boy! I must have been good. He looked scared to death. He's a bad egg!"

"Go easy, Jimmy. Why didn't you report to me? It was my job."

"I — I — didn't know then —" Chester swallowed hard. Harcourt laid his hand on his shoulder.

"I've loved her since I knew her as a little girl."

192

He walked to the other window. "The Commissioner and his deputies will be here any minute now. Coming by plane. Come up to the office." Hand on the door he stopped. "By the way, you didn't by any chance borrow one of my revolvers yesterday, did you?"

Even Jimmy Chester's lips went white. "My God, you don't think I shot Joe?"

"No. When I left my cabin yesterday morning the pistol in the shoulder holster was hanging in its accustomed place. When I returned last night it was gone. Always make all possible inquiries before I accuse anyone of stealing even in my thoughts. I have asked every man here except you. They think they remember seeing it when they were bringing in greens for the cabin."

"Greens! In the H house! Hark! There's the plane now."

"Go up to the field, Chester, and see if you can help in the landing. Pasca is likely to be there alone. Kadyama's struck."

"Struck! For what?"

" 'Much money huntin'.' Bring the Commissioner and his men to the office."

Harcourt looked after Chester as he hurried away. He liked neither Jimmy's color nor his unsteady voice. A very passion of hatred had contorted his face when he had spoken of Hale. His eyes had dilated, narrowed when he had heard of the missing revolver. Nice Jimmy Chester, as Janice called him, wouldn't do that horrible thing. He might threaten, but it was a far call from threatening a man to shooting him. A plane was coming down in the field. Officials. Before sunset the mystery doubtless would be solved.

Martha Samp hailed him from the steps of the H house. Her eyes were tired, her face more deeply lined, the hands with which she pulled at her sweater were unsteady, but her voice held a tinge of pleasurable excitement.

"Is the Commissioner in that plane?"

"Yes."

"He has power to sentence or dismiss a case, just like the Captain of the boat which goes up the coast among the Eskimos, I understand. Where you goin' to hold the inquest?"

"In the office."

"You're right welcome to our sittin'-room."

Harcourt repressed a smile. This case might be cambric tea to the hardened officials about to land, but it would be as stimulating as the blackest of black coffee for her.

"Thank you, Miss Martha, but the office will be the best place. How is Mrs. Hale this morning?"

"I can't make her out. Her pulse is all right, but she just lays there with her eyes closed."

"Where is Janice?"

"I sent her back to her cabin last night. She wanted to take care of M's. Hale, but I wouldn't let her, even if M's. Hale'd wanted her round, which I could see she didn't."

"Is she there now?"

"She was goin' to set out them geraniums she bought — sakes alive, was it only yesterday? Seems as though it must be years ago."

"Any danger to Mrs. Hale in moving her?"

"Not a mite. I was goin' to speak to you about that. Your cabin's no place for her. You send Pasca along to help and I'll see that she's moved."

"And that Janice comes back to the H house?"

Little lines crinkled from the corners of her eyes like rays drawn to indicate the setting sun.

"I'll do my best, but what'd you do to hurt her last night, Mr. Bruce?"

"*I* hurt her?"

"She looked white an' still when I went into the H house. When I told her we'd better leave M's. Hale where she was, she kinder sniffed an' said:

" 'Of course. I haven't a doubt but she'd like to stay here forever,' an' off she marched. I was that troubled about her that I kept runnin' over to the Waffle Shop to stand outside her door. There was a light goin' but it was still as death. Sakes alive, don't go so white, Mr. Bruce, or I'll be sorry I told you. You've got so much on your mind."

"Never be sorry that you have told me anything about Janice, Miss Martha. Tell her to come back. If she refuses, tell her that if she doesn't come I will come after her. I may have much on my mind, but not too much for that."

13

Janice stepped back to get the effect of the red geranium trees in nail-kegs on either side of the Waffle Shop door. Gorgeous against the background of weather-bleached log walls. Perfect day. Air spruce-flavored with a dash of salt. Sky a clear turquoise above a deeper blue sea, lace-frilled waves, which rolled in to break on the shingle. Rails, steam-shovels, ditchers turned to red gold under the Midas touch of the sun. On a rise beyond the cabins a white cross gleamed and disapppeared as a breeze stirred the gigantic fern fronds about it. It seemed heartless to set out these gay blooms in the atmosphere of tragedy which hung over headquarters like an Arctic mist, but the plants would die if they were not potted.

She looked thoughtfully at the Hale cabin. Not yet twenty-four hours since Joe Hale had gone. Where? An hour or more ago the Commissioner and two deputies had landed on the flying-field. She had not seen Bruce since he had lifted Millicent Hale from the floor and laid her on the couch. With a hurried, "Call the Samp girls," he had dashed out. As she had worked over the unconscious woman, she had tried to crush back the memory of her frenzied wail, "I'm free! Free! If you'd only waited!" The Samp sisters had spent the night at the H house, had sent Janice back to her cabin at the Waffle Shop. She had dropped to the edge of the stripped cot. Rigid and still, had sat there listening for Bruce's footsteps, waiting for him to come and tell her that Millicent Hale's insinuation was false.

He had not come. Toward morning she had dozed fitfully. Tubby had entered the deserted kitchen as she was making coffee. Voices hushed, she had asked and he had answered questions. Nothing could be done until the officials came, he had said. Last night he had gone to the Hale cabin with Harcourt. The place had been still, horribly still. Hale lay on the rug. The little dog was chasing something round the room.

"Shot?" Their eyes had met as she had repeated the word. Was Tubby seeing, as she saw, the teasing, laughing group in the Samp living-room, as Miss Martha had read from the newspaper? Was he hearing Jimmy Chester's voice, "There are some men who'd be better for a little shooting"? She had asked Tubby if he had a suspicion as to motive. He had shaken his head. "No, Bruce and I stayed there all night when we were not sending radio messages. Didn't get a clue." He had stopped on the threshold of the Waffle Shop to remind:

"Remember, a man's innocent till he's proved guilty."

A man! Tubby had evidently thought a man guilty. On her knees, Janice stabbed with the trowel at the earth about the roots of a geranium. At intervals since Millicent Hale had burst into the H house, through her memory had echoed the Plop! Plop! Plop! Plop! of beads from a broken string. She saw again a bit of blue glass rolling toward her across the rug. Tatima had been behind the screen. She must have heard Hale's fulsome compliments. From bits she had inadvertently picked up, she knew that the Indian girl had been a worry and care to the Samp sisters while Millicent Hale was in Seattle. Jimmy Chester must have known what was going on. Was that why he had raged at her when he had met her coming out of the Hale cabin? Poor boy. The night of the party his face had been ghastly as he demanded:

"He sent for you, did he? Well, he'll never send for you again."

Janice set her teeth hard in her lips to shut back a cry of horror. Jimmy! Moody, romantic Jimmy Chester! Could he have done it? No! No! It must have been Tatima. It might have been the girl's lover, Kadyama, but it couldn't have been Jimmy Chester.

"Sent for you, did he. Well, he'll never send for you again." The words whirled through her mind like a spinning top. She flung down the trowel, sat back on her heels. Senseless to be

198

puttering with these plants. She would better get at some work in the office. She must shake this hideous suspicion of Jimmy Chester which was stalking her.

Head down, hands thrust hard in his pockets, Tubby Grant approached along the board walk. Tong paced with magisterial dignity behind him, muscles rippling under his tawny coat. Janice called softly. She flung her arms about the dog as he poked his cold nose against her neck. He seemed like a rock in a heaving, tricky sea of doubt. His strength quieted her panic. Grant overturned an empty nail-keg. Seated on it he took one knee into his embrace regarded her critically.

"You wear blue a lot, don't you? I like it."

"Thanks for them kind words. I was low in my mind. Now I'm all sweetness and light."

"I'll say you are. There's a lift in your voice which squares my shoulders and makes me feel like a dragonslayer."

"Why, Tubby!" Janice blinked back tears of surprise.

"That's my story and I'll stick to it. How's the face which launched a thousand ships?"

She touched her cheek with appraising fingers. "So much has happened that is big I had forgotten that little scratch. Have they discovered any clues yet, Tubby?"

"If they have they are not handing them out for publication. Ba-gosh, I'll take off my hat to the Commissioner and his deputies. They are letting the other fellas do the talking."

"Who do you think did it? Kadyama?"

"I wouldn't put it past him. He's talked long and loud and red against Hale, but that doesn't prove anything. The Pekinese must have been among those present when it happened. He would have scented the Indian, would have warned Hale with his bark."

"Whom are they questioning?"

"Haven't begun yet, they've been busy in the Hale cabin. They want you in the office after lunch to take testimony."

"Will they question me?"

"Why not? You were in the H house when Millicent Hale burst in with the news, weren't you? Don't go loco when the Commissioner fires questions at you. He's got eyes like nice, shiny steel drills. You can't tell what's waiting round the corner to pounce, can you? Who'd have thought yesterday as you and I stood looking in that shop window that today we'd be mixed up in a shooting party."

Shop window. The words flashed a picture on Janice's mind.

"Tubby! I never have thanked you for the gorgeous mandarin coat. I wore it to the H house, had just taken it off when Millicent Hale burst in on us and I haven't thought of it since. You're a dear!"

"Says you. Sorry to hand back the bouquet, but I didn't buy it."

"You didn't! Who did?"

"Your boy friend."

"Bruce? How did he know about it?"

"I told him that you'd almost cried your eyes out wanting it."

"Tubby! You should not have let him spend all that money on me when you knew — you knew what a fake that marriage was, that Bruce sacrificed himself to help me."

"Mebbe so. Mebbe so." His face lost its usual expression of cherubic serenity. The pupils of his green eyes contracted as he inquired lightly, "Lady, has it ever occurred to you that you might be a million light-years behind the times? Can't realize that Joe's gone. He wasn't such a bad hombre. Funny, isn't it, how you forget a man's faults after he's stepped out? He got to drinking in the long, dark winters. Books meant nothing to him — they've been food and warmth to Harcourt and me — and his values got twisted."

"Do many of the men drink during the long, hard winters, Tubby?"

"Not so many as you'd think. The radio has been a Godsend, and say what you like about prohibition, it has done a lot of mopping up. There are days in winter when flying conditions are good, when we can break the monotony by a flight to the city. No longer is Alaska — ba-gosh! Who's going out?"

The zoom of a plane drowned his words. The motor thrummed deafeningly as it climbed. It circled like a great bee to get its bearings before it shot for the east. Its wings became shadowy and spectral, its hum a mere vibration. Janice clutched Grant's arm, watched the great bird from hand-shaded eyes till it seemed as small as a fly on an enormous blue windowpane.

"Who, w-who was it, Tubby?"

He patted her hand. "Don't get all excited. I got a jolt at first, as the Commissioner has forbidden anyone to leave headquarters. Then I remembered that he told Parks, one of the deputies, to fly back to the city for an expert he wanted."

"But it was one of the outfit's planes, Tubby."

"Sure. The bus the officials came in had to be tinkered so Bruce suggested taking one of ours to save time. I gotta go. Coming, Tong?" With an apologetic look at the girl the dog trotted off at his heels.

Janice's pounding heart was still getting in the way of her breath. For one horrible minute she had thought that Jimmy Chester was escaping. Flight would be a confession of guilt. He would not leave his sister when she was in trouble. Trouble! The tragedy didn't spell trouble for Millicent Hale, it spelled escape. Escape to Bruce Harcourt? No. She couldn't, she wouldn't believe that. He had bought that gorgeous mandarin coat, not Tubby. Why, why had he spent so much money on a girl he didn't love?

She was still pondering the question when Martha Samp, gaunt and gray, came out of the H house, charged along the board walk. She thrust her rough, big-jointed hands into the pockets of her crimson sweater as she stopped in front of the Waffle Shop.

"My stars, ain't them blooms pretty? When I saw them nodding at me 'twas as though little wings spread under my heavy heart and lifted it. Color's one of God's best gifts, an' we go on day after day acceptin' it as commonplace." She dropped to the nail-keg Grant had abandoned. Pulled off one heavy shoe, grimaced with pain as she flexed twisted toes in their white cotton stocking. "Feet ache like the toothache. I never'd know I had a body if it wasn't for them."

Janice gently massaged the cramped toes. "You do too much, Miss Martha. I would have been glad to take care of Mrs. Hale last night."

"It wasn't the place for you. That feels fine. You've got what my mother used to call, healin' hands. Mary an' I can take care of her easy. Pasca's goin' to bring her to the cabin you had so she'll be near. You pack up the rest of your things an' he'll carry them to the H house. Mr. Bruce wants you there."

"He wants me!"

"Sakes alive, anything surprisin' about that? Those officials are after him every minute. He's takin' the tragedy awful hard. Anyone'd think 'twas his fault it happened."

"Why not let Mrs. Hale stay where she is?"

"Don't talk like a child, Janice, an' you a married woman. Even if it wasn't hard for Mary an' me to be trotting there from here, a man's cabin is no place for a widow."

She cautiously twisted her foot free of the comforting hands. Grimaced as she pulled on her stout shoe.

"I hope the Lord let's me swap my feet for wings the minute I get to heaven. Leave the rest of the geraniums for the boys to plant and come pack up your things. Want M's. Hale settled before lunch time. Those officials being here make more work, but don't they make life thrilling?" Her eyes snapped, her cheeks flaunted red flags of excitement.

"Who do you think did it, Miss Martha?"

"They haven't asked me yet. P'raps they think because my joints are stiff the arteries of my brain are hardening, but they're not. I'm not sayin' anything till I can say it before the right parties. Did you hear that plane go out? They've sent for a finger-print expert. Expert! They'd ought to have questioned me first."

"When I heard the airplane zoom, I thought the criminal was escaping."

"That would be confessing, wouldn't it? The party who snuffed out Joe Hale is too scared or too clever to confess. I haven't made up my mind yet which. I haven't read the newspapers for years without learning something." Her voice prickled with excitement. The girl saw her wince as she entered the Waffle Shop.

"You are doing too much, Miss Martha. If you won't let me take care of Mrs. Hale, let me help in the kitchen. I can cook."

The elder Miss Samp gripped a chair-back for support, held her twinging foot under her to relieve it of weight.

"Mother used to say, 'Marshy, if you really want to help me, do things as I want them done, not as you want to do them.' If you're willing to cook, child, cook for Mr. Bruce. He's been livin' on the greasy stuff Pasca — house-boy, he calls himself — dishes up, when he doesn't come to the Waffle Shop. He's the dynamo of this outfit, spiritual, moral an' mental. It isn't often you come across a man like that. Make it your job to keep him well an' happy an' efficient, an' he'll steady us all through the tryin' time that's ahead."

"Will the investigation take long?"

"If they follow the clue they're trailin' now, I guess you an' me'll be waiting on the angels long before they've got at the truth."

From the dormitory floated a bugle call:

"All you little doughboys come and get your chow!"

"Sakes alive, they're calling the men to dinner and me standin' here talking." She limped hurriedly kitchenward.

In her own cabin, gazing out at the Stars and Stripes floating high and strong in the clear air, Janice faced two alternatives. She could allow Millicent Hale's "I'm free! Free! If you'd only waited!" to fester in her memory until she became a hateful, unhappy person who would be sent out on the next boat amidst a silent chorus of "Thank God she's gone!" — it was human nature to dodge a person with a grievance — or she could take up her life from the time Bruce had said, "I'll get your sandals," — go on from there as though the rest of that evening never had happened.

Once she would have chosen the first way, but one couldn't live for weeks in this northern wilderness, under the protection of that flag, without growing spiritually. She had come north for independence, with a determination to master the imagination which all her life had hobbled her, had set her fear complex to functioning. It would take a big inside resistance to withstand the bitter pressure of Millicent's implication. Could she do it? She must. Trial companionship was a test of good sportsmanship as well as marriage. One didn't whimper, "I won't play!" at the first suggestion of friction.

It was not surprising that the Commissioner had given Miss Martha an impression of inefficiency, Janice concluded as after the midday meal she entered the office. She regarded him from under long lashes, as he sat behind a small table examining papers. He was the antithesis of all the prosecuting officials she had seen on the screen. He was bland and fair. His eyes met hers. Steel drills, Tubby had said. That was a weak comparison. They had seemed to wrench open the secret drawer of her mind. The deputy beside him was small and wiry, with a bristly black mustache at which he gnawed in moments of excitement. Bruce Harcourt was at his desk, Grant at his. Through the open window came the clang of metal, the drill of riveters, the rattle of steam-shovels, the yapping of huskies, the smell of the sea. Business as usual, in spite of that silent, shrouded figure in the Hale cabin. From where she sat she could see the Waffle Shop, the dormitories, and, looming like a look-out tower, the radio station. Far away on the horizon a crater smoked steadily. The sun which gilded the serrated mountain-top paved the office floor with golden flags. The radiant noon was mellowing into shimmering half-tones.

Janice glanced surreptitiously at Harcourt. Two little lines cut deep between his eyes as he bent a supple ivory letter opener back and forth with his strong fingers. Did he know that she had moved the remainder of her possessions to the H house? What he could not know was that upon entering his cabin she had flung open doors and windows to clear the atmosphere of the sophisticated perfume Millicent Hale used, of her personality.

Had the Commissioner spoken to her? She met his gimlet eyes. Perhaps he even knew what she had been thinking. To borrow from Tubby, she wouldn't put it past him. She removed the elastic band from her note-book with a professional snap, ground her pencil in the sharpener on her desk with businesslike proficiency.

Tubby Grant opened the door to the woodshed. Kadyama shuffled into the room. His coarse black hair was greased down, his copper-color face was close shaven. The sardonic slant of one eyebrow, the tilt of his mouth seemed accentuated. His flannel shirt was of fire-department red. A gold-nugget pin was thrust into a blue-and-green tie. Black-and-white suspenders were the visible means of support of his baggy trousers. An exquisitely carved silver belt obviously served no utilitarian purpose. In obedience to a curt word from the Commissioner, he perched on the edge of a chair. Only his eyes moved as he waited, motionless as one of Dallin's bronze Indians.

"You've threatened to get Hale, haven't you?"

Evidently the official believed in the attack direct. Kadyama's eyes sought Harcourt's. He responded to their question.

"Tell the truth. Lying won't help you. You have said you would get Hale, haven't you?"

"Ump. I say that one, two, p'raps tree time."

"Why?"

The Indian's eyes, beady as a trapped rat's, shifted to the Commissioner's face. "He steal Tatima."

"Well? She's not your squaw, is she?"

"She promise to marry on me. She work for Meester Hale. She say she lak dark mans no more, she lak gol' hair."

"Where were you yesterday?"

"Workin' roun'."

"Where?"

"In mornin' cleanin' out hangar. Chief fly off in plane, Pasca say, beeg chance to make order."

"Did that take all day?"

"No sirree. Word come dat chief marry. Mees Samp seesters, they sen' me to woods. I cut everyt'ing green. Bring to H house."

"What did you do then?"

"I put 'em roun' room."

"Yourself?"

"Mees Hale come an' Meester Chester. Bruder, seester, dey work togedder, oder mens come too."

Snap! The ivory cutter in two pieces clattered to the floor. Each occupant of the room started as at a pistol shot. The deputy quivered like a steel spring, protested petulantly:

"Don't do that!"

"Sorry!" Harcourt's voice was apologetic, but his eyes shone with laughter as they met Janice's before he bent to recover the scattered pieces. His smile seemed to clear the air which before had been heavy with tragedy. The Commissioner asked:

"Were Mrs. Hale and Chester in the H house all the time you were?"

"No sirree. Meester Chester go first. Say to her, 'You feenish.' She sen' me for more green. W'en I come back — she gone too."

"Gone, had she? Where were you last night?"

"Squaw-dance."

"Was your girl friend" — he amended — "was Tatima, this girl you expect to marry, with you?"

209

"No. She stay at Waffle Shop for beeg marriage party there." He qualified, "She come to dance late, stay long night through."

"You said first that she wasn't there."

The Indian's scowl was savage. "You t'ink you pretty damn smart fella, catch me, huh."

The Commissioner tipped back in his chair. "I not only think I am, I know I am. Bring in the girl." The order was like the crack of a whip.

Tatima swaggered in, head back. Her face had the curious color dark skin has when drained of blood. Black hair, parted and brought down over her ears, shone like satin. Defiance did not quite camouflage the fear lurking in the depths of her glowing eyes. She flung back the brilliant Yakutat blanket from her shoulders. Her gay print dress clung to her warm body, brought out lines and curves. Her blue beads glowed with the depth and beauty of Burma sapphires. The pupils of the Commissioner's eyes contracted.

"Have a good time at the Indian dance last night?"

Tatima straightened. "Who, me? Me go to Indian dance?" Her contempt was superb. "I stay at Waffle Shop all night, help Mees Samp seesters clear up after marriage party."

14

Silence like a spell settled on the room. The Commissioner's eyes bored into Tatima's smoldering with defiance. The deputy gnawed furiously at the bristle on his upper lip. Kadyama sat in rigid immobility. Harcourt frowned thoughtfully at the Indian girl. Janice nervously drew hieroglyphics on her pad. Grant cracked his knuckles. The deputy jumped.

"Don't do that!"

His petulant voice snapped the tension. The Commissioner grinned at Kadyama.

"Me! Pretty damn smart fella, what? Get out. I'll send for you later." He waited until the glowering Indian had closed the door behind him before he motioned to the chair.

"Sit down."

Tatima favored him with a disdainful glance. "Who, me? I stan' up."

"Suit yourself. You work for Mr. Hale?"

"Who, me? I work for Mees Samp seesters."

"What do you do there?"

"Wait on table. Wash deeshes, sweep, do much t'ings. Work hard."

"Yet, you had time to take care of Mr. Hale's cabin?"

She tossed her head, set her lips in a heavy red line of defiance. Harcourt commanded:

"Answer the Commissioner's questions, Tatima. We all know that you worked for Mr. Hale. Tell the truth."

She regarded him from under lowered lids. Hunched her fine shoulders.

"Who, me? Tell truth? You not like it p'raps much as you t'ink. I tell. I work for Meester Hale." A spasm of feeling twisted her face. She bit her lips. A drop of blood stained her teeth as she went on. "I tak' care of cabin w'ile Mees Hale gone away."

"Been there since her return?"

"One tam, p'raps."

"Remember losing this?"

The Indian girl bent forward to stare at his extended hand. In the centre lay a blue glass bead. She clutched at the string about her neck. Inscrutability veiled the fright which had flamed in her eyes. She drawled:

"Lose bead two days ago. Same tam she there."

With a nod she indicated the girl at the typewriter desk. Janice felt the color mount to her hair as the four men looked at her. The Commissioner laid a restraining hand on Harcourt's knees as he started from his chair. He asked blandly:

"You mean that young lady at the desk?"

"Sure, I mean she. Meester Hale he phone for her to come. Say he have secret letter. First he send Mees Hale to Waffle Shop. Mees Trent come. He tell her letter. He tell her she beautiful. After w'ile he say, 'I kees yo' han's. I —' "

"Tatima!"

With the exclamation, Janice was on her feet. Livid, furious, Harcourt was on his. The Commissioner's voice cut like a razor.

"Sit down, both of you. Don't mess this testimony up by getting on your ear, Harcourt. Sit down and let's get on with it." As they subsided into their respective chairs he suggested:

"Didn't like Hale to tell Miss Trent that she was beautiful, did you?"

"Who, me? I not care. He say to her, 'You run away from marryin'. Kees an' run kin'.' An' she say, to keep to bees-ness. He talk more, much more. Then beads break. I busy peeking them up. I hear no more."

"Didn't hear Miss Trent's voice again?"

"Ask much questions, don't you? P'raps you t'ink Tatima some leetle detector. I hear her speak outside, that all. She speak very mad to Meester Jimmy Chester, 'fore he come in."

"Chester! Did he come into the cabin?"

"Sure, he come. He say very loud, 'W'at you mean sending for Mees Trent, Joe? Try any funny business an' I'll shoot.' An' then Mees Hale come in an' say, 'W'at you doin' with that pistol, Jimmy? Joe's frightened!' An' then she laughed an' laughed 'sthough she didn't know what she doin', an' I went to Waffle Shop an' wash deeshes."

"You didn't see Mr. Hale again alive?"

Tense silence. Silence as haunted as though an impalpable presence drifted in their midst. Outside the clang of riveters, the shouts of men, the bark of a husky, a fly spatting listlessly against the window. Inside tick-tock, tick-tock, the wall clock marking time for the quick procession of the minutes, like a drum-major at the head of a regiment. Tatima cast a terrified glance behind her as though a reminding hand had been laid on her shoulder. Her voice dwindled to a strained whisper.

"Who, me? I not see heem again, never."

"That's all. You may go."

She swung out, head up, the Yakutat blanket trailing from one hand. The Commissioner watched her till the door closed. Made a note on his pad.

"You take stenographic notes, don't you, Grant? Take Miss Trent's testimony."

Harcourt was on his feet. "She's not Miss Trent. She's my wife. Why should she be dragged into this? What possible connection can she have with this case?"

The Commissioner looked up at him thoughtfully. The deputy stopped gnawing his mustache long enough to nod approval as his superior protested:

"Sit down, sit down. We can't play favorites." He looked at Janice. "Sorry to bring you into this, but I want to hear about your visit to Hale's cabin."

"Visit! You mean my business call? Mr. Hale phoned me to come and take a letter from his dictation."

"What was the nature of the letter?"

"It wasn't a letter. It was a strictly confidential matter."

"Mm. I see. Even so, you'll have to tell."

"It was the codicil to a will."

"Codicil! Did he sign it?"

"I don't know. I put it in shape and sent two copies to him by one of the men."

"You have your notes?"

"Yes."

"Make a rough draft for me when we get through this afternoon. While you were at the Hale cabin, what happened?"

"Tatima has given an exact account. She has missed her vocation. She should go in for reporting."

"You are satisfied to let her version stand for yours at present?"

Was the man trying to fasten the crime on her, Janice wondered. His eyes seemed to bore into her brain.

"Quite."

"You met Chester as you went out?"

"Yes."

"What did he say to you?"

"He asked what I was doing in Hale's cabin."

"And you answered?"

"That it was none of his business. The suspicion in his voice made me furious."

The Commissioner was apparently absorbed in the curlicue he was designing. "Did you have any conversation with Chester in regard to the matter later in that day or in the evening?"

"No." Had the relief that she could answer the question honestly in the negative shown in her voice, Janice wondered in panic. The questioner's pencil stopped as his eyes drilled into hers.

"Mm! All the next day you were away from headquarters, I understand. There was a party here in the evening. Did you dance with Chester?"

"Yes."

"Did he mention your meeting of the day before?"

"Yes. He apologized for his manner and I explained why I answered as I did."

"You parted good friends?"

"The best." Thank heaven that was over! She had squeezed by without telling what Jimmy had said in reply.

"Was that all that was said?"

Her assurance crashed. Good grief! She wasn't under oath, she hadn't sworn to tell the truth, the whole truth. She would say nothing which could incriminate nice Jimmy Chester. She smiled engagingly at the Commissioner.

"Anything more would have been anti-climax, wouldn't it?"

His smile was bland, too bland. "You were in the H house when Mrs. Hale came last night, weren't you? Sorry to remind you of what must have been a gruesome intrusion on your happiness, but I want to know what happened."

"I have told you what happened," interposed Harcourt savagely.

"I want her version of the episode. Want all sides of the case. We shall question Mrs. Hale. I understand that she is at present too upset to answer sanely. Go on," he nodded to Janice.

"We were sitting by the fire talking when someone beat furiously at the door. Mrs. Hale stumbled into the room. She was breathless as though she had been running. She braced herself against the wall, tried to speak. Mr. Harcourt said, 'Steady, Millicent. What has happened?' Her eyes were wide with horror as she called out, 'Joe's dead! Shot!' She pitched forward to the floor."

"You can remember nothing more that was said? See who's knocking, Grant."

Janice's eyes met Harcourt's. He must be intensely relieved that she had been reprieved from answering that question. Tubby Grant opened the door. Martha Samp stood on the threshold. The black cat rubbed against her skirts. In the sunlight her rusty-gray hair gave the effect of a sprouting halo. In one hand she held a box. It might have been spun glass so cautiously she carried it. Her faded eyes sparkled. Her cheek-bones burned red as stoplights. Harcourt rose.

"We were to send for you later, Miss Martha."

The woman's grim lips twisted in a smile. "Which's polite for sayin', 'What you doin' here?' Mr. Bruce, I came to save you wastin' the government's time." She stepped into the centre of the room. Her voice quavered with excitement. "Found the revolver that shot Joe Hale? Must be somewhere."

"Obviously." The Commissioner's voice dripped sarcasm. Martha Samp frowned at him.

"What do you mean speakin' like that to me, to a woman old enough to be your mother? I want you should understand that the engineers in this camp didn't leave their manners behind in the States. You et ten waffles for your lunch, Mary told me. I ain't under any obligations to feed you an' your assistants while you're here on this case. If you try to be a smarty with me, you'll eat with the men or the Eskimos understand?"

Tubby Grant camouflaged an exuberant chuckle with a racking cough. Harcourt became absorbed in something outside the window. The deputy plucked nervously at his superior's sleeve. The golden flags vanished from the floor. The black cat seized the opportunity to complete his afternoon grooming. Dauntless Martha Samp belligerently faced the Commissioner. A smile tempered the amazement on his face as he rose. He was decidedly attractive when he stepped outside his official self, Janice decided.

"Miss Samp, if it's a case of love my waffles, love me, I'm eating out of your hand. I never tasted anything so good. Sit down. We'll listen so long as you'll talk."

She sat down, held the box at arm's length, as one might a bomb which had shown symptoms of restlessness. Blot jumped into her lap. She stroked his black coat with her unoccupied hand.

"Sakes alive, I guess you don't know what you're promising. I'm quite a talker when I get goin'. Howsomever, I haven't got so much to say unless I get started on crime or matrimony. Surprisin' how often you'll find 'em related. I've found the pistol." From the box she cautiously extracted a revolver wrapped in a soft white cloth. A revolver with a gleaming mother-of-pearl butt.

The office whirled before Janice's incredulous eyes. Bruce Harcourt's! It was identical with the one he had jerked from its holster when they had met the bear. Would that terrible Commissioner try to fasten the crime on him? He would if he knew what Millicent Hale had sobbed as she leaned against the log wall of the H house last night. Was it only last night? It seemed years behind her. He would never hear it from her. Bruce was leaning forward looking at the pistol as though it were a snake in his path. Tubby Grant was staring at him. What did it mean? Where had it come from?

Martha Samp proudly laid it on the table.

"Thank the Lord I'm rid of that. Expected it to go off any minute. S'pose you'll mark it 'exhibit A'?"

Janice saw the Commissioner's lips twitch as he turned to her.

"The blue bead is 'Exhibit A.' Mark the gun 'Exhibit B.' Now, Miss Samp, tell us where this came from."

Martha Samp grimaced with pain as she slipped off a shoe. She flexed her toes in their white cotton stocking and sat erect. Her usually lack-lustre eyes sparkled like diamonds.

"I found it on the shore when the tide went out. When I heard about Mr. Hale, an' there not being any weapon found, I says to myself, 'First thing'll be done will be to examine and check up on every pistol at headquarters. 'Tisn't likely though that whoever did it will keep it by him, he'll get rid of it. No place I know of better than the shore.' So every chance I had I ran down to the shingle while the tide was low. I had what you call a hunch that it wouldn't be far away, and it wasn't."

"What was behind that hunch, Miss Samp?" The Commissioner's voice cut keen as a blade.

"Sakes alive, what eyes you've got! I guess that's for you to find out. I was flustered when I saw the mother-of-pearl gleamin' an' shimmerin' on the wet pebbles. I didn't touch it with my hands, picked it up the way I've seen folks do in the movies, so's not to disturb the fingerprints."

The Commissioner broke the revolver. "One

cartridge gone." He replaced it on the table. "Ever seen this gun before, Miss Samp?"

"Yes."

"Where?"

"It belonged to my nephew, Archie Harper."

"Where is he?"

Her face aged as she nodded toward a window. Through it was visible the white cross, appearing and disappearing between waving fern fronds. It was with obvious effort that the Commissioner withdrew his eyes from it to ask:

"Who owned the revolver after your nephew — went?"

"Mr. Bruce."

"Did you know that it was missing, Harcourt?"

"Yes." Curtly Bruce Harcourt told of his discovery of the empty holster on his wall, added that he had inquired among the engineers if anyone of them had borrowed it. No one had. He had decided that one of the Indians had taken it. Had intended to pursue the inquiry, but the arrival of the officials had crowded it from his mind.

"Mm. Didn't connect it with the shooting, I suppose?"

"The shooting hadn't occurred at the time I missed it."

"Did you hear a shot, see anything which led you to think that you would find that pistol on the shore, Miss Samp? Did you see Mr. Hale yesterday?"

"Sakes alive, I didn't have a minute to see anybody. After we decided to have a party, I was on the rush. But late in the evenin', after the folks had had their ice-cream, I put some in a bowl an' ran along to the Hale cabin with it — it isn't but a step — I thought it might taste good to the invalid. I never liked him, but you don't hold a grudge against a sick man."

"Had Mrs. Hale gone home when you left the party?"

"I didn't notice. I slipped out through the kitchen."

"Did you take the ice-cream into the cabin?"

"No. Just's I got near I heard Joe Hale roarin'. 'One of his tantrums,' thinks I. 'Millicent's catchin' it for goin' to the party.' "

"Then you did know that she had gone home?"

Excitement welled up in Martha Samp's faded eyes. "I suppose you're givin' me what I've read about in the papers the third degree. It's interestin' but 'twon't get you anywhere. I just assumed he was talkin' to her, 'cause he's the kind who would talk to a wife that way."

"You didn't feel that you should interfere to protect Mrs. Hale?"

"I? No. He'd never struck her nor hurt her to my knowledge. I haven't lived this long without learnin' not to interfere 'twix husband and wife. The wife's the first one to fly at you. Joe Hale was one of those men who has to blame some one for everything that happens. Besides, M's.

Hale has a brother, it's his job to step between 'em."

The door swung slowly open. A man with dazed eyes swayed on the threshold. His face was bruised, his clothing torn. The Commissioner stared at him, open-mouthed.

"Parks! Where the hell did you come from? Plane crackup?"

The man's head achieved a wobbly shake. "Never got off. Fella grabbed me as I was climbing into the cock-pit. He flung me down with such force that I was stunned. I heard a roar an' then I didn't know anything."

"What did he look like?" The Commissioner shook the dazed man in his eagerness.

"Go easy. I fell on that arm. Couldn't tell what he looked like, goggles on. But when he grabbed me I noticed a big black seal-ring on his finger."

15

The monotonous tick of the office clock in the strained silence set Bruce Harcourt's taut nerves twanging like violin strings. He fought a pervading sense of dread. It was not the fact of Hale's taking-off. It had not been the first tragedy of the kind in his experience in this wilderness. Justice was slow. Some men wouldn't wait for it, they administered it. But that Jimmy Chester should be drawn into the mess was unbearable. He was the only man in the outfit who wore a ring. Had love for Janice crazed him? No. Whatever motive was behind his flight it wasn't guilt. He felt the Commissioner's boring eyes.

"Who wears a seal-ring in this outfit, Harcourt?"

"Chester, the second engineer."

"I remember. He's the man who came to help when we landed. Gloomy as hell. Thought he'd probably lost his shirt in the market. Did you suspect he was going to break out?"

"I did not. You forget that I am responsible for this camp, that if the mystery isn't solved and solved quick, I will lose the job toward which I have been working for six years. I would stake my life on Jimmy Chester's innocence — but had I suspected that he intended to leave camp, I would have had him locked up."

Even as Harcourt steadily met the grilling eyes, Jimmy Chester's voice sneering, "He'll never send for you again!" milled over and over in his mind.

"Mrs. Hale is Chester's sister?"

"Yes."

"I'll talk with her next. Where is she?"

"I left her in the big chair in our settin'-room."

"Is she able to see anyone, Miss Martha?"

" 'Twill do her good to rouse out of her daze, Mr. Bruce. 'Course she's had an awful shock, but so've other folks, millions of 'em, who've held their heads up an' carried on. She was afraid of Joe, an' the woman who lives with a man she fears, in time, either turns on him like a tortured animal who can't stand more, or goes to pieces. If M's. Hale isn't roused I'm 'fraid she'll get lower an' lower in her mind. 'Twould be a pity. She's got a lot to live for."

The soft tattoo with which the Commissioner had been accompanying the woman's gruff voice came to a full stop.

"What d'you mean, she's got a lot to live for?"

"Joe Hale was a rich man, I've heard. He didn't need to work, but he was crazy over bridge-building."

"Any children."

"No, more's the pity."

"Mm. And he was dictating a codicil to his will. I'll be over to talk with her." As Martha Samp started for the door with Blot trailing her, he directed, "Don't tell her that I'm coming." He turned to the deputy who had gnawed one side of his mustache out of reach and had commenced on the other. "Shan't need you, Bill. Look after Parks and take care of that revolver. Shan't need the secretary, either. Come with me, Harcourt. The lady may need persuading. I have a hunch, from the way she rushed to you instead of to her brother last night, after she discovered what had happened, that she will talk for you."

Millicent Hale would not talk for anyone unless she wanted to, Bruce Harcourt thought, with his new knowledge of her, as ten minutes later he entered the Samp sitting-room. Eyes closed, head back, she was seated in the wing chair beside the fire. Not a fair hair of the smoothly waved coiffure was out of place, the costly simplicity of her black lounging pajamas, the pearls at her throat reminded him that she would inherit no mean fortune from the man who was now beyond pity and blame. He sensed a change of attitude in the Commissioner beside him. She was appealingly lovely. He remembered her treatment of Janice last night and amended, if one cared for her type. On the heels of the bitter memory came pictures of her through the long, dayless winter when the temperature dropped to thirty below, when radio reception was so poor that even that diversion was cut off. Her home had been a revivifying spot for the engineers and sectionheads. Life must have been a hideous nightmare for her after Hale began drinking, but she had carried on loyally without complaint. Not until this last week had he realized that her self-control was cracking-up.

Millicent Hale's brows drew together in surprise as the Commissioner pulled forward a chair. She looked helplessly at Martha Samp who answered the unspoken question in her eyes.

"They want to talk with you 'bout Joe, want to get the mystery cleared up."

Millicent Hale clenched fragile hands in her lap, sat a little straighter. "What do they want to know, Bruce?" She looked at Harcourt who was standing with one arm on the mantel.

The Commissioner's eyes were sharp but reassuringly friendly as he took command of the situation.

"Mrs. Hale, did you quarrel with your husband before you went to the dance last evening; did he object to your leaving him?"

"Was it only last evening?" She shivered. "He didn't want me to go."

"But you went?"

"Yes. For a short time. The Indian woman who has helped me take care of him has been away two days with a sick mother. The day before he had insisted upon my going out. Said

227

that he would like to be alone for a while, he was bored to death having someone around every minute. He was able to walk about the room, the phone was on the table beside his wheel-chair. He could call for help and get it in a minute — almost. So I left him alone."

"Any indication that he tried to use the telephone?"

"No. I felt quite safe to leave him, he seemed so much better. I had to get away. Just had to. I intended to go air-trotting with Mr. Harcourt and Mr. Grant in the morning. He heard of it and made such a row I didn't dare leave him."

"Did he threaten you?"

"Not more than usual. Said that he had dictated a codicil to his will the day before — perhaps he was telling the truth, perhaps not — leaving me only dower rights in his property, he would sign it at once if I left him."

"Did you know the terms of his will?"

"He told me after we were married that he had made one leaving everything to me."

"Mm. I see. I understand that Mr. Harcourt walked home with you after the dance, that he didn't go into the house, that he said good-night outside. Did you go directly in after he left you?"

Her white throat contracted. "No. I sat on the bench outside the door."

"Why didn't you go in?"

"Go in! Go in! My God, can't you realize what it means to live day after day with a man who tortures, who lashes with words and taunts?" Her

228

voice thrilled. "Go in! I paced the beach, tempted, horribly tempted to lie down and let the incoming tide end it all."

So that accounted for the wet, bedraggled frock, Harcourt decided. The Commissioner probed.

"You heard no commotion, no shot before you went into the cabin?"

She regarded him furtively from under sweeping lashes. "Nothing. I heard only the blare and squeak of the music at the Waffle Shop." Her voice caught spasmodically.

"What did you find when you entered?"

Her eyes dilated with horror. "You know what I found. Why bring it all back to me?"

"Because we must know who shot your husband. Had he quarreled with anyone at headquarters?"

"With Mr. Harcourt. You can't suspect him, you can't! Bruce never quarreled with him. He was at the Waffle Shop every moment till he walked home with me and then he didn't come in."

"But the shooting was done with his revolver."

"How do you know?" The question was a strained whisper.

"It was found on the shore."

She looked up with agonized eyes at Harcourt standing by the mantel.

"Bruce! Bruce!"

The Commissioner became absorbed in the contemplation of his corrugated finger-nails.

"Harcourt is sure that the revolver was in its holster on the wall when he left in the morning, he missed it when he returned at night. You and your brother were in the H house helping decorate it. Did you notice whether the gun was there?"

"The gun?"

"The revolver. Everything's a gun in this country."

"I — I didn't notice."

"Anyone there besides you and your brother?"

"Kadyama brought in the greens. Miss Mary was unpacking some things in one of the bedrooms."

Martha Samp's reaction was a cross between a snort and a sniff. "Sakes alive, you ain't going to drag Mary into this, are you? She's scared to look even a holster in the face."

"We won't drag her in at present, Miss Samp. Mrs. Hale, you said that it was some little time after Harcourt left you that you went into the cabin?"

"Yes."

"What did you find?"

Her hands clenched on the chair-arms till the knuckles showed white. She closed her eyes as though to shut out a picture. Her voice was so low that the Commissioner bent forward.

"Joe was lying face down on the rug. Wheel-chair overturned. I don't know how long I stood staring at him. I felt something tugging at my skirt. It was my little dog begging to be taken up. That broke the spell of horror. I raised Joe's head and shoulders, realized what had happened and rushed for Mr. Harcourt."

"You don't remember seeing a revolver anywhere?"

She shook her head.

The Commissioner fitted spatula finger-tips together with nice precision. "Any theory as to the motive for the attack on your husband, Mrs. Hale?"

Her thin fingers tightened. "No. Unless — unless it was robbery. Joe always carried a lot of cash."

"Mm. When you found him, did you look to see if his money was gone?"

Her long shuddering breath caught in a gasp. "Look! Look! Would I think of anything but the fact that he lay there before me — dead?"

"Why did you go for Mr. Harcourt instead of your brother?"

"Go for Jimmy? Why he hated Joe and —" she stifled a cry with one hand. "You're not trying to make out that Jimmy did it, are you? Bruce! Bruce! You know Jimmy. You know that he's incapable of a thing like that."

She was breathless, colorless. The Commissioner's voice was as sympathetic as a marionette's and about as warming.

"Mm. You saw your brother this morning?"

"Yes. He came to ask me what I wanted done about — about Joe."

"Did he tell you then that he was going away?"

"Away! Where?" She was on her feet, swaying as she stood. Harcourt pressed her back into the chair.

"Take it easy, Millicent. Jimmy went off in a plane."

"Where, Bruce, where?"

"In just one hour he will be on his way to find out. We won't trouble you any more now, Mrs. Hale. Good afternoon. See you in the morning. Come on, Harcourt."

Ignoring Millicent Hale's frenzied appeal to him to stay with her, Harcourt followed the Commissioner out of the cabin. He stopped at the Waffle Shop door to speak to Mary Samp before he joined the official. A drowsy sun was hanging on to a crater-top, like a sleepy child protesting against bed. Overhead spread a limpidly cloudless sky. A faint star or two pricked palely through. Unearthly light flickered above a distant volcano. Far, far to the east stretched fields of Arctic moss palely pink. Against the horizon glittered white mountain-tops girdled by purple valleys. The tide swished softly on the shingle. A little wind whispered along the copper wires of the antennae. Men were sitting outside the dormitories, heads together, talking excitedly. In the centre of another group a bear was being put through his paces: from another came the click of poker chips. The aroma of coffee, the appetizing smell of waffles and bacon scented the air. Out of earshot of the Samp cabin, the Commissioner stopped.

"That woman knows more than she's telling, a whole lot more. We'll let her think we're as dumb as she thinks we are, while we go after Chester."

"Then you really meant that I was to hunt for him?"

"Of course we are going for him."

"We?"

"Sure. I have every confidence that you really want to find the murderer, but you like and trust Jimmy Chester. I'm convinced that he's our man. Meanwhile, have the clerk keep tabs on native expenditures at the Company store. You didn't tell me that Hale's wad was gone when you found him."

"I told you that after lifting him to the couch no one touched him till you got here. We thought you would want everything left undisturbed."

"That's right! That's right! We'll let the robbery theory cool while we go for Chester. You lead the way in your plane. I'll follow in mine with my pilot. Ought always to fly in pairs in this country anyway. Twilight till almost ten, light again soon after two A.M. You must know every field where a plane can land."

"I do. We have three large camps stocked with provisions for two years. They have good fields. Unless Chester had an accident, he must have come down in one of those. He wouldn't go to a city or town of any size. If he is running away, he would know that you would have his description

233

broadcast. Have you forgotten Hale? What is to be done with the body?"

"I'll radio for that expert Parks set out for. After he gets here, and has the information I want, tell Grant to bury it here. It isn't to be taken away — yet. We'll start in an hour. Leave someone in charge with instructions to let Mrs. Hale have her head. Get her out and about if possible. There will be no boat for the States for two weeks. No one will take her by plane. Business as usual. Get 'em all feeling secure, that's the idea. Going to eat at the Waffle Shop?"

"No. At my cabin. I want to talk with Pasca, my houseboy, and leave Grant in charge."

Tubby Grant was strumming a mournful ditty on his ukulele as Harcourt entered his cabin. He flung the instrument to the cot and got precipitately to his feet.

"Ba-gosh, you're white, Bruce. What's up?"

"The Commissioner and I are starting in an hour to trail Jimmy Chester."

"Get that clue from Mrs. Hale?"

"Not from what she said, from what she didn't say. I will take the Tanager. May have to come down in cramped quarters. I'm leaving you in charge, Tubby. Business as usual. And except that she is not to go out on the steamer or in a plane, encourage Millicent to take up her life again. The Commissioner suspects that she knows more than she is telling. She can keep busy packing."

"Shall I have Joe put up on the hill beside Harper?"

"Yes. After the expert gets through. You know what to do. Keep your eye on Janice, will you?"

"What a heck of a honeymoon!"

"Honeymoon! Was it only yesterday that that fat little notary pronounced us man and wife?"

"Suppose the boy friend appears?"

"Paxton? Good Lord, I haven't thought of him since Millicent burst into the H house last night. If he comes, appear as though you took it for granted that he would drop down to see Janice. She must meet him sometime and get over her fear of him. I wish that I were to be here — but keep your eye on her."

"Perhaps you'll be back before he comes. Perhaps he won't come."

"He will come, all right. He won't pass by the chance of showing up the crudeness of this camp, of the H house against his yacht."

"Poisonously jealous of him, aren't you?"

"Jealous as the devil. He is a multi-millionaire, a cosmopolite, remember, and I am an engineer dependent on my job."

"And a wow of an engineer at that."

The lines between Harcourt's brows smoothed out. His eyes flashed with laughter as he mimicked Tatima.

"Who, me? Find Janice, will you, Tubby? I want to see her before I go. I will get a bite at the H house, while I give Pasca instructions. I will bring Jimmy back to clear himself. Don't worry if the process seems unduly long. Between you and me, I think Chester's theatrical get-away was a mere gesture. He may know something but — we must remember that he has a genuis for showmanship."

"He gets his effects."

"He does. By the way, Millicent suggested robbery as the motive of the attack on Joe. No money was found on him or in the cabin, you remember. Kadyama will bear watching."

"Did you get that hunch too? He said that Tatima was at the squaw-dance. She denied being there. Something fishy about that. I put his grudge down to jealousy, I hadn't thought of money. I'll bet that while you and the Commissioner are beating the bushes for harmless Jimmy Chester, the party who shot Hale will be sitting pretty right here."

"Can't take your bet, Tubby. I believe the same thing. But the Commissioner is the doctor. Look for me when you see me."

Smoke rose from the chimney, drifted lazily into the pink afterglow, as Harcourt entered his cabin. He stopped on the threshold. The room seemed strange. It gave a curious impression of order. The pelts on the floor had been re-arranged. Books on the table desk had been slipped between book ends. Where had those come from? The couch — He shouted with laughter. A fresh, bright Yakutat blanket, taken from the wall apparently, had been spread over it, pillows had been plumped up, in the middle

236

of the cover reposed a chair, a chair of size and weight. On his haunches in front of the couch squatted Tong, injured innocence personified. The tawny eyes he turned on his master were wells of indignant grief. Harcourt chuckled as he pulled the wide-apart ears.

"I told you that some day you wouldn't be allowed up there, old fella, but —" Was that really an embroidered cloth and shining silver on the small table laid for two, or was he seeing things? The plates and tumblers of the warranted-to-withstand-wear-and-tear variety were his — he would swear to that. Who was humming to the accompaniment of an egg-beater? He flung open the kitchen door.

"Janice!"

The girl in her gay smock, furiously beating eggs in a bowl bobbed a dancing-school curtsy.

"What are you doing here?"

"Here! Didn't milord send word by Miss Martha that if I did not return to the H house pronto he would come for me?"

"I didn't send for you because I wanted a cook."

"Don't bite. Miss Martha intimated that as a chef Pasca left something to be desired. 'I seen my duty an' I done it.' Look at that asparagus with sauce vinaigrette. I found a basket of gulls' eggs. I'm making an omelette, a plump, yellow omelette, not one of those thin things with a soap-sudsy filling. Something tells me that I have mortally offended your house-boy.

He cares so awfully for himself as a cook. As for Tong, he looked ready to burst out crying when I ordered him off the couch. He is ruining it."

"Jan! You wonderful girl!" He caught her hands. Dropped them. "Have I time for a shower before the banquet?"

"If you hurry."

When he returned to the living-room she had removed her smock. Her simple blue frock had elbow sleeves which accentuated the ivory tint of her arms above her sun-tanned wrists. Pasca in a white coat was placing cups of soup. Tong sat on his haunches on the bear pelt watching surreptitiously.

Harcourt looked gravely at Janice seated across the small table.

"For the first time in my life I understand why my father always said grace at his own table. Mother was something for which to give daily thanks if he had had nothing else." He cleared his voice. "Where did all this elegance come from?" He touched the beautiful cloth with a shining silver spoon.

"I told you that I had not realized quite into what I was adventuring. Thought I might have an occasional afternoon tea."

"And you drew this. It is all wrong, Jan, but we won't go back to that now." He looked at the clock. "I am taking off in just thirty minutes."

"Where?"

"After Jimmy Chester."

"Oh, no! Not nice Jimmy Chester! Does the Commissioner think he did it?"

He told her of the interview with Millicent Hale, while Pasca served the simple supper. Tong followed his every movement with hungry eyes. As the Eskimo set cups of coffee on the table, Harcourt smiled at the girl.

"This has the restaurant at which we dined beaten a mile. Feed Tong, Pasca. Fuel the Tanager. I will be at the field in ten minutes."

As the door closed behind the man and dog, Janice asked:

"Why are you taking that particular plane?"

"Because I can take-off after a run of less than three hundred feet, and come to a complete stop one hundred feet from the spot where the plane first touches the ground. As I don't know where I may have to come down, it's the best bet."

"Will you be away long?"

He rose and stood with his arm on the mantel. "Don't know. If Jimmy is hiding, it may take days to find him. I have asked Miss Mary to stay here nights. Hate like the dickens to leave you alone."

"Alone! With Tubby and Miss Mary and Argus of the Hundred Eyes and Tong? And, of course, Mrs. Hale."

He looked at her steadily. "Do I need to tell you that Millicent's intimation that it would matter to me if she were free is a figment of her crazed imagination?"

Janice was intent on the pattern she was

etching on the cloth with the tip of a silver spoon.

"Imagination! It sounded like the real thing to me."

He caught her shoulders. "You know better. You know that I — Good Lord, is that the Commissioner knocking? Can't he allow me a minute with — with my family?"

He opened the door. The smiling, impeccably dressed man facing him said suavely:

"I was told that I would find —"

"Ned!"

The choked exclamation came from Janice. Harcourt glanced at the clock. Five minutes before he was due at the flying-field. Only five minutes. He looked straight at Paxton, whose eyes were on the girl.

"Come in. Jan, here is a friend from the outside world." As she took a step forward he glanced unseeingly at his wrist-watch. "Sorry that I have to leave headquarters just as you arrive, Paxton, but Janice and Grant will show you the wonders of this north country."

He caught the girl in his arms. "It's like tearing my heart out to leave you, Beautiful!" He kissed her eyes, her throat, her mouth. She struggled for an instant before she relaxed against him. He pressed his lips to her hair. "Dearest!"

"Ha-ar-court!"

The Commissioner's shout outside crashed into his husky voice. Janice caught the back of a chair as he released her. Her long lashes were a dark fringe against her colorless skin. Paxton was staring out of the window, a fighting set to his shoulders.

Harcourt picked up jumpers, helmet, rifle. His blood raced. He had intended to kiss Janice lightly, a mere gesture to impress the late fiancé with the reality of their relationship. The feel of her in his arms had set him aflame. He had kissed her as though he were starved for her — as he was. Would she forgive him?

She followed him to the door in true wifely solicitude. Said in a voice disconcertingly steady:

"Good luck to you, Bruce."

As he stepped to the board walk she leaned forward to whisper furiously:

"Your technic is superb. You must have had heaps of practice. But why martyr yourself to impress Ned?"

He caught her hand. She twisted it free. Stepped back. He heard Paxton exult:

"I'll say that my arrival —"

The door closed. Off shore through a blue sea, against the pink afterglow glided a white yacht. Harcourt heard the splash as she dropped anchor.

16

Janice's angry protest, Paxton's complacence, the sound of the closing door, echoed and re-echoed through Harcourt's mind to the accompaniment of the drone of the engine, as he climbed to cruising altitude. Three hours' flight by compass, then he would descend to make sure that he was nearing the southernmost camp. Why hadn't he gone back to her, held her, kissed her, until she acknowledged that she knew he loved her, knew that he had no sentimental interest in Millicent Hale? Why had he not let the Commissioner shout his head off outside till he had cleared up the misunderstanding between Jan and himself? Two selves warred within him. One scoffed, "Always put your job first, don't you?" The other defended, "Why not? You have been made chief of this outfit. You are morally bound to consider its interests first."

What was the use analyzing motives? It was like turning a knife in his heart. He had not kept his agreement, a gentleman's agreement, with Jan. He had assured her that living in his cabin would be like living with her brother, then he had seized her as though he were about to eat her. Would she think it nothing more nor less than a raid upon her sympathy?

His will steeled. He had not changed, really. The sight of her across the table, the sweetness of her, the intimacy, the thought of leaving her had been getting in its work before Paxton appeared. Then he had decided swiftly that it wouldn't do for Jan and him to part as mere friends, he had caught her in his arms and — had lost his head. The memory set the blood humming in his ears. He would not keep her in this wilderness through a winter if he could. If he really meant that, he would better keep away from her as much as possible when he returned. The invisible wall between them was down. He had sent it crumbling. She had been a sport to return to the H house after Millicent's frantic: "I'm free! If you'd only waited!" Most girls — and justly — would have demanded an explanation of that. She would have, had she loved him. His first big mistake had been to let her remain ignorant of the fact that he loved her. How tragic life could be made by things half said.

He looked at the western sky still ruddy from the pomp of the sun. He was making 105 miles an hour against a light wind. He descended in search of a landmark. The faint sound of a bugle floated up. Taps! He was flying over barracks built around a parade ground. He could make out smudges which were the officers' houses, a white patch which was a cement tennis court. He knew that it was a good one, he had played there. He caught a pin-point of green light in a company window, a spot of red. That would be a lamp in front of the infirmary. In two hours he would make the southernmost camp. He had little hope of finding Jimmy Chester there. He would fill up with oil and gas, talk things over with the section boss, sleep till sun-up and fly on. As he climbed again he heard the far, faint throb of an engine. The Commissioner was following close. Would they find Jimmy Chester, and if they did, would they find him alive? If he had intended to shoot Hale, why borrow a revolver with which to do it? He could have used one of his own and chucked it into the water. But Jimmy had not done it, he would be willing to bet his job he had not. Then why the melodramatic get-away? The more he thought of the robbery motive, the more probable it seemed. Yet the native laborers would know that they couldn't put it across. Would they reason? Many of them had the mentality of children.

He was still stubbornly clinging to the conviction of Jimmy Chester's innocence when on the third day of the search he left the northernmost camp. Not one of the three he had visited had yielded a clue. The Commissioner was irritated and air-worn. He had ordered a return to headquarters, had radioed Grant to expect them that afternoon. As Harcourt climbed to cruising altitude the first uneasiness as to Chester's safety seized him. Suppose he had cracked-up somewhere, had nothing for food but emergency rations?

He gave his entire attention to his surroundings as he piloted through a sea of clouds. They raced by him, weird white phantoms, blotting out the sunshine. Clouds overhead cast shadows on clouds below. He would shoot for a bright spot, only to find himself in a shower of raindrops which pricked like needles. For an hour he flew in an area of magnetic variations, hampered by the storm. Once he thought he heard the vibration of an engine ahead. It couldn't be the Commissioner, must be a sound mirage. He sent the plane up again and came out into the sun. The altimeter registered a mile.

He kept above the clouds till he came into clear sky. Descended to get his bearings. Was that a camp below? Men, looking no bigger than beetles, moving. Digging? Probably archaeologists in search of the first Americans. He looked at the compass. His heart stood still. It had gone dead. Some electric current in that prickling rain storm had done the trick. Where was he? He descended as far as he dared. The water was dotted with bergs, emerald green with snowy tops. Whole colonies of gulls perched on the floating ice drifting swiftly toward the open sea. A black oyster-catcher with long orange beak cackled raucously and took wing. Colder. He had been too absorbed in locating himself to realize it before. The glow, the gleam, the glimmer of sun on ice almost blinded him. On the shore were the low crumbling mounds of what had once been an Eskimo colony. Where was he? He thought he knew every relic on the coast. He dropped even lower to make sure that there was no sign of a plane. Jimmy might have come down here for any one of a dozen reasons. The silence of emptiness brooded over the village.

A buzz in his ear warned him that he must have more forward speed instantly or the plane would stall and spin out of control. As he climbed swiftly he looked round the horizon to get his bearings. Toward the south the sky was black with smoke. Old Katmal tuning up. Now he knew the direction in which to fly.

He mounted into the clouds. They were moving south. They would serve as compass. The drone of an engine? Was he really hearing it? The effect was weird. Suddenly fog caught him. It twisted and coiled like boa-constrictors of the air. The thrum of the phantom plane was lost in its cold whiteness, the sound of his own engine was muffled. Mist clouded his goggles, rolled in drops down the windows, dripped from the wings. The Tanager pitched, wallowed. He peered over. Fog. Nothing to see but twisting, rolling billows of fog. A sense of futility gripped him. He must get out of this. Miss Martha would say, "Find the gate. There's one in every wall." With the thought a series of pictures flashed on the screen of his mind. The weather-beaten cabins. The red and blue and white of the Stars and Stripes floating against a clear, sun-washed sky. Janice smiling at him, Janice looking at him with cold, hard eyes. The last picture had sound effects.

"Your technic is superb."

That settled it. He must get back to her. He would find the gate in this wall and not perish in the attempt either. He dove.

To his astonishment he came out into brilliant sunlight. What an infernally queer world! The berg-dotted sea was over his right wing. In his relief he laughed. The plane had flopped on its side. He righted it and took his bearings. A few islands sparsely wooded, their bases marble-smooth. Water dotted with floating ice, about which mountains lifted snowy peaks gilded with sunlight, patched with purple shadows from the drifting clouds. Dead ahead a great glacier sloped back for miles. Sunshine transformed the frozen cataract into a dazzling mass of glitter, set the blue water sparkling like a sea of sapphires and every scrap of ice gleaming like a huge emerald.

How long had he been flying aimlessly in the storm? He glanced at his wrist-watch. Noon. He frowned at the gas gauge. Couldn't do much more experimenting with that supply. He peered over the side of the ship. An ice-floe. Big as an able-bodied island with acres of plateau. He wing-slipped nearer, wires humming. Dot's! Three of them! Two moving. One inert. A plane on its side! The phantom of the clouds

247

cracked-up? Could one of the dots be Chester? No. Jimmy went alone.

Engine shut off, he side-slipped down. Landed, bumped and skidded over the rough surface to a stop. The floe stretched away illimitably, not a collection of cakes but acres of grinding, heaving ice-fields, their smoothness broken by an occasional crevice choked with loose fragments, by swiftly running rills. He pushed back his helmet. The crippled plane! Good Lord, what a wreck! Propeller smashed, one wing gashed into fringe by the ice. Where was the pilot?

A yell of horror cracked in his throat. He seized his rifle, climbed down from the cockpit, stumbling, slipping, raced toward the man wielding a gun like a club as a great polar bear charged at him. Another, smaller, bleeding, roaring horribly, was struggling up from the ice.

Harcourt stopped. Raised his rifle. Fired. His gun cracked again. Again. Both animals crumpled into mounds of white fur. The man who had been defending himself jumped back, turned. The world whirled into a glinting mass of blue and green and white. Out of its midst shot Jimmy Chester's yell.

"Bruce! Bruce!"

The universe steadied. Panting, bleeding, ashen, dripping with moisture, Chester stumbled forward. His eyes were the eyes of a man who has stared death in the face. His voice came in rasping sobs.

"Just in time! I shot — the — cub — didn't know there was another and — and —" he swayed. Harcourt caught him.

"Take it easy, Jimmy, till I can get you into the cockpit." He shut his teeth tight as he saw the long gashes made by the bear's claws, half dragged, half carried the dazed man to the plane.

"Climb up. Help yourself, boy. We've got to take-off quick. Father bear may come to look after his family."

With moans, Chester pulled himself up. Tumbled in. Rifle in hand, watchful eyes on the snowy ridges of the ice island, Harcourt transferred fuel and emergency rations from the smashed plane to his. It was common enough for polar bears to be caught on ice-floes. Eskimos watched for them for their pelts, he had heard them tell weird stories of their experiences. He stopped once to listen. The air was still and faintly tainted with gas fumes. He could hear cautious, creaking sounds in the ice, his heart pounding heavily, nothing else. Better keep going. He stepped into a crevasse, lost his rifle. With an ominous roar one of the bears struggled to its haunches. That settled it. He would take-off with the fuel he had.

As he climbed into the cockpit, Chester opened tortured eyes. Mumbled deliriously:

"Take me — back — Chief. Crazy stunt to — run — away. Milly heard — me — threaten — Joe. I'll — come across with —"

His face contracted in pain. His eyes closed.

17

"That's that!"

Grant's usually clear voice was toneless, quite in keeping with the crawling gray mist through which flapped and winged wildly screaming gulls. A low-spirited wind shook the shutters of the office, moaned in the firebox of the great Yukon stove. Shadows in the room grew distorted and dim. Impatiently he snapped on the light. Janice's brown eyes were velvety with sympathy.

"Was it harrowing, Tubby?"

"Harrowing! Ba-gosh, it was terrible. The fog was copper-color. It twisted into eerie shapes. We could barely make out the grave at our feet. Stephen Mallory's voice as he read the burial service was muffled, and when the black cat rubbed against Miss Mary's skirts — a D. W. Griffith touch — it stuck. Mrs. Hale's sobs as she clung to Miss Martha were ghoulish. They seemed the real thing, but how can she sincerely mourn for a man like Joe? Praise be to Allah, that's twenty-four hours behind us. I haven't had a minute to look in on this office since. Did you get those notes typed?"

"Yes."

He picked up the sheets she indicated. Looked them over. "You're good, you are certainly good. When you leave us you'd better take a turn at the reduction of the Public Debt."

"Leave! What do you mean?"

"Don't like the way this guy Paxton has been hanging round since Our Hero left. He and his 170-foot yacht, with its twin 550-horsepower engines, make headquarters look as bare and unlovely as a plucked chicken. I went aboard yesterday. It's a wonder. It's even equipped with radio sets of high and low frequency, for sending and receiving. The Modern Mariner! The name fits it. It's modern, all right. I'll bet Bruce would be fit to tie if he knew that bozo was here."

"Ned arrived before he started."

"He did! And he went off and left you?"

"Of what importance am I in comparison to his job?"

"Says you." Grant's always ruddy skin took on a deeper tint. Anger darkened his greenish eyes. He perched on the high chair in front of Harcourt's desk. Fog drifted by the window. Through it stole the yelps of huskies, the ring of steel on steel, hollow and unreal. Tong balanced precariously on his hind feet to lay his forepaws on his knees. He rubbed the dog's ears.

"Now listen. Do you suppose for a minute that Bruce was thinking of his job when he went through that marriage ceremony with you? I have a hunch that Hale's bumping off will be the end of women in this camp."

"But a woman had nothing to do with it."

"Mebbe so. Mebbe so. Just the same I bet an edict goes forth, 'Married men not wanted.' "

"It would be cruel for Bruce. It would break his heart. Didn't you hear him say at the inquest that he had been working toward his present position for six years'?"

"I heard him. That wouldn't cut any ice with the Crowned Heads. They have the hearts of robots, all springs and switches to keep the machinery going."

"In that case the sooner I depart and get the marriage annulled, the better. I will ask Ned to take me back on his boat — properly chaperoned of course — perhaps Mrs. Hale would like to join us."

Grant regarded her with cutting scorn. "Trying to be funny, aren't you? For Pete's sake, don't go getting things on your mind."

"I haven't anything on my mind."

His chuckle was the triumph of temperament over fog. "You've said it. I'm sorry I suggested Bruce might lose his job. He's a wow at it and the Crowned Heads know it. I'll bet they would let him have two wives if he wanted them. It isn't only his brains. It's what he stands for in a wilderness like this. He is all for the beautiful and high things of life. He's firm as a rock against the bad and ugly temptations, not because he is a prude or an ascetic, but because something inside him hates and rejects the unclean, physical and moral."

"Tubby! I didn't know you could think or talk like that."

Grant's grin was sheepish. "I can't, except on one subject. Evidently Bruce hasn't told you that he pulled me out of Hades — I wasn't born there — and alternately licked and praised me till I stood steady on my moral pins. Pick up, we'll call this a day."

"But it is not four yet."

"Can't help it. I've got to go the rounds of the section bosses. Make sure that all orders for supplies have been sent out. The goods must get here before we are shut in by winter ice. The old-timers are prophesying that the Arctic waters will close earlier than ever before." He leaned over her desk. Said softly:

"I've just found out that Kadyama didn't appear at all at the squaw-dance the night Hale was shot."

"He told the marshal that he was there after nine."

"He sure did. But he wasn't."

"Where was he?"

"That's what I mean to find out. You're the only person I've told. Don't breathe a word to anyone."

"I won't. I'm all excited. Anything I can do to help?"

"Be friendly with Mrs. Hale."

"I will. It will be terribly hard. She has the effect of nettles on me. Whenever I meet her I come away prickling."

"Do your darndest. The Commissioner and Harcourt are sure that she knows more about the late unpleasantness than she is telling. They radioed that they would be back at headquarters tomorrow. Didn't say whether they were bringing Chester. Get her up to the H house for a cup of tea this afternoon, can't you? I'll drop in. Philo Vance stuff. If your former fiancé comes, all to the good. I suspect that the sunshiny presence of a multi-millionaire might help dispel her gloom."

"You don't like her any better than —"

" 'I do.' Don't bite off a sentence like that. Finish it. I don't like her, but, I have a profound respect for her. She stood by her husband as faithfully as those mountains guard the inlet, and a woman who will do that with such a man is entitled to temperament. Let's go." He locked the office door behind them. "Will you ask her to tea?"

"Of course, Tubby. Pasca will be all smiles. He is eager for indoor work, it keeps him from hard labor outside."

"When you get a chance, tactfully lead him on to express any conviction he may have as to who took the revolver from the holster on the H house wall."

"Tubby! Do you think?"

"I never think. Run along, little girl."

As she walked the short distance to the Samp cabin, Janice marshaled her memories. Where had Pasca been the evening of what he called the marriage-party? He had welcomed Bruce and herself when they landed on the flying-field. She couldn't remember having seen him even for a moment during the festivities. That didn't prove anything. The day had been so hectic it was a wonder she had remembered that she had a new name.

She paused abruptly on the threshold of the Samp living-room. Ned Paxton was beside Miss Mary at the table from which books and lamps had been removed to make space for a profusion of unmounted photographs. Martha, in the wing chair, white-stockinged feet on a stool, shoes on the floor beside it, peered from behind a newspaper.

"Sakes alive, aren't you through work early, Janice?"

The black cat, dozing on the hearth, arched his back into an interrogation-point as Paxton took a step toward her. Janice observed her one-time fiancé thoughtfully. His ash-blond hair had the gloss of satin, his eyes held in their intense blue depths the mocking light she had feared and hated, his full red lips, under his slight mustache, were set in a line which boded no good to the person who crossed him, and yet she sensed an indefinable change in him. If it were not too improbable, she would think that he had lost a grain of self-assurance. Her suspicion slunk shamefacedly into the background as she met his eyes. He had not changed. She leaned over the back of Miss Martha's chair as she answered her question.

"Mr. Grant closed the office early. I had finished the work he left. I suspect that he didn't want to be bothered with me. Immediately I thought of a tea-party. Where is Mrs. Hale?"

"Gone back to her cabin."

"Alone?"

"I promised I'd go over and stay nights. She wants to get packed up. Says she'll go out on the next boat."

"Is she less dazed, more cheerful?"

Martha Samp's voice was grim. "She isn't what you'd call cheerful. I kinder think Millicent's goin' to enjoy widowhood like some folks enjoys poor health. She's talkin' an awful lot about missin' Joe. Now, makin' allowance for the shock, an' all, everyone knows she was terrible unhappy with him."

"You don't understand folks who aren't hacked out of Plymouth Rock, as you are, Martha."

If one of the scarlet-coated Hessians on the hearth had slashed with his gold sabre, Janice wouldn't have been more surprised than she was at the younger Samp sister's outburst. Miss Mary's eyes sparkled, her cheeks were a deep pink, the work-worn hand which held a photograph trembled. Martha stared at her with faded agate eyes.

"Mary Samp! What foolish talk! Have you gone plumb crazy?"

"Crazy! I've just come sane. I've spent over two years of the precious few I got left cookin' waffles up in this wilderness, where you don't ever see anybody, when I might have been seeing places, real places, an' having clothes, real clothes. Great things are goin' on in the world, an' all I know is waffles an' then more waffles."

Martha Samp opened her lips.

"Now don't you say a word till I get through, Martha. You've told me what to do all my life an' I have done it, because first place it was easier than settin' up against you, an' second I didn't know there were such things in the world as I've found out since I came here."

"Mary Samp! Your head's been turned readin' those fashion magazines. Foolish things."

"They ain't foolish. They're like fairy tales to me. When I read 'bout slim, slithery women in trailin' silver dresses an' ermine capes an' emerald bracelets glitter-gleamin' on their arms, I'm them. You an' I are not poor. You like to pile up money. I don't. I'm going to spend my half. I'll stay here till the last boat goes out, then I'm through with pots and pans and waffles."

She sank back, visibly shaking. Her sister's voice was as sharp as a razor, though Janice saw the glint of tears in her eyes.

"Sakes alive, Mary Samp! I didn't know you had so much spunk. An' here I've been layin' awake nights wonderin' what would happen to you if I died. I guess I'm not so important as I thought I was. You'd probably get on a heap sight better without me. If that's the way you feel, you needn't wait for the last boat. Go as soon as you like. I don't need you."

Paxton, who had been standing by the mantel smoking, flung his cigarette into the fire. He laid his hand on Mary Samp's heaving shoulder.

"Call her bluff. I will take you down the coast in my yacht. I'll give you the time of your life. I will take Mrs. Hale too if she'll come."

Mary Samp wiped misty eyes with a shaking hand. "I'd like it, Mr. Paxton, but — but I'm not a very good sailor."

"You'll think the sea a mill-pond in my boat. We'll do some cruising before we leave so that you will get used to it. I shall not start for a couple of weeks. Perhaps by that time I may have persuaded another person to join us." His eyes met Janice's. He smiled before he added, "Miss Martha may decide to come."

"Huh! When I go, I don't go in a slow boat. I'll fly. Janice, if you're set on a tea-party, you'd better get it going. Mary will come. She'd better get in practice for city life an' silver dresses an' ermine capes. Try to get M's. Hale out. 'Twill do her good."

At Miss Martha's direct command, Janice roused from the state of mental coma into which Mary's rebellious outbreak had plunged her. With a murmured, "I'll expect you all in an hour," she dashed out of the cabin. The fog dripped from the roofs like rain, ran in rills down the window-panes, drenched the brim of her soft hat. Would Ned Paxton follow her? She listened for footsteps on the board walk. Evidently he was staying behind either to placate Martha Samp, or to make further plans with Miss Mary. What had been behind his offer to take her back to the States? He had an ulterior motive, she was sure of that. He had suggested taking Mrs. Hale too. Had he been attracted to her? She might have thought so, if she hadn't met his eyes a few moments ago. For an instant they had flamed with triumph. What had he been thinking? He would not have appeared quite so exultant had he known the relief which had surged through one person's mind at thought of his departure.

Millicent Hale was seated at a desk littered with papers when Janice entered her cabin. In her black frock she seemed passionless, remote, intangible as a shadow. The beady eyes of the Pekinese curled up in her lap glittered through a mop of hair. The sombre gown accentuated her pallor, the lustre of the pearls about her white throat. The fire cast rosy shadows on her skin without warming it, flashed reflected flames into the strained eyes without lighting them. Janice felt her color rise in the face of her well-bred surprise.

"Did — did you wish to see me?"

She resisted the temptation to answer impudently, "No. I came to gather ferns." Instead she explained. "I have an afternoon off. I've been craving a tea-party for weeks. I'll be ready in an hour. Will you come?"

Mrs. Hale touched her black frock. "You are inviting me to a party?"

Her pained surprise made Janice feel like a worm. "I didn't mean a real party. Merely a cup of tea. I thought coming to the H house for a while might shorten the day for you. It must seem horribly long."

Millicent Hale's shudder was slight, quickly under control.

"This day is neither longer nor harder than many other days have been in this horrible country. Has Bruce been heard from? Poor boy, he so hated to leave me, but that hateful Commissioner dragged him away."

"They radioed that they would leave the northern camp early tomorrow. Would reach headquarters in the afternoon."

"Have they found Jimmy?" Mrs. Hale's voice was hoarse, she clenched the back of her chair with a fragile, white, knuckled hand.

"Nothing was said about Mr. Chester. At least Mr. Grant told me nothing."

With a sob, relief perhaps, Millicent Hale laid her face on arms outflung on the desk. The little dog clawed at her skirts. She put out a hand and pulled him up into her lap. Janice tried to comfort her.

"I wish that I might help you."

"Help!" The woman rose with a haste which catapulted the somnolent Pekinese to the rug.

Her voice shook with anger. "Help! You! You've snatched all the good in life there was left for me. You knew Bruce years ago, I hear. Met him again, ran away from the man you were to marry, disguised yourself as a boy, brought a truckload of seductive clothes and came hotfoot after him, didn't you?"

"And got him!"

18

Janice banged the door behind her. Humiliation succeeded fury. If moments of crisis revealed one's true self, she and Millicent Hale had not shown up well under the late pasage-at-arms. Two tenement-house women fighting over a man would have stripped down to the same basic frenzy.

"And got him!" The words chased one another round and round in her mind, like a cat in pursuit of its tail, as she hurried to the H house. Raw, terribly raw. What would Bruce think if he heard what she had claimed? The question which haunted Janice's waking hours, intruded on her dreams, bobbed up again: "Was Bruce in love with Millicent before I came?"

As she opened the H house door she heard a thud. Pasca, his plaid shirt of a blinding brilliance, was laying a log on the fire. The red coals thrust out orange tongues to lick it greedily. Tong, on his haunches in front of the couch, yawned prodigiously. She laughed as she patted his head.

"Bad boy! I heard you jump down." She

plumped up the pillows. A sudden inexplicable ache of loneliness seized her, the bat-like wings of depression brushed against her spirit. Was the fog creeping into her heart? Her voice reflected her mood.

"Don't put any more wood on, Pasca."

"Aw right." His usually stolid face crinkled in concern. "You trouble? Much sunshine not in your speech, no sirree."

Janice smiled. "It's the fog. It is my proud boast that my spirits are never affected by the weather, but this day got me. It won't last. I'm having a tea-party. Set up the card table. Lay the cloth and arrange the Chinese pewter tray the way I showed you. Be sure that the water for the tea has been freshly boiled. Grate cheese on crackers and brown them, put others together sandwich fashion with guava jelly and chopped nuts."

The man's stolid face brightened in a childish smile. "How many tea? One? Two? Tree?"

"Four cups. Put on your white coat." As she removed a faded flower from the bowl on the table desk which had been full of red roses the first time she entered the cabin, she asked casually, "You like the white coat, don't you? What do you wear when you go to dances? Feathers and blankets or just ordinary clothes? Perhaps you don't dance? Perhaps you weren't at the squaw-dance the night the Samp sisters had the party for me?"

He stiffened into immobility long before she

had finished speaking. Why? Had she spoken too rapidly for him to understand? Or had something she said put him on guard? Before he answered he shuffled across the room, removed the embroidered tea-cloth from the dresser drawer.

"I not go to dance, no sirree. Work all time at Waffle Shop. Tell Kadyama, 'You help. Then I get through much quick, then we two go squaw-dance.' He say no. He plenty lazy all time." He spread the cloth carefully and pattered into the kitchen.

Later, seated on the spavin-legged stool before the crooked dressing-table, Janice thoughtfully buffed her already polished nails. In spite of a refreshing shower, the gayest print frock of her colorful wardrobe, that curious sense of depression, almost of impending danger, persisted. She patted her ruddy hair which already lay in smooth, glossy waves close to her head, appraised the effect of the lace collar and cuffs of her blue-and-jade gown in the mirror. They were becoming, took several years from her age. Her eyes were deep and clear as pools.

She nodded approval. Not too bad. She couldn't justly hold her ensemble responsible for her gloom. It must be the fine black dust which settled on everything. Neither was the outside world responsible now, for in spots the sun was wearing through the clouds, revealing blue, scintillant patches of sky. The wind had changed. Elbows on the unsteady table, she sank

264

her chin into her pink palms. Eves on the gleaming circlet on her finger, softly advised the mirrored girl.

"Face it, my dear. Get it off your mind."

What had Bruce meant when he had crushed her in his arms, had kissed her and kissed her as though never would he let her go? "It's like tearing my heart out to leave you, Beautiful!" The recurrence of the husky words set her heart beating suffocatingly. Had his leave-taking been merely good theatre, just good theatre to impress Ned Paxton?

"Ooch!" The sound escaped from between clenched teeth. She sprang to her feet. She burned up with shame when she thought of the manner in which she had flung herself on his protection. What could he have done but ask her to marry him after her silly lie? Fool performance, that hasty ceremony. Instead she should have taken the first boat back to the States. She might have found a position as secretary somewhere on the coast. She didn't wonder that he had scoffed that night in New York:

"Girls! What would we do with a girl in our outfit!"

No one knew how much Tatima, possibly Mrs. Hale, had been indirectly responsible for the late tragedy. If Millicent hadn't been at headquarters, who would have suspected nice Jimmy Chester of shooting Joe Hale? Probably he wouldn't have been shot.

She prowled restlessly about the living-room,

straightened the white cloth on the small table, brushed a fleck of soot from it. How little she had realized the sort of life into which she was adventuring when she had packed that delicate thing! She wasn't sorry that she had brought it any more than she regretted bringing her smart clothes. Frills kept one from going savage. Dear Miss Mary had learned that. Who would suspect her of becoming clothes-conscious? She would get her fill of luxury if she returned to the States in Ned Paxton's yacht. How crude this room must have seemed to him.

Hands clasped lightly behind her, she viewed it with his fastidious eyes. Home-made chairs, most of them with swollen knee-joints. A couch which sagged from Tong's occupation, pillows with dingy covers. The pelts on the floor were above criticism, the Russian samovar was an exhibition piece, the fan-back chair a gem, and the old Chinese pewter tea-service probably couldn't be duplicated in any antique shop in the country. She crossed to the shelves, filled not merely with books, but with literature as well. Bruce must read French and Spanish, there were numberless volumes in those two languages. She moved on to the window. The fog had lifted. The ceaseless din of machinery, men's rough voices drifted from the plateau. Someone called "Pick up!" and the sounds stopped instantly. The faint stroke of a ship's bell drifted across the water from the long, white boat lying at anchor off shore. The Stars and Stripes floated from its stern, a yacht club pennant fluttered from a masthead. Seaworthy for outside requirements, with draft shallow enough for inside waters, Ned Paxton had planned to take her around the world in it. He had had the spacious interior re-decorated as a surprise and she never had seen it. What had attracted her to him? Had she been flattered by the attention of a man whom mothers with marriageable daughters were pursuing? For how much had the magic glamour of millions been responsible?

Why think of that? Terrible waste of gray matter to keep dragging up the past. She could see the red blooms of the invincible geraniums in front of the Waffle Shop, could make out the line of the far horizon. What worlds lay beyond it? What secrets did those mountains, rearing sharp and black against a mass of blood-red clouds, hold? Her problems which seemed of immense importance dwindled to midget proportions in the immensity of her surroundings. Restlessly she looked at the clock. Ten minutes before the party would arrive. She turned the dial of the radio.

"*Ich ha — be muth.*" An enchanting soprano rendered the phrase of Leonora's hymn of heroic daring from Fidelio. Immediately followed a guttural translation.

"Fear have I none." The words were as clear as though spoken in the room.

A German-English lesson coming across the Pole from Berlin. Janice hummed "Fear have I

267

none," as she twisted the dial. A crisp American voice announced:

"This program is coming to you from the New York studio of the National Broadcasting Company. The orchestra will render selections from Verdi's Aïda."

New York! The words were a magic carpet which transported her thousands of miles in the sob of a violin. To the martial blare of trumpets, the melody of strings, she slipped back into the world she had known all her life. It was evening there. Summer though it was, some members of the smart world, girls whom she knew, would be in the city for the première of a play — it was the season for try-outs — for dancing on a floor like glass, for Contract, perhaps for a prizefight. They would wear lovely, floating frocks, jewels even on their incredibly high-heeled slippers, gorgeous. Doubtless they had made a day of it motoring in, after a tray breakfast in bed, for an hour of gymnastics at the latest fashionable studio. They would have lunched at Pierre's or Sherry's or the Colony Club. She could smell the exotic scent of gardenias, the spiraling cigarette smoke. After that they would have made the round of the important galleries, making smart, more or less — generally less — intelligent criticisms of the paintings exhibited. Then tea with the man of the moment to the accompaniment of music, challenging, seductive, jazzy, as the mood dictated. Dressing at the town house or the Club for evening. Back to the country at midnight or early star-spangled morning, for sleep, golf, tennis, swimming, cards and still more cards. She knew the program. She had been round and round the treadmill half a thousand times.

She snapped off the radio. If she lingered another moment in the past, she would begin to be sorry for herself. Sorry! Why? Had she been urged to come to Alaska? She laughed. Urged! Good grief! Hadn't she fairly stuffed herself down the throat of the outfit? Wasn't every moment of her life here interesting? Perhaps she had a small-town mind, perhaps that was the explanation of her contentment in this wilderness. "It's like tearing my heart out to leave you, Beautiful!" She put her hand to her throat. Her heart seemed to be beating there. Was Bruce the explanation? Of what had she been thinking when his voice crashed into her thoughts? About New York. Would she go back if she had the chance? She would not. Would she have the chance?

She curled up in the fan-back chair, eyes on the leaping, crouching flames, visualized Ned Paxton's expression as he had invited Mary Samp to return to the States in his yacht. He had meant it. He would give her the time of her life. He was unbelievably thoughtful of older persons and children. Would Millicent Hale sail on the Modern Mariner? Would she be allowed to until the mystery of her husband's death was cleared?

Had the party come? Janice flung open the

269

door in response to a knock. Her smiling lips stiffened. Ned Paxton. Alone. She feigned enthusiasm.

"Come in. Where are the others?"

"Coming. I'm the vanguard. As the relations between the Samp sisters seemed a little strained, I left them to fight it out." Back to the fire, he lighted a cigarette. He might have been the Well Dressed Man stepped from the pages of *Vanity Fair*. The engineers would pale with envy could they see his blue coat, gray flannel trousers and accessories. One of their favorite indoor sports was to plan outfits for their return to civilization. Janice was conscious of his critical scrutiny of the room as he inhaled and exhaled a long breath of smoke. His cynical eyes came back to her in the fan-back chair.

"So you chose this in preference to what I could give you?"

His amused incredulity stung her. She struggled to keep her voice as lightly contemptuous as his.

"But, you see, I didn't have to take you with it."

"*Touche!* Score one for you."

Janice asked with honest curiosity:

"Why did you want to marry me, Ned? I am different in all my tastes from the girls with whom you play round."

He frowned as he regarded her with appraising eyes. "You'd be surprised if you knew how many times I have asked myself that question. I went out of my way to meet you. I was curious. I had heard that in spite of the fact that you neither smoked, drank, gambled nor petted, men hung round you in smitten swarms, that you had more friends than any girl in your set. I didn't believe it, but I fell for you like all the rest."

"Smoking for some inexplicable reason makes me dizzy and cutting out the whoopee stuff was no virtue in me. I tried it all. I don't like the ugly and sordid, and more particularly the cheap things of life. They leave tarnished memories. My inhibitions ought to prove to you that I wouldn't fit into your scheme of living."

"What do you know of my scheme of living? I want a woman at the head of my house, for the mother of my children, who has an infallible instinct for the fine and beautiful things of life and the courage to go after them. And I'm going to get her. You must have thought me an easy mark when we met at the hotel. I was dazed by the news of your marriage. As the day wore on I grew suspicious. Asked a few questions. Discovered that you married Harcourt after you met me that morning. Why did you do it?"

She had almost liked him again, trusted him as he confided his ideal of family life. The savage contempt of his question hardened her heart.

"Continue sleuthing. Find out."

She looked at him with steady, cool eyes. He might have been a stranger for any power he had to quicken her pulses either to fear or love. She couldn't even keep angry with him.

"I have it on rather good authority that Harcourt was not in love with you — he is as popular as a talkie head-liner with the ladies of Alaska — I suspect it was a clear case of knight errantry on his part. Girl announces that she is married to him. What could he do but come across with the ring?"

He might not have power to inspire fear or love but he had power to hurt her unbearably. Every word was true, that was why it cut. And he said it after witnessing Bruce's impassioned leave-taking on the day he had started off to bring back Jimmy Chester. He had recognized it for what it was, a touch of drama for his benefit. Anger burned out the hurt as caustic burns out poison. She shrugged.

"You will have to answer that question yourself, Ned. But after all, how can you? What do you know of the ambitions, struggles, sacrifices, self-discipline which lie behind what you call knight-errantry? You see. You want. You buy."

His face was dark with anger. "You said that once before. I don't like it. I'll prove to you that I can earn one thing I want — that's you. Think I don't know that this marriage stuff is a bluff to save your face? Harcourt's theatric farewell the other day was more bluff — though it was too mighty well done to suit me — he would make a fortune in the talkies — you are no more his wife than you are mine. Acknowledge it." He drew her close. She protested sharply:

"Ned! Let me go!"

The kitchen door banged open. Tong dashed into the room. Head lowered, brush drooping, one corner of his lip snarled to reveal a fang, baleful eyes watchful, he stood as motionless as a creature in bronze.

Paxton released Janice. His laugh showed a tinge of strain.

"My mistake." His hand was not quite steady as he lighted a cigarette. The dog crouched back on his haunches, alert as a sentinel on guard.

Pasca shuffled into the charged silence. Balanced on one hand, high above his head, with the grand manner of a Pullman waiter, he carried the Chinese pewter tray. The flame from the small alcohol lamp streamed out behind like an orange pennant in a brisk breeze. Janice visualized the perfection of tea-service on Paxton's yacht and suppressed a nervous giggle.

"You ring? Yes sirree?"

Pasca looked at her as he set the tray on the card table. She had not rung and he knew it. Had her protest been loud enough to reach the kitchen? She glanced at Paxton. He was frankly comtemptuous of the man's clumsy effort at service. Pasca was childishly oblivious to criticism.

"Look good. Like million dollars, yes sirree. Tatima in kitchen with deesh. Mees Samp seesters send her."

"Aren't they coming?" Janice's voice dripped disappointment. "Tell Tatima to come in, Pasca." Grant entered by the front door. "Tubby, I'm glad you have arrived to swell the list of those present, it looks as though my party might be a frost."

"Says you. How are you, Paxton? Where's Mrs. Hale? Well, what d'you know! See who's here!"

Tatima had come in from the kitchen. Her bronze face showed lines of suffering, but her eyes sparkled, a self-conscious smile twitched at the corners of her mouth. Her sleeveless red georgette dress, designed by a mail-order house for a perfect thirty-six, accentuated the supple curves of her ample thirty-eight figure. Exquisitely carved silver earrings touched her shoulders, two broad bracelets of incredibly wrought links adorned one arm, her blue beads still served as a necklace, her fingers were laden with rings. She set a doily-covered plate on the table, removed the cover and revealed flaky scones, indented with wells of ruby strawberry jam.

"Mees Samp seesters send plate. They say, sorry they can't come to party."

"Tell them that I am terribly disappointed." The girl lingered, twisting her bracelets in conscious expectancy. "I never saw so much lovely silver jewelry. Something tells me you've had a present."

Tatima assumed indifference. "Who, me? Kadyama geeve to me. He geeve me much more. I marry on him. He chief's son. Some day I beeg chief's squaw."

Low as it was, perhaps because her subconscious was simmering with suspicion, Janice heard Tubby Grant's hushed "Ba-gosh!" She glanced at Paxton perched on the corner of the table desk. The speculative gleam in his eyes as he appraised the Indian girl made her a little sick. She looked back at Tatima who was regarding Grant with a superior smile.

"I no sell my beads. I keep w'at I have an' get more an' more an' more." Her eyes glittered. Her fingers clutched at her red dress.

There was a thread of excitement in Grant's laugh. "Mebbe so. Mebbe so. Kadyama's struck pay-dirt, has he? Where's his gold mine?"

"He noding like gol' mine. Money owe him long time for card game. Yesterday man pay. Kadyama buy silver from Ossa."

"Who's the rich stranger? I'd like to get up a little game with him myself."

Tatima sniffed scorn. "Stranger! Pasca pay heem. Pasca have beeg fat roll of money, Kadyama say."

19

Coming aboard Ned Paxton's boat had set old memories twanging unbearably. Even if Tubby Grant's argument had seemed water-tight, she should not have stepped foot on it, Janice reflected uneasily, as, back to the rail, she regarded the group under the awning of the deck lounge of the Modern Mariner. Mary Samp's eyes were big with wonder, her cheeks pink as Delicious apples, partly from excitement, partly from heat generated by the heavy drab woolen dress and thick shoes which were Miss Martha's conception of the proper costume for yachting. She perched on the edge of the seat like a plump pigeon on a ledge ready to take-off at the slightest warning. Millicent Hale, in a deck chair, had removed her black hat. Her fair hair seemed fairer in contrast to her sombre frock. From her regal air she might have been Cleopatra voyaging in a gilded barge, under outspread sails of purple, to the rhythmic pulse of silver oars. Janice sniffed. Cleopatra was too snappy a comparison. Her face was as maddeningly complacent — when one didn't see her evasive eyes — as a sculptured goddess in a gallery. Why had the fragile woman in black such power to hurt her? Whenever they met she left a barb of innuendo rankling like a thorn which one cannot see but which pricks irritatingly. Unless Millicent Hale was a smooth and convincing liar there had been more than friendship between Bruce Harcourt and herself.

Was Ned Paxton intrigued by her? He sat on a high cushion at her feet, hands clasped about his white flannel knees as he talked. His conversation had the true cosmopolitan flavor. Why not, when he spent his life in the gayest, largest capitals of the world? The sun brought out the gloss of his smooth hair, patterned his navy serge coat with gold. Was that her own turquoise blue self grotesquely broadened in the shining ball of brass? Janice regarded the reflection thoughtfully. Life was a jolly joker. She had ordered this very sports frock to wear on this very boat before she had given Ned back his ring.

Good grief, she hadn't a minute to spend on the past with the present and future tangled into mystery. Perfect afternoon. Warm as a Long Island summer day, fragrant as a forest-rimmed harbor in Maine. Raucously screaming gulls soared and dove about the boat. The sky was clear sapphire softened by an opal haze which settled in a light film on the deck, lava dust from the volcano which they were sailing forth to see at closer range. The distant shore was emerald green. Dense woods of birch, spruce and hemlock rose gently into slopes patched with moss, dotted with junipers and alders, reared sharply into fanglike summits holding mouthfuls of snow. To the south a wild light hung over the water. It seemed to rise from a mammoth deep-sea reflector which cast curious, macabre patterns on the helmet vapor clouds.

Admitted that it was a glorious day, that fact did not explain her presence on this boat. Tubby Grant had been responsible. That was unfair. She alone was responsible for what she did. She was white, free and considerably over twenty-one, quite old enough to make her own decisions. Had it all been Tubby's insistence, or had she been glad of the chance to be away when Bruce returned? She pigeon-holed the question for future examination. After supper last night, Tubby had held her up outside the Waffle Shop — while men, sourdoughs with gold teeth, workmen with no teeth at all, Indians and Eskimos, passed and re-passed, for all the world like extras on the silver screen, while the aroma of coffee and sizzling batter scented the air — had begged her to second his efforts to have Millicent Hale away from headquarters when the Commissioner and Harcourt arrived the next afternoon. From the fact that his name had not been mentioned in the radio message, there was every reason to believe they were bringing Jimmy Chester. He had asked Paxton to cooperate by inviting a party on his yacht for a nearer view of the erupting volcano. He had caught on at once. Said he had promised Miss Mary a trial trip or two, that he would invite Mrs. Hale.

Grant's plan had seemed sound. Now, on thinking back over the conversation, she wondered that he had not referred to Tatima's startling disclosure as to the source of the money which Kadyama had lavishly expended on silver jewelry. Where could Pasca get so much cash so suddenly? Was it part of that taken from Joe Hale when he was shot? Apparently no one had suspected Bruce Harcourt's house-boy. Because of that very fact, had the events happened in a detective story, he would have been proven to be the perpetrator of the crime. It would account for Bruce's revolver having been used, for Pasca's absence from the squaw-dance. What would have been the motive? Not Tatima. Money? Tubby had said that it was public knowledge that Hale carried a fat roll.

The mystery would be cleared up soon, then what would happen? Would Bruce and the Commissioner be at headquarters when the yacht returned? Would the boat approach near enough to the volcano for her to get a picture of it? Had the opal haze thickened, or was the sky clouding over? The sea was running smooth, the day had been made for Miss Mary's first trip. A ship's bell struck. She counted. Eight bells. Was it possible they had been sailing three hours? Tea time. She joined the group under the awning. Paxton rose.

"You stood so long staring over the rail, we

decided that you were making up your mind for a swim."

"Not in this icy water. I was wondering if we could approach the volcano near enough to get a picture. I brought a movie camera."

"I'll talk with the Captain and the native pilots. We have two aboard. Meanwhile, will you show Miss Mary the interior of the boat? You know every crack and cranny of it, though you haven't seen it since I had it re-decorated — for you."

The last words were so low that Janice wondered if anyone but herself heard them. Miss Mary admitted half-heartedly:

"I'd like real well to see it, but I'm not much of a sailor below stairs. You coming, M's. Hale?"

"No. I am really not equal to the exertion. Don't feel that you must stay with me, Mr. Paxton."

"Miss Mary will enjoy the tour of inspection much more if there isn't a man trailing round. I will interview the Captain."

Janice slipped her hand within Mary Samp's arm. "We'll begin our sight-seeing tour with the hydraulic steering apparatus. It is the last word in its class. As the mechanic's cell was left out when my brain was assembled, auxiliary engines, synchronized Diesels mean nothing in my young life. We'll get the second officer to explain them to us."

Mary Samp's eyes shone, her cheeks reddened with excitement as she passed from one part of the yacht to another. The silver and blue, black and rose and gold of the staterooms reduced her to a state of thrilled speechlessness. On the threshold of the main lounge she clasped ecstatic hands.

"Well, now! I suppose this is what folks call modernistic!"

Janice, accustomed as she was to the latest vogue in furnishing, gasped at the sheer daring of the room. The ceiling graded down in equally proportioned tiers of pearl and silver. Lights cunningly concealed radiated a soft glow. In lieu of a fireplace for a focal point the decorator had set in one wall panes of opaque glass, illuminated from the back, through and over which water gently trickled. The fountain gave the effect of moonlight on a silver sea. It glowed with beauty. Blues, turquoise and peacock tones, white, silver and black were repeated in the hangings and furnishings. Mary Samp drew a long, unsteady breath.

"Isn't it beautiful! Martha's right. One half the world doesn't know how the other half lives. Don't seem like a man's room though."

The blood throbbed in Janice's temples. The ghost of her old self whispered:

"This was planned for you." As in a crystal she saw the crude living-room at the H house. No doubt but that was a man's room. Miss Mary touched her arm.

"What's that?"

Janice's eyes followed the pointing finger

toward a corner which was occupied by a broad shelf, before which were stools of polished metal, behind which were wall cabinets.

"That is a bar, Miss Mary."

"You mean, like they used to have in saloons for *drinks?*"

"Yes."

"Well, now! That standing there as bold as brass, an' only last week a captain of one of the coast boats was sent to prison for selling liquor to a native! It don't seem fair, somehow. Let's go on deck. Lookin' at that made me kinder sick."

Two Filipino boys were bringing the tea things when they returned to the lounge deck. Janice's lips twitched with laughter as she remembered Pasca's high-held tray. That reminded her, where had the Eskimo procured the money to pay Kadyama? The moment she reached land again she would begin sleuthing. Suppose — Her imagination took the bit in its teeth and galloped. She had Pasca safely behind prison bars, Jimmy Chester free as air once more when a voice crashed into her reflections.

"Janice!" She looked up. Paxton was standing before her fastening a holster belt. "That's better. You were a hundred miles from here. I'll bet you couldn't tell whether you've had tea or not. You have. The sea is running smooth. If you want to get near enough to the volcano to take a picture, the Captain says that it will be perfectly safe for the native pilots to take you in the launch."

Janice's premonition nerves tingled. Darn her imagination. Here was the opportunity of a lifetime. Would she let her fear-complex rule? She would not.

"I'm all excited! Am I to go alone?"

"No. I'll go to make sure that you don't fall out of the boat in your excitement. The sky is not quite so clear as it was, we'd better get a move on. The yacht will follow. We will turn back the moment you say the word."

Seated in the launch, Janice waved to the two women and the Captain bending over the rail to watch them start. Miss Mary's eyes were troubled, Millicent Hale's inscrutable, the Captain's complacent as he listened to the purr of the motor, rhythmic as a kitten's breathing, observed the skill of the native pilots who had shed their coats and caps, gold braided with the yacht's insignia, and had stolidly wriggled into kamalaykas, which looked like waterproof overshirts with a hood. When at a proper distance, Janice focused the camera on the group on the deck. She cranked until the faces were dim.

"There! I wonder what Tubby will say to that. He is teaching me the motion-picture art. I've even learned to develop films. When I return to civilization I will be equipped to go on the lecture platform."

"Then you expect to return to civilization?"

Apparently absorbed in the intricacies of the black box she held, she answered abstractedly:

"Return! Of course. Then some day we are going to South America to build a bridge."

Paxton laughed skeptically before he crouched down behind the engine to light a cigarette.

From whence had that iridescent bit of fabrication bubbled, Janice demanded of herself in dismay. From the rows and rows of Spanish books in the H house? Had those spelled South America to her subconscious?

Paxton went forward to consult the man at the wheel. The Modern Mariner had dwindled to Lilliputian proportions. The launch was running parallel with a green shore from which twin mountains lightly clothed with alders and willows, arid, with volcano ash, rose in a graceful sweep to taper into dazzling white cones. Beyond towered higher peaks like purple shadows. She could make out an abandoned Indian village, its tumble-down huts shining weirdly white in the distance. Were those uprights carved totem poles? She turned eagerly to Paxton as he came aft.

"See that Indian village, Ned. I wish —"

The sentence died on her lips as a rain of tiny rocks showered upon the boat. They burned as they struck her hands, hissed as they fell into the water to float away like dingy snow-flakes. Orange and scarlet flames fired curling vapor, belching smoke, till the sky seemed one frightful conflagration.

"Hol'tight! Hol'tight!"

Janice hadn't needed the hoarse shouts of the

pilots as a warning. Instinctively she had gripped the side of the launch.

"Come about! Make for the yacht!" Paxton shouted.

Too late. With the roar as of all the thunderbolts forged in Vulcan's workshops let loose, with a crash which rocked the world, the volcano blew up. Fascinated eyes on the spectacle, Janice saw what looked to be the back of a great sea monster rise to the surface. An island being born? Paxton caught her in one arm, clung tight with the other hand. A wave which seemed mountains high rolled toward the launch, caught it as though it had been a chip in a puddle, swept it shoreward with incredible speed. Sweat ran down the bronze face of one pilot as he strained at the wheel. The eyes of both bulged with terror. Overhead feathery, scooting clouds merged. The world which had been all sapphire, emerald and crystal went dreadnought gray. Stinging white foam flew back in drenching spray. Smoke rolled and twisted like a boa-constrictor in the throes of acute indigestion. The boat climbed a huge roller, lunged sickeningly in the trough, staggered and shuddered when a fresh wave struck it. The sea snarled and hissed under a shower of hot stones. Spray blurred Janice's eyes as she strained them in an effort to see what lay ahead. Another mighty smash and shock of water, greater than its predecessor, lifted the boat like a toy and flung it on the shore.

For a dazed instant she sat with eyes tightly shut. She had thought that last plunge would end everything. Paxton touched her shoulder.

"We're safe, Jan. Don't, don't go to pieces now that the danger is over."

"Go to pieces!" She blinked, forced a smile. "I was merely orienting myself, that's all."

The launch was stranded on a pebbly beach, not so far up, she told herself, but what another tidal wave would either land it in the tree-tops or carry it out to sea. If she had her choice she was all for the tree-tops. Coppery coils of smoke obliterated sea and sky twenty feet from shore. No escape that way. The native pilots were huddled in the bow. Paxton, livid, tense, was standing over them. With a final word he came back to her.

"We'll have to camp here until the yacht picks us up. The men say there is a hunter's shack somewhere on this shore. They are dumb with fright. That was all I could screw out of them. We'd better find it before another wave catches us."

The girl's heart stopped for an instant. A mammoth wave rolled in. She jumped into water when she left the boat. The three men were holding the bow. The tide was sucking at it, trying to drag it out. She helped pull the launch farther up shore. An uncanny howl from somewhere inland rose to crescendo, slid into diminuendo and died away.

"What's that?"

The teeth of one of the pilots visibly and audibly chattered as he answered Paxton.

"That a wolf cry, yes sirree. Smoke an' fire drive dem to shore. Dey no lak fire. Not much ever come oder time. Hunters come here. Shack up by trees."

Paxton's voice showed strain. "Come on, Jan. We'll find it. Don't lose your nerve over that howl, it was miles away."

"It is not my nerve I've lost, it's my knees. There is nothing but all-goneness where they should be."

"You've clung to your camera, I see. We may wish it were something to eat before we get through. There are two cans of crackers in the launch, that's all. If only this infernal smoke would lift, we'd get back to the yacht. The men were right. There's the shack."

Janice's heart went into a tailspin. On a little hill, a spur on the side of the mountain, sagged a cabin of warped, weather-beaten boards. It leaned tipsily between two spruces like a blowsy woman in the grip of austere law-enforcers. Into her mind flashed the remembrance of the night she had lost her black satin slipper from the roadster. Ned had been unbearable then. To be sure, he had been drinking. Why, why should that memory bubble to the top now when she needed confidence, trust in him?

She didn't know how long she and Paxton stood there staring at the distant hut. He wheeled at sound of the put-put of an engine starting. With a startled oath he ran back to the water's edge. Janice stumbled after him. As they reached it, the stern of the launch vanished into the mist, where smoke and sky merged with blackish green water flecked with boiling white. There was a blur of red, white and blue, then that also slipped into the phantom world.

"Come back! Come back!" Paxton shouted. Only the fading throb of the engine responded. He drew his revolver and fired into the air. As though in answer, a wild wail was relayed by echo after echo through the woods. Janice caught his arm. Her voice came raggedly.

"Ned! Ned! Save your ammunition. Remember that ghastly howl."

20

A shower of hot stones pelted the man and girl standing motionless as Indian gods, peering into an impenetrable wall of smoke and mist. Rain splashed. Paxton turned.

"Come on, Jan. We'd better make for that shack while the going is fairly good. I'll bet it leaks like a sieve, but it will be some protection. Those infernal quitters threw out a can of crackers. I'll take that along."

He picked up the tin. With cocked revolver poked ahead of him, he started up an almost obliterated trail along the bank of a rushing, foaming brook. Janice followed him with her eyes. A flash of lightning zig-zagged through the murk; thunder bumped like a mammoth ball from the hand of a giant bowler. A wild night ahead. She was cut off from the world with Ned Paxton. Swift, upleaping fear shook her. She wanted to scream, to run. She did neither. So much for ancestors who had met life as it came, with heads high and smiling lips. Her voice gave no hint of her inner turmoil as she caught up with him.

"I'm all for the shack. If a few more hot pebbles hit my face, I'll look like Oliver Herford's spotted Le—o—pard."

He was too intent on the trail to heed her poor attempt at humor. She passed great patches of blue lupin. Wild raspberry bushes, higher than her head, clawed at her wet clothing, as though to direct attention to the dead ripe fruit hanging in maroon clusters. She gathered handfuls, carried them in her hat which she had lined with a damp but spotless handkerchief. The woods rustled with the motion of unseen life. A porcupine rattled across the trail ahead. An otter swam down stream, two martens scuttled into a tangle of brush. A fox trotted by, stopped, one foot raised, looked back before he dashed off as though pursued by furies. A fat ptarmigan rose with a whiz which sent Janice's heart into her mouth. A few blood-thirsty mosquitoes buzzed about her head, before drifting smoke sent them winging. Did everything living feel the pervading imminence of danger? Did Ned Paxton? His face was gray, when he turned to warn her of a mouldy log across the trail or a treacherous hole.

Even when they stood together before the shack he made no comment. Wind whistled through the cracks left by the shriveled moss calking, moaned mournfully among the spruces, set the bullet-perforated door a-squeal on its one rusty hinge. Rain drilled like a riveter on the roof of moss and rotting branches. A log, green and rusty as oak leaves veined with bronze, provided a step to the splintered sill. The entrance yawned like a cavernous mouth upon the eerie starkness of desertion.

Paxton's eyes were inscrutable as they met Janice's. Something about the grimness of his mouth set her heart thumping. He waved his hand toward the hut.

" 'Will you walk into my parlor —' "

"Don't finish. Please! I — I — loathe spiders." She balanced on the wet slippery log. "It smells musty. Something tells me that we will be more comfortable outside."

"Let's investigate. I have a light. I was trained by an old sea-dog never to leave the ship without a flash, a gun and matches." He pulled an electric torch from an inside pocket of his soaked blue coat. Its glow revealed a room high enough for a man, a tall man, to stand upright without hitting his head. A bunk against one wall was heaped with dried boughs of spruce. A loose-jointed pipe, one end poking through the roof, acted as smoke-conductor between a rusty cook-stove and the outer world. A degenerate chair and a rickety stool kept dissolute company. A table whose legs sprawled outward like those of a teetering new-born calf, supported two tallow streaked bottles and a dirty pack of cards. A rusty kettle and a frying-pan burned black hung from a crude shelf. Against the wall leaned an axe with a long handle and nicked blade.

Sordidness unbelievable. Janice camouflaged a shiver by a shaky laugh. She pointed toward the pile of wood and brush beside the stove.

"Shall we switch on the electric range?"

"Let's set the incandescent blazing first." He snapped a gold lighter. After several futile attempts succeeded in producing a small flame which he applied to a candle stub in one bottle. "We will save our matches for the fires. My knowledge of camping is all laboratory stuff, no field work, but I know enough for that."

They hung over the table breathlessly till the wick caught and a flickering flame set ghoulish shadows astir on the walls. Paxton snapped off the electric torch, laid his revolver on the shaky table, a card of matches beside it.

"Those must be kept dry. Think you can start the fire in the stove while I collect brush for a signal to the yacht? Wrecked on a desert island stuff."

He flung his wet blue coat over the chair-back. Axe in hand he smiled at her from the threshold. Good, but not good enough. Did he think she didn't know that the outside fire was more to keep off marauding animals than to signal the boat, that she had forgotten those banshee howls? She steadied her lips and smiled back at him. This last hour had aged him unbelievably. It had set deep crow's-feet at the corners of his eyes, etched lines between his nose and lips. Except for war service, all his luxurious life he had played hard and worked little. His once immaculate buckskin shoes oozed mud; his soaked white flannel trousers were criss-crossed with black lines, where wet shrubs had lashed at him; little green rivulets, sponsored by his necktie, were cavorting down the front of the silk shirt which was plastered to his body. His eyes with a laugh in their blue depths met hers.

"I don't like the suggestion of criticism of my appearance in your expression. You're not so hot yourself."

The liking she had felt for him during the first weeks of their acquaintance, which had flamed into love — or fascination — crumbled into gray ashes of doubt and distrust, stole back. It warmed her voice.

"I'm a sight. I feel like a rag doll which has been left out in the rain."

His eyes widened with surprise, he took a quick step forward, wheeled and jumped from the sill. Stopped to warn:

"Use those matches as though they were gold dust."

She heard the crackle of brush under his feet. Had her change of heart been apparent in her voice? Her breath had caught when he had started toward her. She would better watch her step.

She lifted a rusty cover from the stove. Her thoughts raced on as she laid a fire of dry leaves and brush. Billy and Bruce had taught her wood-craft when they had taken her with them on their fishing expeditions. If only Bruce were with her instead of Ned Paxton. What a gorgeous adventure they would make of it. He was the most companionable man she ever had met. She didn't love him, her pulses didn't quicken a beat when she saw him, it was just that being with him was like sitting in the sunshine after being cold. Had he returned to the H house? Had he found Jimmy Chester? Had the yacht gone back to headquarters to report about the missing owner? What would Bruce say when he heard? Would he be anxious, or would he feel that she was safe with Ned Paxton?

"It's like tearing my heart out to leave you, Beautiful."

His husky voice was in her ears, his lips on hers. Resentment surged. If only he had not said that to impress Ned Paxton. Ned had appraised it for just what it was, good drama.

She struck a match to escape the memory which set her heart pounding unbearably. She watched the dry leaves ignite before she clapped on the rusty cover. She listened. The fire roared. Had she put in too much fuel?

How the pesky thing smoked. She wiped her smarting eyes as she hunted for a damper. Her throat stung. It was humiliating not to be able to start a dinky little fire, but she would have to ask Ned to help. She stepped to the entrance for air. Brushed away smoke tears. She had not realized that it was so light. Was the mist lifting? Where was Ned? He had said he would be outside. She hadn't heard the axe. Could he have fallen, hurt himself?

She stepped down to the mossy log, laughed in

relief. Her imagination really ought to be harnessed to a scenario department. He was sitting on a stump trying to sharpen the axe with a stone.

What was that? Good grief! What was that behind the tree near him? A dog? A gray dog? A dog's eyes wouldn't be green. A wolf! What was hanging from the creature's cruel mouth? Cloth! A piece of plaid cloth caught on one yellowed fang. Sickening! She tried to call a warning. Her tongue dried to the roof of her mouth. Her body prickled with horror. The animal took a stealthy step toward the man on the stump. Stopped. Not a muscle rippled under its skin. Ned would have no chance to save himself.

Eyes on the motionless creature, Janice backed to the table, seized the revolver. On the doorsill she dropped to one knee. "Steady! Steady! Remember Jimmy's instructions," she warned herself. She took careful aim. Fired.

Man and beast leaped simultaneously. The wolf soundlessly slunk into the shadows. Paxton ran toward her, caught her shoulder. Shook her.

"Why in heaven's name did you do that?"

She steadied trembling lips. "It was a wolf — just back of you — he — he was watching you — hungrily. I thought — I thought —"

She dropped her head in her hands. Shuddered uncontrollably.

"A wolf! You shot him?"

"I shot at him." There was a touch of hysteria in her laugh. "I'm not too good."

295

"God, we'll have the whole pack down on us."

Indignation steadied Janice's nerves as no commendation would have done. "I call that darned ungrateful. You would have been torn to shreds if I hadn't fired."

"Why didn't you yell?"

"Yell! I was dumb with horror. I came to the door to ask you to help with the stove, saw that terrible creature moving toward you, and fired."

He loosened the fingers still clutching the revolver, laid it on the table.

"Did you care when you thought me in danger, Janice?"

Her heart flew to her throat. Blue eyes aflame could be more terrifying than fierce green eyes.

"Care! Wouldn't you care if you saw a human being in peril of his life? Isn't the smoke stifling? Can't you do something to stop it?"

"I —" He coughed, sneezed, wiped his eyes. "What's the matter with the infernal thing?"

Lids half shut, tears marking grimy furrows down his cheeks, he poked about the stove. Tears brimming from her smarting eyes, Janice tried to help. He shook what seemed to be a damper. The portion of the pipe which pierced the roof fell with a clatter which set her already taut nerves twanging like violin strings under the fingers of an impassioned virtuoso. A vicious orange-red fang shot from the standing smoke-stack, licked at the rotting branches of the roof. Damp as they were, they ignited. Fire ran from twig to twig.

The man and girl stared incredulously.

"We've done it now! Quick! Out of this!"

Paxton pushed her to the door, caught up the revolver as he dashed by the table. Janice grabbed her camera, snatched the tin of crackers. As they jumped to the mossy log she heard the crackle of wood. The walls of the shack were on fire.

Side by side they watched the lurid light inside flicker, flame, wane. Heat poured out as through the door of a furnace. Janice turned her back.

"I'm thoroughly toasted on one side. ' 'Tis an ill wind, etc.' It would have taken hours before an ordinary fire to dry our clothes. What is the next feature on this peppy program? It ought to be announced over a coast-to-coast hook-up."

Paxton's eyes shone blue and clear in his smoke-grimed face. "Janice, you're the best sport in the world. You set a great pace." He steadied his voice. "The fire's dying down. We'll have a warm, charred shack at our backs. That will be some protection."

"Protection from what?" She hated herself for the terrified catch in her voice.

"From prowlers. You heard the native pilot say that the volcano smoke would drive animals to the water. They will come down the bed of this brook from the interior. We are quite safe with that sooty ruin back of us and a fire in front. I'll get some water from the stream before all the light goes. There was a kettle in the shack —"

"You are not going into that furnace to get it.

We'll use the cracker tin." She peeled off paper, opened the box. With infinite care piled the crackers on the cover. "Miss Martha says there is a gate in every wall." In a sooty hand she held out the box. "Behold the gate!"

Hours passed. Hours filled with nerve-racking suspense, listening, listening for the sound of a boat which did not come, with the drip of rain, the pelt of hail, flash of lightning and detonations of thunder. Janice dropped to the mossy log in front of the shack which gave out an acrid odor of smoldering wood. It also gave heat and a sense of protection. Nothing could steal up behind them. The red light from the fire illumined mossy, lichened tree-trunks, was reflected in the shining rivers of rain which rilled from the tips of spruce boughs. Through strained, smarting eyes she looked at her wristwatch. Midnight. The woods were weirdly quiet. Even the tinkle of the brook seemed hushed. Only a few hours before daylight. It didn't seem as though she could carry another armful of wood. They had collected everything burnable within a safe distance. Piece by piece they had fed the furnishings of the shack to the flames.

Paxton carefully laid a heap of brush beside him as he dropped wearily to the log. The fire had died down to red coals.

"That's all I could find. We'll feed it stick by stick. We are safe enough now. Haven't heard a howl for an hour." He opened a gold cigarette case. "One left." He snapped it shut. "Glad you don't smoke. Otherwise I would have to sacrifice that on the altar of chivalry. Any crackers?" She drew one grimy piece from her pocket. "The last?" She nodded. "Put it back. I have indulged in too many calories already. I'll lose my boyish figure if I don't watch out."

"What's that?"

"What? Where?"

Janice gripped his sleeve. Pointed. Two lambent green dots glowed between low alders.

"Eyes?"

He crushed her fingers under his.

"Listen!"

She sensed rather than heard a swift noiseless movement in the darkness beyond the fire. As if in response to the touch on an electric button, a semi-circle of twin yellow-green sparks flickered and steadied. As though controlled by a master-hand on a switch-board they closed in.

With a muttered inprecation, Paxton threw on the pitifully inadequate pile of brush beside him. The fire flared. The sinister points of light retreated. A howl tore through the distance. From near at hand the blood-curdling wail was answered.

Janice shivered. "I'm not crazy about the sound effects with this picture, are you, Ned?"

He didn't answer. He was staring at the fire which had died down again. She looked beyond, strained her eyes till they became accustomed to the blackness. Her heart turned turtle. The unblinking, uncanny circle of yellow-green had contracted. Drawn closer. Paxton rose swiftly.

"I'm going for more wood."

"Where? You mustn't. It isn't safe."

"It is safer than staying here with the fire dying. With those great gaps in the base boards, the shack instead of being a safety zone might prove a trap. As we came up the hill I saw a big log by the side of the brook. It will last till dawn if I can get it here. It's not far. There are no eyes glaring from that direction. Keep between the shack and the fire."

"I'm going with you."

"Janice. If you want to help, do as I say." His eyes burned like twin blue lights in his soot-streaked face. His shirt sleeves hung in rags, his trousers were scorched in holes. His shoulders sagged. He looked unutterably weary. This night must have been a grueling, muscle-racking experience for a man who had for years lived softly. She capitulated with sympathetic understanding.

"I will do wherever you say, Ned. I'll keep the home fires burning."

"That's the stuff. See those two humps on the trees that look like misshapen heads hoisted on petards? The log is under those. I noticed it when we came up the brook. Hang on to the revolver but don't waste a shot. Watch out. If you see points of light between me and the fire, yell like a maniac but don't shoot."

"Ned, before you go I want to take back what I said about your never having earned anything.

Tonight you have earned my unwavering respect and friendship."

"Friendship! Think I'll be satisfied with that?"

She valiantly disciplined the little shiver his rough voice sent twanging along her nerves. He gripped the axe handle like a bludgeon. Into her mind flashed the memory of King Arthur wielding his sword, Excalibur. She followed him with her eyes till his figure was lost in the blackness.

Slow seconds dragged into interminable minutes as she waited, watched, listened. The rain had stopped. Drip from branches, the squeal of the rusted door-hinge, the faint crack of a branch under a cautious foot were the only sounds which broke the spooky stillness.

A warning howl rose from beyond the fire. Heart in her mouth she sensed swift, stealthy movement, green eyes shifting. The beasts had discovered Ned. Suppose she yelled. What help would that be to him? Fire, only fire would keep them back. Wood! Wood was what she needed. Could she pull a board from the shack? No. She might bring the whole wobbly thing down and be buried in the ruins. The door! She seized it. Within her welled a terrific physical impulse. She wrenched the bullet-riddled thing from the one rusty hinge. Dragging, lifting, jerking, she dropped it on the coals. It flamed like a piece of pitch pine.

Thank God for that. Instinctively she looked up. Were her eyes deceiving her or were those stars? Stars, like a million lighted windows. They gave a sense of home glowing through the darkness, sent her courage soaring like a captive balloon let loose. All her life lighted windows had fascinated her. In the city at twilight she would pass them slowly, imagining what was going on behind them. Always to her they suggested home-coming men, someone calling, "Is that you, dear?" That had been her mother's gay, tender greeting to her men-folk. Mother. She seemed very near out here under the stars.

Would she ever have a home again? A close-up of the H house flashed on the screen of her mind, she could see the imprint of Tong's head on the forbidden cushions, could see Bruce standing with arm on the crude mantel looking at her. His disturbing eyes met hers, they seemed to drag her heart from her body. A surge of longing such as she never before had known shook her. Regardless of the sinister sentinels beyond the fire, she dropped to the mossy log, covered her face with her hands.

Millicent Hale had been right. She had pursued Bruce. His smile, the touch of his hand, the rich tenderness of his voice had drawn her half across the world. Had she loved him all these years deep down in her heart? Did he care for Millicent? Millicent couldn't have him. Tatima had boasted, "I keep w'at I have an' get more an' more an' more." She would keep what she had of Bruce's — she couldn't call it love — affection and get more and more and more.

A touch on her shoulder. She started to her feet. A sob of relief tore up as she looked into Ned Paxton's grimy, weary face.

"How did you get back?"

"After you threw the door on the fire we didn't need that log. Crawled back. There is a pink light in the east. The wind has changed. It's blowing the smoke away. They will find us soon. Meanwhile —" he cleared the huskiness from his voice to suggest practically, "let's sit on the log. You may feast on that broken cracker. I'll smoke the last cigarette."

She smiled at him tremulously. "Ned. I like you better than ever before. You seem so — so different!"

His mouth was grim. "Different! I have been different since you told me that I bought everything I wanted. Don't care for that word 'like'. I want your love, Jan."

She laid her hand on his. Could she make him understand?

"I love Bruce Harcourt."

The undisciplined spirit of the man to whom she had been engaged flamed in his voice. "He can't have you. Think what I can give you. Jewels, travel, sables, homes anywhere you want them."

"A home means more than a house, Ned. Somehow I've learned that in these last weeks. I feel terribly old and wise tonight. A home is built by mistakes and struggles as well as by love. It means mutual sacrifices, mutual responsibilities, spiritual companionship. You can't buy a home." She felt the hand under hers clench. "I didn't mean that you were trying to buy my love now, really I didn't. You will believe me, won't you?"

He looked down at the scorched, bruised fingers. His haggard eyes met hers. "I believe you. We'll have no tarnish on the memory of this night, Jan."

"Tarnish! It will shine as clear as — as that sliver of silver moon on the brook."

"Jan darling, I can't let you go!"

A creepy wail rose from beyond the fire. Paxton released the hands he had caught tightly in his. Said with an attempt at lightness:

"A timely reminder that we are still chaperoned. Let's smoke and eat."

21

Bruce Harcourt looked down at Chester lying on the cot in the cabin which had been built for Janice. Were they really back at headquarters or was this a continuation of the nightmare of the last hours? No. Stephen Mallory bending over the unconscious man was real, so was the smell of antiseptics in the air. The coast missionary gave a final touch to the bandaged arm and straightened.

"He'll be stiff for days, but nothing more serious unless inflammation sets in. I would feel better if he were under the care of a surgeon. The gashes were ugly but not deep. I've treated the Eskimos for bear wounds. They are everlastingly paddling round ice-floes in their kayaks, on the chance of finding what you and Chester found, and they're just as everlastingly getting mauled as they attack the bears with spears and knives. Lucky you had a rifle. Better get to bed, Harcourt, you look all in."

"All in! You don't know the half. I've had hair-raising adventures and escapes since I came into this north country but nothing equal to the hell of these last hours. Came down twice on the

305

shore. Had to risk it, though I knew if my self-starter went on the blink I was done for. Radio wouldn't work. Compass useless. Chester half dead, I thought. Good Lord! Why am I living over that? It's behind me. If you are sure Jimmy is all right, I'll turn in."

"I'll stay with him."

Harcourt's tired eyes narrowed as he stepped out upon the board walk. Lights, voices in the dormitories at this time of night! What had happened? Grant had not met him when he had come down in the flying-field. Pasca and an Indian had come running at sound of the plane. He had been intent on transferring Chester, on getting hold of Stephen Mallory, who was as much of a doctor as he was a minister, to take care of his wounds. The sky was clear, spangled with stars. Moonlight dappled the sparkling with silver. What did he miss? Paxton's yacht! Gone! Janice!

He flung open the door of the H house. In the fan-back chair, shoes on the rug beside her stockinged feet, sat Martha Samp. Her face was deeply lined, her eyes seemed to have been pushed back into her head with a sooty finger. The black cat brushed against her skirt. His purr and the crackle of the fire were the only sounds in the room. She rose as he caught her arm.

"Where's Janice? Where's Grant? What's happened?"

She patted the hand on her sleeve. "Sakes alive, Mr. Bruce, don't get scared yet."

"Scared! What do you mean? Where's Janice? Has she gone with — with — are you here to tell me?"

He dropped his head on an arm outflung on the mantel. Martha Samp explained quickly:

"She's gone with Paxton, if that's what you mean, but not the way you think. That's better. Your eyes are gettin' alive. They was so dull when you came in, I was frightened."

"Where is Janice? Where the devil is Grant? I left him in charge here."

"He's gone in the launch huntin' for Kadyama. That sneaky Indian is out in his kayak an' Mr. Tubby is sure he knows somethin' about the shootin'. Paxton took M's. Hale, Mary and Janice out for a sail. They were goin' to get as near that belchin' volcano as they safely could. It was a beautiful day when they started. Along about four a storm came up, sudden. There was a great rumblin' an' then a wave which seemed mountains high swept up. Almost reached this plateau."

"Go on! Go on!"

"Sakes alive, boy, give me a chance to draw breath. Even then we didn't get anxious about the boat, 'tis such a big one. About two hours ago the radio station picked up a message from the Captain."

The color went out of her face. Her fingers picked nervously at his sleeve.

"Well? Well?"

"He said that the yacht was all right an' M's.

307

Hale an' Mary, but that he was cruisin' round to pick up the launch."

"The launch! The Modern Mariner's launch! Who was in it?"

"Janice and Paxton and two native pilots."

"That message came two hours ago! Pasca!"

The Eskimo swung open the kitchen door in answer to his shout. His beady eyes bulged in their slanted slits. His bronzed face was curiously colorless. "Fuel the Sikorsky. Quick! Be ready to take-off with me."

"Yes sirree. Meester Grant say to tell you he out huntin' for Kadyama, the minute you come. I see Meester Chester near dead. I forget."

"Get a hustle on."

"Yes sirree, I hustle."

The swing-door closed with a force which brought a yelp of pain from Tong who was passing through. He stopped to lick his tail before he jumped on Harcourt in effusive welcome.

"Down! Down, Tong! Miss Martha, I'm going for Janice. Have everything ready here in case — she's — she's chilled or — or hurt." He pulled off his wet jumper. Went into his room for a fresh one. Martha Samp followed him to the door.

"Now, Mr. Bruce, don't you worry. You won't find anything the matter with her, that child has a head on her shoulders even if her imagination does get to gallopin' at times. She thinks she's a terrible 'fraid-cat. I think she's the spunkiest little thing I ever saw. Don't know why I call her little, she isn't, it's something 'bout her makes you feel's though you couldn't keep from puttin' your arms round her."

She wiped away two big tears. Sniffed. "Sakes alive, I didn't know I could feel so sentimental. Got all worked up 'cause Mary didn't come back. Now I know she's safe I'm kinder crackin'-up. I've got hot chocolate on the stove at the Waffle Shop. You can't fly right if you don't take care of yourself. You stop there an' have a cup. I'll fill a thermos bottle and pack a basket with food. When you find Janice, she'll be hungry as a bear, prob'ly. Now don't you worry. Remember there's a gate in every wall."

A gate in every wall. Harcourt repeated the phrase over and over as the amphibian climbed. It kept at bay thoughts which almost drove him mad. The overturned launch! Janice hurt. Janice suffering. Janice on some lonely shore with Paxton.

"You fly up play tag with stars, yes sirree." Pasca's guttural voice came through the ear-phone in warning. "Gettin' day quick. Look — see. We fin' dem now."

"Watch the shore for signs of a fire, Pasca."

The rising sun was tinting the cloud, delicate as marines, unsubstantial as a colorful dream, which trailed along the far horizon. In its midst a pale star flickered and went out. Below, the white yacht steamed slowly, like a fabled bird floating on the breast of the water. Still searching. From a volcano-top in the east a column of smoke rose languorously, as though the force within the mountain was too exhausted from its orgy to do more than send out a puff of hot breath.

"Look! See!"

Harcourt leaned over the side to follow Pasca's shaking finger. Listed at a precarious angle, a launch was piled up on a beach under a cliff. He sent the Sikorsky wing-slipping down for a closer view. The launch from the Modern Mariner! Each foam-tipped wave set the contents awash. Life preservers floated out with the receding tide. The staff from which flew the Stars and Stripes was broken off short, the flag rose and fell with the motion of the boat.

Harcourt strained his eyes till they seemed starting from their sockets, flew low over it. Not a sign of life. No smoke rising from the woods near. That wrecked boat didn't mean necessarily that Jan had been in it when it struck. Paxton might have thought it wise to go ashore before. Paxton! He visualized the man's intense blue eyes, heard his incredulous laugh, his voice.

"I am the man she was to marry. Is to marry. Just who are you?"

"She's safe! I know she's safe!" Harcourt told himself savagely and climbed into the air. On toward the mountain. Pasca, who had been leaning over, looking down, clutched his arm. Pointed. Above a clearing on the shore hung a blue haze. Wood smoke! No mistaking that. He leaned over. Shouted directions to the Eskimo. Could he land on that shore? He must. The great winged creature obeyed his lightest touch, came down and settled on the water with the ease of a mammoth swan. On the edge of the shore Harcourt touched the control which released the landing wheels. It taxied smoothly up the sloping beach.

He flung helmet and goggles to the seat before he climbed out. Revolver in hand, he gave a few curt directions to Pasca. His voice cracked from the strain.

"I do w'at you say. Your face white as crater-top. You fin' 'em pretty quick now. All fine an' dandy. Yes sirree."

Harcourt nodded. His throat ached unbearably. If Janice were under that smoke haze she would have heard the plane. She would have rushed to the shore long before this. Perhaps she was hurt. Paxton could have come. Paxton! He'd better keep him out of his mind. Footprints in the mud along the side of the brook! He was on their trail. What a racket the rushing water made! Had every bird in the Alaskan world suddenly burst into song? If only they would be quiet, so that he could hear voices. The underbrush had been trampled, crushed. He leaned close to the ground. Footprints of animals. Wolves.

Horror clutched at his throat, he stumbled into a clearing. Stopped. Caught at a scorched spruce to steady himself. Were those real persons on the threshold of that blackened shack? Their clothes were scorched brown, their faces smooched as stokers'. The girl's head rested against one side of the doorframe which leaned like the Tower of Pisa. The man was huddled against the other. Were they — Before his parched tongue could formulate the word, he had his hand on her shoulder.

"Janice! Janice!"

Paxton lifted heavy lids. Closed them. Mumbled sleepily "Damn you, Saki. What'd you wake me for?"

He tumbled over flat as the girl sprang to her feet. She held out her hands. Sobbed.

"Bruce! Bruce! I knew you'd find us."

He caught her close in one arm. His hand tightened on his revolver. "Look up at me, Jan."

She leaned her head back against his shoulder. The grime about her mouth was dented with dimples, laughter shone through tears in her sleep-clouded eyes.

"Look at you! You don't have to growl that command. I never was so glad to look at anyone in all my life."

"Thank God!"

His heart swelled in a passion of gratitude. She was living safe, unharmed. He slipped the revolver into its holster. The arm which held her tightened. She pressed her face against his breast before she confided with unsteady gaiety:

"I hate to seem grossly material at this climactic moment but you don't happen to have a broiled live lobster or sea-food Newburg up your sleeve, do you?"

Harcourt's voice shook. "Nothing up my sleeve, dear, but eats in the cockpit."

"And smokes?" Her voice broke betrayingly. "Ned has suffered untold tortures since his last cigarette. He has been wonderful, Bruce, but he is so exhausted I was frightened. Thank God, you've come. You're so — so staunch, so brown, so — so heartwarming."

22

Bruce Harcourt tapped on the door of Janice's
room. No answer. He glanced at his wrist-watch.
Ten o'clock. He tapped again. Dead to the world
probably, tired child. Immediately upon landing
on the flying-field soon after dawn, she had gone
to the H house, two of the men had rowed Paxton
out to his yacht. He hated to waken her, but the
Commissioner wanted to push the investigation.
Chester was up, bandaged, grim-lipped, ashen.
They needed Jan to take stenographic notes. He
lifted the latch, entered the room. A breeze from
the two open windows swayed the chintz hanging,
sunlight emphasized certain color values, sub-
dued others. The rose brocade spread had been
folded on a chair. He could see the outline of the
girl's body under the blanket. She lay as in a rosy
cloud, bare arms outspread as if she had flung
herself face down in utter exhaustion. Her hair
which waved to the shoulders of her orchid
pajama blouse still showed damp traces of a
shampoo. Her hands were scratched and burned.
On one a circlet of diamonds emitted tiny sparks.
His ring. What did it mean to her? Dark lashes like

a shadow on one colorful, smooth cheek. She was so still that he bent nearer to make sure she breathed. He touched her shoulder.

"Jan!"

With a sudden surge of love and longing he pressed his lips to her bare arm. He spoke softly twice before she stirred. She opened the one visible eye, gazed up at him unseeingly, as though her spirit were struggling back from a far country, sat up with a start. A delicate flush spread to the little damp curls at her temples.

"Bruce! What are you doing here?"

He felt his color mount to match hers. "I knocked and knocked. You didn't answer — so — I walked in. The Commissioner wants you to take notes. Feel equal to it?"

She was pulling on a satin coat colored like a Persian amethyst. "Equal to it! I? The silly season must be on when you ask me such a question. I'll be with you in just ten minutes." As he lingered at the foot of the bed, she added crisply, "that is, unless I'm detained by callers."

He laughed. "I'm going." He stopped on the threshold. "Come to the Samp cabin. We took Jimmy Chester there last night."

"Do they still think he did it?"

What would she do if he kissed her troubled eyes? "It looks black for him. Come as soon as you can. Let's get it over."

As he strode along the board walk he relived the few moments before the charred shack, when he had held Janice in his arms. Did her emotion at seeing him come from any deeper feeling than relief at being rescued? Evidently she had emerged from the terrifying experience with a new-born respect for Ned Paxton. Would that respect flame into love again?

The question lay like an undertone in his mind as he conferred with the Commissioner and his deputy in the Samp living-room. The Hessians on the hearth, gold sabres drawn everlastingly on the march which got them nowhere, the open Bible on the table, the heaped-up work-basket, the melodeon in the corner, the black cat curled in the sunny window in precarious proximity to the flower-pots, he had seen hundreds of times. Was it the presence of the livid-faced man with closed eyes leaning against the pillows on the couch which made them seem strangely unreal and unfamiliar? Jimmy Chester appeared unconscious of the black-robed woman beside him who clutched at his hand with its dark seal-ring. The Commissioner sensed her appealing loveliness if Jimmy didn't, Bruce Harcourt told himself, as he noted the official's furtive glances in her direction. The eyes of Martha Samp were on the same business, as she sat stiff-jointed as a marionette in the wing-back chair. Miss Mary, in a low rocker, was darning a sock. She looked up as Janice entered in a navy blue frock with collar and cuffs of exquisite fineness.

"My dear! My dear! I lived centuries last night. I didn't know how you had grown into my heart — until — until —" she wiped her eyes.

"Martha was right when she said where you were was home for her and me."

Janice left a kiss on her soft gray hair before she took the chair with a broad arm which the deputy fussily placed for her. He tiptoed back to his superior, confided in a hoarse whisper:

"All set."

"Where's Grant? He's got information for us. Why in time can't people be prompt?" The door opened. "Here he is with his witnesses. Let's get going. Quick!"

Grant pushed Pasca and Kadyama into the room ahead of him, backed up against the closed door. Chester's face hardened into a chalky mask. Millicent Hale looked at the Eskimo and the Indian with terrified eyes, laid her other hand over her brother's. Had Jimmy told her the truth, Harcourt wondered. Martha Samp's mouth settled into grimmer lines as she frowned at Kadyama.

The Commissioner looked up from his notes. "Bring in the Indian girl."

Miss Mary padded out of the room breathlessly, her usually serene face crinkled with anxiety. Only the snap of the fire, the tick of the clock, stirred the silence of the room. From the plateau drifted the snort and hiss of a steam-shovel lumbering inland like an early neolithic dragon. Men shouted. Huskies yelped.

Tatima swayed in on the heels of the younger Samp sister. Her practical work-dress was a maze of brilliant color, her blue beads were her

317

only ornament. Her great dark eyes smoldered, she tossed her superb head as she met the Commissioner's grilling eyes.

"Hear you've had a present lately."

"Who, me?"

"Yes, you. Who gave you that silver jewelry you were swaggering round in?"

"Who tole you I — w'at you say, swagger?"

"Answer my question. Who gave you the silver?"

"Kadyama."

"Is that true?" He turned to the lowering Indian, who stood awkwardly twisting a soft hat in his hand.

"Yes. I geeve it. She marry on me."

"Cost a lot of money, didn't it? Where'd you get the cash?"

Kadyama shot the inquisitor a murderous glance before he motioned with his thumb.

"Pasca pay money he owe."

Harcourt stared incredulously at his house-boy. Pasca with money! He was a confirmed gambler, an unlucky gambler, he was always asking for an advance of his pay. Was Kadyama lying? He watched the Eskimo's face, a trifle less florid than usual, as the Commissioner demanded:

"Is this true? Did you pay Kadyama money?"

Pasca looked furtively at Chester. Did he answer with a slight nod or was it a figment of his own hectic imagination, Harcourt wondered.

"Yes sirree. I pay Kadyama much money.

Leetle game we had, I lost. He want long time I pay."

"Where'd you get it?"

"He geeve it me." All eyes followed his nod toward the couch.

"Mm. You say that Mr. Chester gave it to you. Know where he got it?"

Was the Commissioner trying to pin robbery as well as the shooting on Jimmy? Didn't he realize that as second engineer he had a fat salary which he had mighty little chance to spend? Would it help or harm Chester's cause if he came out with that information now? Into the turmoil of Harcourt's thoughts trailed Pasca's lazy drawl.

"How I know where he get it? He mak much money p'raps. All engineers mak much money."

"Why did he give it to you?"

This time there could be no doubt of the interchange of glances before the Eskimo answered.

"Meester Chester, he say to me, 'I geeve you two hun'ed dollar — you help me.' He nice fella. I say 'Sure.' "

"How did he want you to help him?"

"He say he must mak quick get-away in plane the fella you sen' for finger-print man go in. I help your man, honest lak, then Meester Chester pull heem out hard. I help Meester Chester get off, den lock up your man. Meester Chester pay me two hun'ed dollar. I pay Kadyama. Yes sirree."

"Is this true, Chester?"

"Yes."

"Where'd you get that money? Hale's roll?"

A contemptuous smile touched the corners of Jimmy Chester's blanched lips. "No. I've never needed to steal from my brother-in-law."

"Then where —"

"Just a minute, Commissioner. I wish next you'd ask Kadyama why he wasn't at the squaw-dance the night Joe Hale was shot. Why he was hanging round the back door of the Hale cabin." Grant's voice caught in a gulp, his green eyes blazed with excitement. Kadyama started to bolt. Grant caught him. "Come across, Kadyama."

The Commissioner sat forward in his seat.

"Yes, Kadyama — come across."

A speck of foam bubbled at the corners of the Indian's lips, his eyes burned deep ruby lights.

"Aw right, I tell. I went to Hale cabin — good chance — one, two dance goin', everybody there, he alone, to tell heem Tatima my squaw."

"Did you tell him?"

"Never had no chance. I go in back door. Look round screen. Meester Hale sit in wheel-chair countin' roll of money. I tink, now's my time. I step out — not quick enough — front door open, slow — slow —"

Kadyama's voice dropped to a hoarse whisper. He leaned forward as though he were seeing again Hale in his chair, the slowly opening door. Chester dropped his head into his hands,

Millicent Hale gasped. The Commissioner's voice was taut with suspense.

"Go on! Who came in that door?"

Kadyama pointed to the couch.

"Chester! I thought so. What did Hale do when he came in?"

Kadyama sniffed contempt. "You tink you pretty smart fella, catch me, huh? Not Meester Chester come in. She, Mees Hale." He pointed to the woman who sat, fair head bent, clutching her brother's hand.

Millicent! She had said that she had found Hale dead! Harcourt crushed back dismay, to listen.

"*Mrs. Hale.* Are you sure?"

"Let me speak."

"Sit down, Chester, your turn will come. Go on, Kadyama, what happened next?"

"Meester Hale, he begin to talk loud an' hard. Vera fast. Mees Hale say nothin'. She open table drawer, tak out somethin'. She laugh, she say:

" 'See this revolver, Joe? I borrowed it. Bully in you skulk when Jimmy t'reaten you. I try it. If you say one word more, I fire.' He curse, jump for her, he catch revolver way from her han', it fire, he fall. I go."

The occupants of the room sat as still as though under the spell of a necromancer. A log broke apart with a loud snap, sent a shower of sparks up the chimney. Startled, the black cat leaped from the windowsill. A flower-pot fell with a crash. The deputy jumped from his chair, dropped back. The Commissioner roused from a state of coma, scowled at Kadyama.

"Where does Chester barge in on this?"

"He — he — doesn't come in!"

With the hoarse defense, Millicent Hale rose, caught the mantel shelf to steady herself. The sombre black of her gown emphasized her slenderness, the brilliance of her violet eyes which were too feverishly bright, the strained lines of her mouth which was too pale. The nails of her clutching fingers showed white.

"Kadyama is telling the truth. I had seen my husband cringe before my brother's threat. I thought, 'Perhaps I've been too easy, perhaps Joe will have more respect for me if I defy him.' I had been frightfully unhappy. It seemed as though I couldn't go on another day. I was crazed with despair." Her voice, which had been broken, steadied. She straightened, cast off confusion, fear, like a princess discarding a tattered cloak. "Believe me or not, I had not the slightest intention of shooting my husband. I didn't even know the revolver was loaded. I had never had one in my hand before I took Mr. Harcourt's down from the wall and hid it in our cabin. Before I could make my grandstand play of aiming it, Joe had caught it. It went off. He fell. Terrified, I tried to lift him. Horrified, I realized what had happened. I would be accused of shooting him, I, who never in my life had hurt anything. What should I do? A roll of money lay at his feet. I tucked it into the bosom of my gown. Crazed, I picked up the revolver, stole down to the shore, flung it into the water. I raced and stumbled to the H house to tell Bruce Harcourt what had happened. He would advise me what to do. When he opened the door — I remembered that — that — he was married — I called out something, then the room went black." She dropped to the couch. Her brother put his bandaged arm about her.

The Commissioner's eyes were points of steel as he regarded them.

"If that's true —" he held up his hand as Millicent Hale opened her lips. "I believe you. Only a fool would doubt your story — why in the devil did you make your get-away, Chester?"

"It was a dumb move. When Harcourt told me that his revolver had been stolen, the remembrance of my sister's laugh after I had threatened her husband flashed through my mind. I remembered the questions she had asked, the interest she had shown in the holster on the H house wall the afternoon we were decorating for the party. I was certain that she had shot him. I felt responsible. I had put the fool idea into her head. I didn't realize it was an accident. I thought if I got away you would think I did it. It would give us time to figure out the best thing to be done."

The Commissioner glared at Kadyama. "Why haven't you told of what you saw?"

The Indian bared yellow teeth in a wolfish smile. "Why I tell? Much obliged to Mees Hale. She save me much trouble — p'raps prison. I help her. W'en you say I shoot heem den plenty time to tell w'at I see."

"It didn't occur to you that coming across with the truth was the best thing to be done, I suppose, Chester?"

"Sakes alive, Mr. Commissioner, it occurred to me." Martha Samp's agate eyes sparkled as though flecked with mica.

"You — you — suspected the truth all this time?" The Commissioner's diction suggested a skipping motor-engine.

"I did. I told you I heard her and her husband quarreling. I didn't try to hear what they said. I slipped away as I told you, thinkin' that while ice-cream might be coolin' to the tongue, 'twouldn't do much to tempers. That night when I went to the H house an' found her skirts all wet and draggled, I suspected; when I found this tucked in her bodice — I knew."

She drew a roll of bills from her pocket, tossed it to the table. Color darkened the Commissioner's face. His fingers twitched with anger.

"You've let us sweat blood over this when all the time you knew! Why didn't you tell, woman? Why didn't you tell?"

Martha Samp rose in impressive dignity. "You came here like a lord. Just thought I'd see how a real live official handled a case. I've got my knowledge from the papers, an' I'll say right now, reports are much more interesting than the real thing as conducted by you."

The Commissioner showed symptoms of apoplexy. "You could be jailed for holding back testimony."

"Sakes alive, could I? Because I waited for M's. Hale to tell herself. She's been a loyal wife. She's been through hell without whimpering. I knew when she got to thinking she'd straighten things out. The world's just bubblin' with stories of man's loyalty to man, but there isn't so much said about woman's loyalty to woman, an' letting her tell her own story was my idea of loyalty to her."

"Suppose she hadn't told?"

"She did, didn't she? But I provided against that. When I've read about trials it's seemed to me that testimony rehashed months after the crime took place couldn't be very accurate. The morning after the shootin' I wrote down everything I'd heard and seen. Sealed it. Took it to the radio man. He stamped it with place and date just as he does letters that go out. Here it is." She handed the Commissioner an envelope. He turned it over in his hand. Conferred with the deputy. Rose.

"My associate and I agree that the late Joe Hale met his death by accident. The inquest is closed."

23

"All you little doughboys come and get your chow!" The ringing call of the bugle pierced Bruce Harcourt's absorption as he left the Samp cabin. Would he find Janice at the office, or would she have gone to luncheon? She had slipped away directly after the Commissioner had pronounced a verdict of accidental shooting. Paxton, immaculately attired, with deep lines of exhaustion about his eyes and an apparent stiffness in every joint, had come in, had announced an afternoon departure. He had offered to take any one who wanted to go back to the States. Millicent had been tearfully eager to get away, Mallory advised expert surgical treatment for Jimmy Chester, the Commissioner had decided to send his deputy back by plane and return himself by water.

Why hadn't Millicent come out with the truth at once, Harcourt fumed! As for Jimmy's fool get-away, and his pursuit of him, he saw red every time he thought of it. No use milling over what was behind. What lay before? His jaw tightened. He knew what lay directly before him. He stopped to look down at the shore. Paxton was stepping into a small boat. He watched the flash of oars as two sailors pulled toward the yacht which looked like a mammoth white swan resting between a blue sky and a bluer sea. Far away snowy mountain-tops shone spotlessly, dazzlingly. The black dot on the horizon he knew to be a trading schooner Siberia bound. Not long now before the ice would close in solidly. The realization steeled his purpose. Had Paxton come from the office? Had he been persuading Janice to join the party back to the States? If he had, the task he had set himself would be easier.

She was hooding her typewriter as he entered the office. Her cheek still bore faintly pink evidence of Blot's mercurial temperament, but her eyes and smile were radiant.

"Now that the cyclone of excitement has passed over, I hope to accomplish something. For weeks and weeks one day was so like another I would get mixed on the date. Then one morning I start air-trotting. Something snaps like one of those Christmas bombs which bursts and showers sparks, favors and candies over the table — we're caught up and swept along in a cloudburst of adventure, humorous, tragic, thrilling."

Harcourt picked up a letter from his desk. "This is Alaska. You mustn't expect life here to be like life in New York. It's a different story in this wilderness."

"Not such a wilderness when within flying dis-

tance one may buy roses and mandarin coats."
She took a step toward him. "Tubby told me
that you bought that gorgeous coat for me,
Bruce. I love it."

The tenderness of her voice almost smashed
his self-control. He said curtly:

"Paxton's yacht goes out this afternoon with
Mrs. Hale, Chester and the Commissioner
aboard. I want you to go with them."

Amazed consternation wiped the happy radiance from her face. "I! On Ned Paxton's boat!
You advise that?"

"Two days ago I would not have permitted it,
but he has proved himself trustworthy. This
letter is from your brother Billy. I wrote him
after I discovered the identity of Jimmy Delevan.
I've told you before that I will not let you spend a
winter here. As soon as I can get leave I will join
you and we'll — well, we will talk things over. I
will cable Billy to meet the yacht at Seattle."

"Just like that!" Her eyes were brilliant with
anger, he could see her throat contract. "You
needn't trouble to cable Billy. I'm not going.
Tubby Grant hired me to work for the outfit. I
shall keep my position here. You talk about my
going back as though it were as simple as setting
out for dinner and dance. How am I to earn my
living when I get to the States? It isn't so easy to
pick up a job. Perhaps you think I'll live on my
brother. Absolutely not!"

Indignation swept him like a red hot wave.
"My wife does not need a job. You'll have half

328

my salary, more if you need it."

"Your wife! I'm not your wife. I'm merely a companion on trial. Money doesn't figure in that agreement. Do you think I would accept it from you? You can't give me even understanding. When you made good my silly lie to Ned Paxton, I saw myself as I was, always at the mercy of my imagination. I determined that I would do my utmost to make you happy. I didn't know then that 'if you'd only waited' you would have married Millicent Hale."

"Jan!"

"That whitens your face, doesn't it? You can have her now. Better go along in the yacht yourself and start annulment proceedings. Once you told me that when you mushed back behind the dog-team and saw the H house through the falling snow, it seemed like coming home, although you knew that only a husky and a house-boy waited for you behind those lighted windows. I had thought that next winter you might be glad to find me there too. My mistake."

The picture she conjured of her lovely self waiting for him to come in through the snow-filled darkness set Harcourt's blood afire. With all his strength he resisted her charm. If he touched her again he would never let her go. She should not be subjected to the strain of the long, dark winter. He kept his voice under rigid control.

"That means that you will go — this afternoon?"

Her breath was a straggling sob. She caught her lips between her teeth. From the threshold she defied him. "Iceberg! I'll go, but only from the H house. Now that the one person to be impressed by convention is leaving — I will return to Argus of the Hundred Eyes and Miss Mary. They'll be glad to have me back with them." Grant pushed open the door. "Thank heaven you've come, Tubby. You almost lost your secretary. Your superior officer was giving her notice. Don't ruffle up like a turkey-cock. She wouldn't accept it." The door closed behind her before Grant emerged from a stupor of surprise. He glanced at Harcourt surreptitiously as he made his whistling way to his own desk. He dropped his brief case with a bang.

"Ba-gosh, our hair-raising mystery busted up like a pricked balloon when Mrs. Hale broke loose, didn't it? When I remember how I steamed up the inlet and dragged Kadyama back by the hair of his head, sure that he was the criminal, I feel as useful as a flat tire. Accident! She didn't know the revolver was loaded! Old stuff. Seems to me I've heard that somewhere before. Beware of taking unto oneself a wife ignorant of the use of firearms. Weren't you flabbergasted at the denouement?"

"I was. Yet, thinking back, there was one moment at the inquest, when Kadyama told of Millicent decorating the H house, when a dull suspicion flickered in my mind. It was speedily pushed out by later developments. New orders

330

for us came by plane this morning. No bridge-building this winter. Retrenchment all along the line. We are to push the tracks from here south while the weather holds — the Crowned Heads are all excited about pulp-wood possibilities — then keep the repair shops at headquarters humming till spring."

"Headquarters for us all. Janice will be crazy about the winter here. We'll teach her to pilot, to handle a dog-team."

Harcourt crossed to his desk. "I want her to go out on Paxton's boat with the others this afternoon."

"Says you!" The words bubbled with indignation. "What'll she do for a job when she gets there! I happen to know that her capital is fifty dollars besides what she has saved of her pay."

"Do you think I can't support my wife?"

"Mebbe so, mebbe so, but I can't see her taking money from a man who returns her as stolidly as he would an unsatisfactory pair of shoes."

"Tubby!"

"It's true, isn't it? Why go dark red and glare at me? Granted you're a wow of an engineer, as a married man you're a total loss. Isn't he, Miss Martha?" he demanded, as the elder Miss Samp entered the office. The black cat raced by her to pounce on a scrap of paper skipping across the floor.

"Isn't he what? I heard you shoutin', Mr. Tubby, as I came from M's. Hale's cabin —

she's pretty near packed up — an' dropped in to see if you were tryin' to talk with Fairbanks without a wire."

Grant's grievance was too acute to permit of appreciation of her humor. "You'll shout when you hear that the chief wants Janice to join the party on Paxton's yacht."

"Sakes alive, has the excitement turned his brain?" Miss Samp dropped into a chair. "Course 'tisn't any of my business any more than 'tis Mr. Tubby's, but why are you sending that child away, Mr. Bruce?"

"You have been so kind to Janice that it is your business, Miss Martha. I don't want her to experience the hardships of a winter here. Remember what this life did to Millicent Hale."

Martha Samp's gnarled fingers stroked the glossy coat of the black cat circling in her lap. She regarded Harcourt with shrewd eyes.

"Did to her! It made a woman of her, didn't it? Think back. She came here just an ordinary, spoiled, flighty young married girl. At first she fretted. Then she kinder found herself. Never complained. She developed the heart, the endurance of a noble woman."

"And how did it end?"

"You mean about her kinder flyin' off the handle at the last? I've got a pretty good idea of what caused it. She got to leanin' on you, Mr. Bruce, you were all her husband wasn't. When Janice came along, so pretty an' gay an' attractive, she got to broodin' on her troubles an' thinkin' life played favorites, an' something snapped. She hadn't any notion of hurtin' Joe. Course she shouldn't have threatened him, but who doesn't do a fool thing or two in the course of a life? Doesn't it restore your faith in human nature to find an officer of the law with the common sense to recognize an accident when he sees one, an' not try to make a criminal out of a female who hasn't enough sense to leave a revolver hangin' in its holster?"

The black cat slid to the floor as she stood up. "I must be running along. I left Tatima alone in the Waffle Shop. That Indian girl is about as much use since she got that jewelry as one of them slinky paper women in the magazines Mary's always lookin' at. I didn't know but what I'd be packin' for my sister, she flared up so 'bout wastin' her life cookin' waffles. Perhaps she's right, but we'll both stand by so long as Janice stays."

She laid one hand on Harcourt's arm, with rough-skinned fingers gently touched his temple. "That hair wasn't white when you left to hunt for Jimmy Chester, boy."

"Last night was a thousand years long, Miss Martha."

She patted his sleeve. "This winter'll be a million years long if you send Janice away — for you — for us all." She coughed to clear her voice. Hand on the latch of the door, she stopped. "If Millicent Hale could grow spiritually in this wilderness, seems to me you might trust a girl like

Janice. Course if you're afraid of her gettin' so homesick that she'd shoot you, you could lock up your guns. Blot, don't you know that's nothin' but a piece of paper you're hectorin'? You're as short-sighted as the rest of your sex. Can't see two inches in front of your nose." The door banged.

Grant grinned. "And that's that. Let's eat."

Martha Samp's argument seethed like an undercurrent in Harcourt's mind during the afternoon as he packed for Chester, sent messages, helped the Commissioner with his reports. Not until she came to the shore to embark in the launch which was to take her to the yacht did he speak to Millicent Hale. Her hand clung to his, her violet eyes were tear-filled.

"I wish I were the one to stay with you, Bruce."

He smiled and shook his head. "You have forgotten the long dark winter. I'm willing to bet that with the first sight of the lights of Vancouver, you'll be thanking all the gods that be that you're back in civilization."

"Boat's waiting for you, Mrs. Hale," Grant reminded. The Commissioner took her hand, steadied her into the launch. Chester, pale, gloomy-eyed, leaned against Stephen Mallory's broad shoulder in the stern.

Side by side Harcourt and Grant watched the launch as it shot like a brown streak for the yacht. Indians and Eskimos stood in groups on the shingle behind them, section bosses and engineers, with unconsciously wistful faces, waited for The Modern Mariner to hoist her anchor. Men were at headquarters flagstaff. Gulls circled and dove about the prow of the yacht. An occasional berg dotted the water. The broken mouth of the crater across the bay blew out filmy scarfs of pastel colors in farewell.

Harcourt glanced up at the cabins. White handkerchiefs were fluttering from the doorway of the Waffle Shop. He could see Janice on the step of the H house. What was she thinking as she stood there?

"Hi! There she goes! She's dipping the colors in response to our flag!" Grant's voice caught in his throat. "Ba-gosh, gives you a queer feeling in the pit of the stomach to see a boat going — going home, what?"

Harcourt let the question go unanswered. His intent eyes were on the yacht as it moved majestically toward the south. Across the water drifted the measured stroke of a ship's bell. He could distinguish the figures at the rail. Paxton with glasses at his eyes, Millicent Hale waving a handkerchief, the Commissioner beside her flourishing a cap, Jimmy Chester braced against Mallory. Grant linked his arm in his.

"Bad luck to watch them out of sight. Come on, let's cheer up the Samp girls. I'll bet that home-bound boat laid their spirits low for a minute. I'll suggest a tea-party for those of us left behind. Preparations for that will pep them up. Hope that Janice is with them."

"She is at the H house. Let me know if we are to have the party and I will bring her."

He walked on rapidly. If that out-going boat had made him, who had spent years in the wilderness, desperately homesick, what must it have meant to Janice. He had been brutal to leave her alone. He had deliberately kept out of her way. He couldn't trust himself with her. He honestly wanted her to go for her own sake. If she had loved him — well, she didn't.

She was leaning against the H house, eyes on the pale blur which was gliding into an opaline mist. Her long lashes were wet, but she faced him with gay bravado.

"Sorry not to have been moved out before you came back, but Pasca was so busy helping the travelers off that he had no time for me."

He caught her by the shoulders. "You're not going back to the Samp cabin. You will stay in my house."

She defied him flippantly. "Big Chief! Heap bossy! You tried to push me out of headquarters, and now you are dictating as to where I shall live. I am working for Tubby Grant, not for you."

His hands tightened. "Jan, my dear, don't you know what it means to love a person so much that you would tear your heart out if you thought it best for her?" He cleared his voice of huskiness. "I know that you are forcing yourself to stay, triumphing over what you think is a fear-complex, what I know to be imagination. I know, also, that if you stay here you are bound to be miserably unhappy."

Angry tears drenched the eyes which made him think of bronze pansies. "How do you know that I would be unhappy? You and Tubby and the Samp girls think Mrs. Hale a marvel of sweetness and light because she carried on. Why shouldn't she? It was her job. You talk about love. A lot you know about it. I can see you following a person half across the world. Not a chance!"

"Jan!" The incredulous whisper brought her eyes to his. Even his lips whitened. "Jan!" He caught her up in his arms, kicked open the door. His laugh was a caress. "This time I'll carry my bride across the threshold as big, strong men do in the movies and points south." He set her on her feet, gently raised her chin till her head rested against his shoulder, demanded softly:

"All right with you, Beautiful?"

Eyes valiant, lovely color tinting her soft skin, she answered with an unsteady attempt at raillery. "I never did think much of that trial companionship idea of yours. If you care —"

"Care! If I care!" In a fury of passion he kissed her eyes, the hollow in her throat, her mouth. Kissed her vehemently, thoroughly. Said with a husky, reckless laugh: "That's how I care."

Tubby Grant pushed open the door. "First call for tea in the dining-car! You —" His voice dwindled to a gurgle. He blinked something suspiciously like tears from his wistful green eyes. With a softly breathed, "Praise be to Allah!" he gently closed the door from the outside.

The employees of G.K. Hall hope you have enjoyed this Large Print book. All our Large Print titles are designed for easy reading, and all our books are made to last. Other G.K. Hall books are available at your library, through selected bookstores, or directly from us.

For information about titles, please call:

(800) 257-5157

To share your comments, please write:

Publisher
G.K. Hall & Co.
P.O. Box 159
Thorndike, ME 04986

DATE DUE

JAN 2 7 2015	

DEMCO, INC. 38-2931